P9-CLJ-762

ALSO BY FREIDA MCFADDEN

The Housemaid's Secret
The Housemaid
Never Lie
The Inmate
Do You Remember?
Do Not Disturb
The Locked Door
Want to Know a Secret?
One by One
The Wife Upstairs
The Perfect Son
The Ex
The Surrogate Mother
Brain Damage
Suicide Med
Baby City
The Devil Wears Scrubs
The Devil You Know

THE
COWORKER

FREIDA McFADDEN

Poisoned Pen
PRESS

Copyright © 2023 by Freida McFadden
Cover and internal design © 2023 by Sourcebooks
Cover design by *the*BookDesigners
Cover photos © Ground Picture/Shutterstock, Yeti Studio/
Shutterstock, FabrikaSimf/Shutterstock

Sourcebooks, Poisoned Pen Press, and the colophon
are registered trademarks of Sourcebooks.

All rights reserved. No part of this book may be reproduced in any form or by
any electronic or mechanical means including information storage and retrieval
systems—except in the case of brief quotations embodied in critical articles or
reviews—without permission in writing from its publisher, Sourcebooks.

The characters and events portrayed in this book are fictitious or
are used fictitiously. Any similarity to real persons, living or dead,
is purely coincidental and not intended by the author.

All brand names and product names used in this book are trademarks,
registered trademarks, or trade names of their respective holders.
Sourcebooks is not associated with any product or vendor in this book.

Published by Poisoned Pen Press, an imprint of Sourcebooks
P.O. Box 4410, Naperville, Illinois 60567-4410
(630) 961-3900
sourcebooks.com

Cataloging-in-Publication Data is on file with the Library of Congress.

Printed and bound in Canada.
MBP 10 9 8 7 6 5

To my family

PROLOGUE

To: Seth Hoffman
From: Dawn Schiff
Subject: IMPORTANT

To Seth,

    A sensitive matter has come to my attention that I must discuss with you urgently. I would like to request a scheduled meeting with you in your office at your earliest convenience.

Sincerely,
Dawn Schiff

To: Dawn Schiff
From: Seth Hoffman
Subject: Re: IMPORTANT

Okay, sure. Come by my office.

To: Seth Hoffman
From: Dawn Schiff
Subject: Re: IMPORTANT

To Seth,

    I would prefer to have a scheduled appointment to ensure that you will be present at the time of the meeting and that we have adequate time to discuss some potentially upsetting information that I feel compelled to share with you. I do not wish to have an in-depth discussion interrupted by a prior commitment, or worse, arrive at your office only to find you are not there at all. I would feel much more comfortable with a scheduled appointment. I can check your calendar and cross-reference it with my own and come up with six potential appointment times in the next 48 hours when it would be convenient for both of us to meet, and you can highlight two of those times that work best for you, and we can agree on a final time that is mutually convenient.

Sincerely,
Dawn Schiff

To: Dawn Schiff
From: Seth Hoffman
Subject: Re: IMPORTANT

How's tomorrow at 2?

To: Seth Hoffman
From: Dawn Schiff
Subject: Re: IMPORTANT

Here are the details for our scheduled meeting:
   Location: Seth Hoffman's office
   Time: 2:00 PM
   I have added it to my calendar.

Sincerely,
Dawn Schiff

PART I

CHAPTER 1

PRESENT DAY

NATALIE

Dawn isn't at her desk this morning when I walk into the office, which means the world is coming to an end.

I'm joking. Obviously, the world is not coming to an end. But if you knew Dawn, you would get it.

For the last nine months, Dawn Schiff has occupied the cubicle next to mine at Vixed, the nutritional supplement company where we both work. You could set your watch by her routines. 8:45, she's at her desk. 10:15, she takes a bathroom break. 11:45, she goes to the break room and has her lunch. 2:30 is another bathroom break. And at 5:00 sharp, she shuts down her computer and leaves for the day. If there were some sort of apocalyptic event in which all timepieces in the world were lost, we could all get back on schedule just by watching when Dawn went to the bathroom. Down to the *second*.

I usually arrive at work somewhere in the thirty-minute window between eight thirty and nine. Well, nine-*ish*. If all the stars align, I make it by 8:30. But even though I swear I put my keys in the exact same place every day, on the table right by the front door, sometimes during the night, they get up and walk away somewhere. And then I have to look for them.

Or else I hit traffic. So much traffic. Dorchester Avenue is a parking lot during rush hour.

This morning, the lights were not in my favor, but the traffic was sparse, so at ten minutes to nine, I step into the large office space that houses Vixed. I walk through the rows of identical cubicles stuffed into the center of the room, my red heels clicking against the lino-leum floor, the fluorescent lights flickering above my head. As I pass by Dawn's cubicle on the way to my own, my hand already raised in greeting, I stop short.

The cubicle is empty.

As strange as Dawn's schedule is, it's even stranger that today she isn't following it. I can't help but think that Dawn's absence must signify something ominous. After all, Dawn is never late. *Never.*

"Natalie! Hey, Nat! Guess what!"

I rip my eyes away from Dawn's cubicle at the sound of Kim's voice. She's skipping down the aisle of cubicles, her tanned face glowing.

Kim Healey is my best friend at work, which sadly means that she's my best friend in general since work has increasingly become my entire life. She got back from her honeymoon two weeks ago and has the most spectacular tan as well as highlights in her formerly dark brown hair—she even still smells slightly like sand and sunscreen. She looks fantastic and I'm so happy for her. And I'm only like 10 percent jealous. Really—I genuinely wish her all the happiness in the world, as I said in my slightly drunken wedding toast.

I rake my eyes over Kim's black-and-white patterned Ann Taylor dress, noting a telltale bulge. "You're pregnant!" I gasp.

The smile instantly drops off her face. "*No*. I'm *not* pregnant. Why would you say that?" She tugs at the tie cinched above her waist. "Do you think this dress makes me look fat?"

"No! Oh, Kim, of course not!" In my defense, the way she said *guess what* really made it sound like she had a baby announcement. Women my age seem to be announcing pregnancies left and right lately—it seems like the only exciting news anyone has to share—and she *did* recently get back from her honeymoon. "Not at *all*. I'm *so* sorry I said that. I just thought…"

Kim is still tugging at her dress self-consciously. "You must have said that for a reason."

I mentally smack myself in the head. "I didn't—I swear. And anyway, *everyone* puts on a couple of pounds on their honeymoon. It totally suits you."

But she isn't even listening. She's too busy craning her neck, trying to look at her own butt.

I clear my throat. "So, um, what did you want to tell me?"

"Oh." She manages a tiny smile, her initial enthusiasm dampened. "The T-shirts came. I put them in the conference room."

Ooh, that *is* good news! I follow Kim to the conference room, and sure enough, there's a slightly dented brown cardboard box waiting in the corner. I run right over and pry open the flaps. "Did you look?"

"I sifted through. Didn't do a full count."

I rifle through the box stuffed with T-shirts and pull one out. It's teal in color, and all the necessary information is there. 5K charity run. Benefiting cerebral palsy research. The shirt in my hand is a medium, and it looks about right. I was nervous about the timing— the T-shirts were supposed to arrive last week, and it's already Tuesday. The charity run I'm organizing is on Saturday.

"They look gorgeous, Nat," Kim breathes. She has been such an amazing cheerleader in organizing this run—I couldn't have done it without her. "We can pass them out later in the morning, when everyone is here."

I nod, relieved this is coming together as planned. "By the way," I add, "do you know if Dawn called out sick?"

Kim holds a T-shirt up to her chest, smoothing it out over her abdomen, which still looks a bit like a baby bump to me. "No. Why?"

"Well, she's not here."

"So? She's running late."

"You don't understand." I drop the T-shirts back into the cardboard box. "Dawn is never late. *Never.* Not once the whole time she's worked here. She's always here at 8:45."

Kim looks down at her watch and then back up at me like I've lost my mind. "So she's twenty minutes late. So what?"

It's strange behavior for Dawn. On top of that, there's something else I haven't shared with Kim. Yesterday afternoon, Dawn sent me an odd email asking if I could talk to her at the end of the workday about a "matter of great importance." But I was out on a sales call most of the afternoon, and when I got back to the office, she was already gone.

A matter of great importance. I wonder if that was about…

No. Probably not.

"I hope she's okay." I shake my head. "Maybe she got into a car accident."

Kim snickers. "Or maybe she was finally committed."

"Stop it," I murmur. "That's mean."

"Come on. She's a weirdo and you know it as well as anyone. You're the one who has to sit next to her."

"She's not so bad."

"Not so bad!" Kim bursts out. "It's like sharing the office with a robot. And what's with her obsession with turtles? Like, who is that into *turtles*?"

Okay, I'm not going to say Dawn isn't a little strange. Or even *very* strange. There are times when people at the company make fun of her behind her back. And yes, she does like turtles more than any fully grown adult rightfully should. But she's a very nice person. If they got to know her a little better, they would be nicer to her.

Not that I know her very well. I always meant to ask her to dinner sometime, but I never got around to it. A couple of weeks ago as we were riding down in the elevator on Friday evening, I casually asked her if she had any plans and she looked shocked by the question. *Just having dinner at home. Alone.* I would have asked her to join me for dinner, but I was meeting my boyfriend, and it would have been weird if she tagged along.

I'm going to invite her out to dinner. For sure. Just as soon as the 5K is over.

"Anyway, I better get back to work." Kim glances down at her watch. "I'm not Miss Saleswoman of the Month like somebody else here."

My cheeks color slightly. My sales are admittedly better than anyone else at the company, but I work my butt off for it. "You got married this month. You have an excuse this time for the low sales."

"Yeah, yeah." Kim shrugs because she doesn't really care that much. Her new husband is loaded. At some point in the near future, she'll be pregnant for real, and when that happens, she'll quit and never look back. "Anyway, good luck with the T-shirts. I'll see you later."

After Kim takes off, possibly in the direction of her cubicle, but more likely in the direction of the break room to get her third or fourth cup of coffee of the morning, I close the flaps of the box of T-shirts and head back to my cubicle. When I get there, I notice something on my desk that I hadn't seen before.

It's a turtle figurine.

It's small—no longer than the length of my index finger. It's green and blue in color, the geometric patterns on its shell shining in the overhead fluorescent lights. Its head is lifted, and its beady black eyes stare up at me.

A while back, Dawn excitedly presented me with a turtle figurine for my cubicle. It was so sweet of her, and I felt terrible when the turtle she bought me toppled to the linoleum floor and shattered into a dozen tiny pieces. But that turtle was never replaced. And it was different from this turtle on my desk right now.

I pick up the turtle figurine and roll it between my fingers, feeling the smooth surface. What is this turtle doing here? Who put it here?

Was it Dawn?

But it couldn't be. When I got back to the office yesterday at the end of the day, she was already gone. And she doesn't seem to be here yet. So how could she have put this turtle on my desk?

When I rest the turtle back on my desk, there's a stain on my fingers. Something dark red rubbed off on my hand when I picked up the turtle. I stare down at my palm, trying to figure out what I just touched. It can't be paint, since the turtle is green. Ketchup?

No, it couldn't be. It's too dark in color and not sticky with sugar. And it doesn't have that sweet smell. It smells almost...metallic.

What *is* this stuff?

As I'm examining the dark red material that has caked into the grooves of my fingerprints, I am vaguely aware of a phone ringing nearby. Coming from Dawn's cubicle.

I return to Dawn's cubicle, hovering by the entrance. It's still empty. Is it possible she came in earlier this morning and is in the bathroom or something? She must be here, and she must've been the one who put this little turtle on my desk, even though her jacket isn't hanging on the back of her chair. And her computer screen is dark—no screensaver, just black.

The phone on her desk is still ringing. Usually, the caller's number flashes on the screen but not this time. It's a blocked number.

I snatch the phone off the hook. It isn't my job to answer her phone, but if she is out sick today, I could at least try to take care of any issues that have come up. I'm sure Dawn would do the same for me. She always tries to help other people, almost to a fault.

I wonder what it was she wanted to talk to me about yesterday. *A matter of great importance.* Coming from Dawn, that could mean just about anything, from a dirty milk carton in the fridge to a terminal cancer diagnosis. There's no reason to worry.

"Dawn Schiff's desk," I answer.

There is silence on the other line. It almost sounds like ragged breathing.

"Hello?" I say. "Is anyone there?"

More silence. Just when I'm about to hang up, two words are spoken in a tortured female voice that send an icy chill down my spine:

"*Help me.*"

And then the line goes dead.

CHAPTER 2

I stare at the dead receiver, a sick feeling growing in the pit of my stomach.

Help me.

It sounded a lot like Dawn, although I can't be absolutely sure from just two words. But whoever it was, they sounded hysterical. Panicked.

Help me.

And then the dead line, which has now turned into a dial tone.

I toyed with the possibility that something was wrong when Dawn was late this morning, but I didn't genuinely believe it was anything serious. Was I wrong? Has something terrible happened to Dawn?

Is she in danger?

I reach into my purse for my phone. I select Dawn's name from my contacts and click on her number. It rings several times and then I hear the monotone of her voice:

You have reached the cellular phone of Dawn Schiff. I am not available to answer your call at this time. At the beep, please leave your name, a callback number, an alternate contact number, and your reason for contacting me.

I decide against leaving a message. Instead, I shoot off a text message:

Hey Dawn, everything okay?

I watch the screen, waiting for the little bubbles to indicate she's typing. They don't appear.

I've got to do something. I've got to talk to Seth.

Seth Hoffman has been the manager of the Dorchester branch of Vixed since before I started working here. Seth and I have an understanding—he gives me a long rope, and I kick ass at sales. It's nice having a boss who isn't up in my business all the time about every penny I spend on my customers or who makes me account for every nanosecond of my time. I'm sure it would be different if I didn't get results, but Seth trusts me.

I rap on the door to Seth's office, which is already partially ajar. He does have a secretary, but she's sort of the secretary for everyone, and she doesn't monitor who goes in and comes out of his office. So when he calls out for me to come in, I go right on in.

When Kim and I started working here, we used to giggle about how cute our boss was. Seth is now in his midforties—fifteen years my senior—but he's got a youthful look. He has lines around his eyes that crinkle when he smiles, a sprinkling of gray hair in his temples that suits him, and while he always wears a tie, it's never quite cinched all the way to his throat.

"Hey, Nat," he says when he sees it's me. "What's up? Everything okay?"

"Not exactly." I hover in front of Seth's desk, wanting to share my concerns with him but not wanting to sound too crazy. "Did Dawn call out sick today?"

His dark eyebrows shoot up. "No. She didn't. Why? She's not here?"

Like me, Seth must know that Dawn operates like she's controlled by a master clock. "I haven't seen her."

"Huh," he says.

Damn. I had been hoping she had called him. Told him she had a sick grandma and she wouldn't be in for the day. "I called her and she didn't pick up. And also…"

He frowns. "Also what?"

"Dawn's phone was ringing and I picked it up. And the person on the other line said, 'Help me.'"

Seth nods. "Okay, so what did they need help with? Did they need information on one of the products? Was it a customer complaint?"

"No, you don't understand. It sounded like they were in trouble and needed help. I…I think it was Dawn."

"So…she's having car trouble or something? Did she tell you what she needed help with?"

"No." I squeeze my hands together. "She just said 'help me' and hung up."

"Oh." The expression on his face betrays a distinct lack of concern. He doesn't look even the slightest bit worried. "Well, just call her back and ask what she needs help with."

"I have. She's not picking up."

He shrugs. "I'm sure she's fine. What could have happened?"

17

"I don't know." I start to bite on my thumbnail—an old bad habit when I'm nervous—but I stop myself. I spent a lot on this French manicure, and the last thing I want to do is wreck it. "Maybe she was in an accident."

"Let me give her a call."

My shoulders relax slightly as Seth picks his cell phone off his desk and scrolls through the numbers. Now that I can see his hands, I notice the wedding band he always wears on his left fourth finger is gone. Recently gone—there's a visible tan line. My eyes stray to the photograph he always keeps on his desk of him and his wife, Melinda, but that's gone too.

Hmm. That's interesting.

I'm itching to ask Seth about the missing ring and picture of his wife. But it's none of my business. He's my boss, after all. And there are more pressing problems at the moment.

Seth places the call and we both wait while it presumably rings on the other line. After a few seconds, I can hear the muted sound of Dawn's voicemail message. Seth drums his fingers against his desk as he waits for her irritatingly long voicemail message to run.

"Hey, Dawn," Seth says. "We haven't seen you at work today, and I wanted to know what's going on. Is everything okay? Give me a call as soon as you can." He disconnects the call and places his phone down on his desk. "Not picking up. But she'll call back."

"Oh."

"You know what?" He snaps his fingers. "I just remembered—Dawn and I were supposed to have a meeting today at two. She made a big thing out of how she needed an appointment and it was so important."

"Important?" My stomach flutters, remembering the similar email she sent to me. *A matter of great importance.* It must have been at least a *bit* of a big deal if she scheduled a meeting with the boss about it. "What was so important?"

"No clue. Probably something ridiculous, knowing Dawn." He cracks what feels like a very inappropriate smile, given the circumstances. "Anyway, she made such a big deal out of it, so I'm sure she'll show up at two to talk to me."

I shift my weight between my bright red Louboutins. I always wear heels, and red is my favorite color for shoes, but these are pinching my toes like crazy. I should've gotten a size 8. "Maybe we should call the police?"

"Call the police?" Seth blinks at me. "Are you *serious*? She's an hour late to work and you want to call the *police*?"

"She called asking for help!" I remind him.

He blows air out between his pursed lips. "Are you sure it was even Dawn on the phone? Maybe it was a customer who needed help."

"It *wasn't* a customer."

"Are you sure?"

I start to say yes, but now he's got me questioning my own memory. I picked up the phone and the other person on the line said "help me." And they did sound upset. But then again, some customers do sound upset when they call. Is it possible that it wasn't Dawn calling, and it really was just a customer? And maybe they hung up when they heard my voice instead of hers?

"There are a hundred things that could've happened to her," he points out. "I don't think we need to call the police. They would laugh at us."

That could be true.

Seth's eyes soften. "Are you okay, Nat? You look kind of frazzled."

"Gee, thanks."

"I'm just saying. You've been working your butt off lately. Your sales have been through the roof, and you've been organizing this 5K. I don't even know how you have the time. You should relax a little."

The beginning of a lump forms in my throat. "I make time for things that are important."

"I know."

I swallow down the lump. "You're showing up to run on Saturday, right? I'm counting on you."

"I'll be there." He places a hand on his chest. "I promise. And don't worry—I bet anything Dawn will be in my office at two. She's always on time."

As soon as I get out of Seth's office, I return to my cubicle. That turtle figurine is still on my desk, staring up at me with its vacant black eyes. Seth's comment about how I look frazzled is still ringing in my ears, so I pull out my compact. Despite the expensive face cream I smeared over my cheeks this morning, my skin looks sallow. Usually, I have great skin. It's one of the things that helps me sell our product. But I didn't sleep well last night. And my blond hair looks uncharacteristically limp and lifeless.

I just can't stop thinking about that phone call... I can't stop hearing the frantic edge in the caller's voice.

Help me.

It didn't sound like somebody asking for customer assistance. It sounded like the cries of somebody who was truly in trouble.

But Seth is right. I can't call the police to report that my coworker is an hour late to work. I'm sure Dawn will show up to work soon. This is surely all a big misunderstanding.

CHAPTER 3

NINE MONTHS EARLIER

To: Mia Hodge
From: Dawn Schiff
Subject: Greetings

Dear Mia,

Today was my first day at my new job that I was telling you about.

I wish I could say it was easy, but you know me. You know I'm shy. I have that in common with turtles—they are naturally shy animals. Not to say that they don't have any personality, because they certainly do, but most turtles prefer to stay in their own environment. They don't want to be played with. And when faced with any kind of threat, their first reaction isn't to attack. It's to retract into their shells and hide. Sound familiar?

My life would be easier if I had a shell like a turtle does. Remember when you helped me build that shell out of cardboard boxes? I gathered the rocks at the park and we glued them onto the boxes together in my living room. It didn't look real, of course—we were only seven years old. But when I was having a bad day, I had a place to hide.

How long did that shell last? A week? Two? I just remember coming home one day and it was gone. My mother had dismantled it while I was at school and threw it in the trash. She ripped it to shreds so there was no chance of possibly reconstructing it. She said to me: *This is why you only have one friend, Dawn.*

As if I need another friend besides you. I just wish you didn't live across the entire country right now.

The closest thing I currently have to a shell is my round tortoiseshell glasses, which I purchased about a year ago. I don't think you've seen them. Don't worry—they're not made of real tortoise shells.

The company I'm working for is called Vixed. They sell natural vitamin supplements or some such items. I'm sure I'll learn more about it soon, although all I'm doing is accounting so it's not necessary to know the details of all their operations. I received a three-inch-thick packet in the mail about the company's products, although it was sadly lacking in data about their efficacy. Perhaps I could suggest some randomized controlled studies along those lines? I'm trying to think of ways to make myself more useful.

My new boss, Seth, took me around to meet everyone in the morning. I only met Seth once before today, when he interviewed me. When I met him, I got a good feeling about him. He's fortysomething, very friendly in a way that a turtle is definitely not, and he seemed as enthusiastic as he possibly could be about me coming to work as the company's accountant.

But today Seth seemed different. He was more charming the day we met—all smiles and excited about every little thing I had to say. Today, he seemed distracted. He rushed me around the office, not giving me a chance to remember anyone's name or do anything more than wave a quick hello. He looked at his watch five times while taking me around. Also, when I asked him questions, he didn't seem to know many of the answers. It was rather disappointing.

For example, I asked him how often the refrigerator was cleaned. He looked surprised. So I explained to him that many bacteria such as listeria can easily grow at cold temperatures. I had quite a lot of data on it, but when I tried to share this data with Seth, he didn't seem to be interested. He just mumbled something about asking the janitorial staff. Then he said, "Jesus, Dawn."

I was beginning to feel like Seth was annoyed at me because that's what my father always used to say when I would do something to annoy him. *Jesus, Dawn*. He said it a lot. Practically every day.

The last stop on our tour was my cubicle. At my last job, I had my own office, although it was tiny and didn't have a window. Still, that was preferable to this tiny cubicle. There isn't anywhere to hide in a cubicle. Also, the chair they provided me didn't look very comfortable. It did not have adequate lumbar support. I'll have to ask Seth about alternate seating options.

Seth introduced me to the woman working in the cubicle next to mine. I'm glad he did, because I have trouble introducing myself to people. I always feel awkward about it, and then if I wait too long, it's too late. You can't introduce yourself to somebody when you've been working with them for a month. So I was happy that Seth did the introductions.

He told me her name is Natalie. And she's our best salesperson. He told me if there was anything I needed to know, Natalie would be the person to ask.

I committed her name to memory. *Natalie, Natalie, Natalie.* She was wearing headphones with a microphone attached, but she pulled it off for the introductions. She even stood up, teetering on a pair of striking red pumps that neither of us would ever even consider wearing. She's about our age, maybe 30, and extremely pretty. The thing I liked best about her was her hair. It was yellow, like the color of corn silk, and went all the way down to the middle of her back. It looked so soft and silky, I almost wanted to reach out and run my fingers through it.

Remember when I reached out to touch Becky Doyle's hair, and she scratched my face so badly, I had a red mark there for months? Now I know better.

Instead, I touched my own hair. That wasn't nearly as satisfying. My hair is the same dull brown color it's always been, and these days, I've been keeping it cropped close to my head. I'll have to attach a photo. But even if I had long hair, it wouldn't be soft and silky like Natalie's, and the truth is, I don't like the way my hair feels on the back of my neck. It makes my skin crawl, which is why I keep it so short.

Natalie gave me a huge hi. Her smile made her look even prettier. She said, "Welcome to Vixed!"

She had a nice smile. A friendly smile. She also

25

had a very pretty voice. She sounded like she could be a singer or do voice-overs. Natalie seemed like a really sweet person. She was the first person today who didn't make me feel like hiding in my nonexistent shell.

I could tell from the way Seth was looking at her that he likes her a lot too. She must be excellent at her job.

Natalie gushed about how much I'm going to love working at Vixed. And the more she talked about it, the better I felt.

I really like Natalie. In my whole life, you're the only person I've ever clicked with, and believe me, I know I'll never be close to Natalie the way I'm close to you, but it would be nice to have a casual friend to have a cup of coffee with or have dinner with after work. You always said I should try to make more friends, so I'm trying. I really am.

Sincerely,
Dawn Schiff

To: Dawn Schiff
From: Mia Hodge
Subject: Re: Greetings

First off, congratulations on your new job! I know making friends is hard, but this Natalie woman seems really nice. Just remember to be yourself, okay?

XXO
Mia

CHAPTER 4

PRESENT DAY

NATALIE

"Natalie, I just want you to know, I love your products."
I've got Carmen Salinas on the phone from Happy Healthy, a local wellness store in Quincy. Even though her store is tiny, she's a valuable customer. I do whatever I can to give her discounts on products because full price is hard for her.

"I'm so glad," I say.

"Collahealth is the best," Carmen continues. "I've been using it myself the last few weeks, and I swear to God, I look ten years younger!"

"I know!" I say. "I think it's absolutely a miracle. I wouldn't go a day without using it!"

"Me either!"

Collahealth is our newest product, which is a capsule containing a special formulation of collagen. I swear, this stuff is magic. I barely even have to sell it. It sells itself.

Actually, that's not entirely true. I still have to work pretty hard.

"So you'd like another box then?" I ask.

"Make it two!"

I scribble down the details for the sale and arrange for another box to be sent to Carmen's store. All the while, the little turtle figurine stares up at me. I rubbed off a little more of that dark red material that was adhering to its surface. If it really was a gift from Dawn, I'm surprised she wouldn't have cleaned it off. She's obsessed with cleanliness. I'm tempted to toss it in the trash bin, but if it was a gift from Dawn, I don't want her to be offended and think I don't like it.

Except I *don't* like it. It gives me the creeps. And what on earth was that dark red material that stained my fingers? It almost looks like…

Like blood.

Ugh, I can't let my imagination run away from me. There is *not* a blood-stained turtle figurine on my desk. It's probably just…I don't know, paint that rubbed off from some other figurine that was packed with it. That makes way, way more sense than blood.

Still, the turtle is creeping me out.

Finally, I nudge the turtle with my pinkie over to the corner of my desk and turn it so that it's looking away from me, at the wall of my cubicle. There—that's better.

It's almost noon, and Dawn still hasn't shown up at work. I've called her two more times. Sent yet another text message. I don't know what to do. She mentioned her mother lives out in Beverly, but I don't know how to contact her. Steve in HR probably has the number. I don't know if he's allowed to give it out, but I'm sure I could charm him into handing it over. But am I overreacting? Dawn is a few hours late to work. But there was that urgent email from her yesterday—she was upset enough about something to contact both me and her boss about "a matter of great importance." And then that strange phone call…

Help me.

At the time, I thought she sounded hysterical. But now that several hours have passed, I'm not so sure anymore. Maybe Dawn is fine. Maybe it was just a customer on the phone. And she's got that meeting with Seth at two, so I'm sure she'll turn up by then.

Anyway, I can't think about this right now. I've got a podcast interview in fifteen minutes that I've been preparing for all week.

After I hang up with Carmen, I grab my personal laptop that I brought with me to work this morning and head for the conference room. Just as I'm exiting my cubicle, I run smack into Caleb McCullough, who was coming to see me.

"Hey, Nat. Lunch?"

Caleb is his usual slightly rumpled but incredibly cute self. Caleb never wears a tie, and I don't think that white dress shirt has ever seen the hot end of an iron, but it's not like he's in sales and has to deal with people. Seth hired Caleb a few months ago to work on updating our website and setting it up to drive sales through the website itself. He comes to the office a couple of days a week and usually works in an empty cubicle.

Also, we've been dating for nearly two months.

"I'm kind of busy." I smile apologetically. "I've got that podcast interview in fifteen minutes."

"Oh, right." Caleb nods. "Good luck with that. You'll be great."

29

He smiles at me when he wishes me good luck. Caleb is just slightly above average in looks—tall and lanky with baggy eyes—but when he smiles, it transforms him. He is movie star-level handsome when he smiles. The first time he smiled at me, I was gone.

But in the last (almost) two months, I have discovered a lot of other qualities about Caleb that I adore, besides his dazzling smile. He's a hard worker, a whiz at computers, funny as hell, and most importantly, he's a good guy. Whatever else you can fake, it's hard to fake being a genuinely kind person. It's also exceedingly rare.

Although what I like best about Caleb is the way he looks at me. Like he can't quite believe his luck.

I've dated a lot of guys in my life. Too many, probably. And my last relationship was a complete disaster that made me seriously worry for my safety. But for the first time in thirty years, I feel like I might have met *the one*. We've only been together for a short time, but sometimes you don't need long to know. My grandparents dated for only one month before getting engaged. And they were married for sixty years.

Not that Caleb and I are getting engaged any time soon. I mean, we haven't even slept together yet. But I could see it happening. I could see myself spending my life with this man. And I'm ready to make that kind of commitment. Caleb is ready too. His father died when he was young, and it's made him eager to start a family. He told me he's just waiting for the right woman—*hint, hint*.

So I allow Caleb to pull me closer to him, pressing his lips against mine under the flickering fluorescent lights. It's an office kiss, but it's enough to make me tingle down to my toes. Sometimes the most chaste kisses are the sexiest ones.

"I had a great time last night," I murmur.

He beams at me. "Me too. You have no idea."

Caleb came over for dinner last night at my place. I ordered in Chinese food, and then we had a pretty steamy make-out session. But he was a total gentleman and didn't push me to go further or spend the night. Which was pretty classy, considering I absolutely would have said yes if he did. Caleb is *respectful*. It's another rare quality.

Even though I was a *little* sad when he went home at only 9:30.

"Hey," I say to him. "You haven't seen Dawn today, have you?"

"Who?"

"The woman in the cubicle next to mine." He's still looking at me blankly, so I add, "The one with the really short hair—like a military cut? Really into turtles?"

"Oh." He snaps his fingers—everybody knows about Dawn and her turtles. "Right. No, I haven't. Why?"

I consider telling him about Dawn being late this morning and the strange phone call. But I'm trying to show him my best side at this point in our relationship, and I don't want him to think I'm a worrywart. Plus I'm going to be late for my podcast interview.

"Nothing," I say. "Never mind."

He reaches for my hand and laces his fingers through mine. Then he gives me a squeeze. "Knock 'em dead, Nat."

"I'll do my best." Before I forget, I reach into the box of T-shirts and pull out an extra large that I earmarked for him. "Here's your T-shirt for Saturday, by the way."

I hold it up against his chest to make sure it's the right size. Caleb is tall, but it doesn't look like the shirt will be too short on him. It looks perfect.

"Appreciate it," he says. "I can't wait to run circles around you."

I smack him playfully on the shoulder. "You wish. I've been training."

"And I'm just *naturally* great at running."

I laugh, and he winks at me as he tugs the T-shirt out of my grip and then returns to his workstation. I truly wish I could go to lunch with him today. I've been feeling strung out all morning after that strange phone call, and it would be nice to go out for a bit and forget my troubles. But I've got to do this interview. It's really important.

When I get to the conference room, I take out my compact from my purse and give myself a once-over before starting the interview. I realize it's ridiculous to worry about how I look for a podcast interview, but I always feel more confident when I know that I look good. Sure enough, my lipstick is still intact from this morning, my mascara isn't caked in the corner of my eye, and my skin looks pinker and healthier than this morning.

I angle the compact to get a quick look at my hair—my roots are starting to show. For my entire childhood, I had perfect golden blond hair, then sometime during my early twenties, it evolved into this washed-out dirty blond color. But it's nothing a trip to the salon won't fix—Magda works wonders. I hope I have time to go before the race on Saturday.

Just as I'm shoving my compact back in my purse,

the call pops up on my laptop. The name flashing on the screen is Sherri Bell. I connect the call and plaster a smile on my face, even though Sherri can't see me. Again, it doesn't matter. When you're smiling, people can hear it in your voice. I always smile during my sales calls—*smile before you dial.*

"Natalie!" Sherri sounds like she's smiling too. She has a great voice. Very perky, like the girl next door. "Are you ready?"

"So ready," I say.

I've done several podcast interviews in the past, so I feel relatively experienced with them. Usually, I find a quiet place to set up, like the conference room, and I invested in a decent mic so listeners can actually hear me. This is the fifth podcast interview I've done to promote my 5K, so I shouldn't be nervous at all.

But something about this entire day is making me edgy.

"Today we have Natalie Farrell joining us," Sherri's voice pipes up through the speakers. "Natalie has organized a 5K run this Saturday to benefit a foundation doing research in cerebral palsy."

"That's right, Sherri."

"Now, Natalie, I hear you have quite a few people participating in this charity run?"

I clear my throat. The key to talking on podcasts is not to go on too long. You want it to be a conversation, not a monologue. "Yes, that's right. I work at a fabulous company called Vixed, which sells nutritional supplements, and almost all my coworkers will be running, as well as many people in the community. We've raised a lot of money so far and are still soliciting donations."

"And this is not the first time you've done this, right?"

"It's my fifth time. And we have more people participating this year than any other year previously."

"Amazing." Sherri pauses. "Now tell me a little bit about this charity. I hear it's very meaningful to you."

I am vaguely aware that Sherri has asked me a question and I need to answer it, but something has distracted me. Before starting the podcast, I put my phone on silent and placed it on the conference table next to my laptop. Now the phone is vibrating with an incoming call. I looked down at the screen—the call is from a blocked number.

Like this morning.

Help me.

"Natalie?" Sherri's voice startles me out of my distraction. "Are you okay?"

"Yes, yes." Thank God she can edit this prior to the broadcast. I'm desperate to take the call, but I recognize how incredibly rude it would be, so I let it go to voicemail. "Sorry about that. What was your question?"

"I was just wondering why this charity is so close to your heart."

"Well…" I close my eyes and take a deep breath. I always get choked up during this part, but at least it takes my mind off the mystery phone call. "My best friend growing up had cerebral palsy. She struggled with it a lot. Unfortunately, she's no longer with us. So this is in Amelia's honor."

"Oh my. I can hear how much you must miss her. I'm sure she's looking down on you and grateful for what a good friend you were and still continue to be."

"Yes. I…I hope so."

I take another deep breath, struggling to get my composure back. It's hard to talk about Amelia, but she's the reason I'm doing this. That always needs to be said.

We spend the next fifteen minutes talking more about the charity itself and the details of the run. This Saturday is promising to be a beautiful day, and we're going to have a great showing at Florian Hall, which is the start and the end point of the run.

I expect it will go off without a hitch.

CHAPTER 5

One thing I love about my job is that I'm not stuck in the office all day. I would lose my mind if I had to spend nine to five in that cubicle Monday through Friday. But fortunately, Seth allows me to travel to vitamin and health stores in the greater Boston area, because he knows that the personal touch can help to make sales.

Soon after a quick sandwich in the office, I travel to a sales call at a nutritional store in Quincy. Quincy is a commuter town on the transit system's Red Line, largely made up of an eclectic mix of people who want to live near the city but can't afford to pay the steep Boston housing prices. And it has an amazing Chinatown, where I could seriously eat dinner every single night.

There are also a large number of vitamin stores, and by now I have sold products to nearly every single one of them. I like to think of myself as Quincy's official Vixed girl. Today I visited one of the stores I've never made a sale with in the past, but I managed to leave with an order for three boxes of our products. And the owner informed me that if they sold well, he would be requesting more.

As I climb back into my car with the paperwork for the new orders, I check my phone. There's a text message waiting for me from my mother:

Coming to dinner Sunday night?

My mother invites me to Sunday night dinner well in advance nearly every weekend. It's a bit of a tradition in our family. She told me once that she (not so) secretly hopes one day I will show up with a serious boyfriend, but unfortunately, I have not yet dated a guy who is worthy of the Sunday night dinner. After all, whoever I bring is going to get grilled like crazy.

But for the first time, I consider inviting a guest this Sunday: Caleb. I really feel like he could be the guy. At the very least, he could withstand my mother's incessant questioning. And if I invited him, he would say yes.

I type into the phone:

I'm bringing...

Before I can type the rest of that sentence, I rethink it. What Caleb and I have is great, but it's still very early. I don't know if I want to subject him to my mother yet. And if things don't work out, I'll never hear the end of it. *What happened to that nice Caleb? Why wasn't this one good enough for you?* So I revise my text:

I'm bringing salad.

Bringing salad is a much smarter choice than bringing Caleb. After all, my mother only cooks greasy, fatty meals.

I scroll through the messages on my phone. I checked my voicemails right after my podcast, but the blocked caller didn't leave a message. And now it's nearly 3:00, and there has still been no word from Dawn. She is the kind of person who always responds to text messages within five seconds, so no response the entire day is extremely strange. I shoot off a quick message to Seth:

Did Dawn show up for your meeting at 2?

Immediately, those little bubbles appear on the screen. A second later, his response pops up:

No. I guess she forgot.

Dawn—forget a meeting? That seems highly unlikely. Although now that I think about it, there were a few meetings a bit ago where she showed up just when the meeting was ending and seemed confused when she realized she was an hour late. But that problem resolved itself, and lately, Dawn has been back to her almost scarily prompt self. In fact, if Dawn appeared even a millisecond after the scheduled start time for a meeting, I would faint dead away from shock.

And of course, there was her request to meet with me as well, about that "matter of great importance." And in a very uncharacteristic fashion, she left early and blew me off. And then that phone call this morning...

Help me.

This is not like her at all. Something is wrong. I *know* it. Maybe everyone else at the office blew it off, but they didn't hear the way Dawn sounded on that phone call. She's in trouble.

It hits me that Dawn lives in Quincy. Not so far from here, if I recall correctly. I picked her up once when her car was being repaired. She was going on and on about how she didn't know how she was going to get to work, so I volunteered to chauffeur her back and forth, thinking we might get to know each other better, although it didn't work out that way. She mostly talked about turtles the whole time, even when I tried to press her for details about her life.

In any case, the address is still stored somewhere in my brain. She lives at…

Lake Street? Was that it?

No. *Lark* Street. Like the bird.

I enter Lark Street into my GPS, and it's a tiny street not far from Quincy Center and my absolute favorite hot pot sushi bar. It's less than ten minutes away from here. I don't remember her house number, but the street is small enough that if I drive there, I'll probably recognize it. And then I can make sure she's okay.

Before I can change my mind, I click on "start" in my GPS, and a clipped British female voice instructs me to make a right at the next light. Even though I vaguely know where her house is, I don't dare travel anywhere without my GPS. The streets in the greater Boston area simply don't make sense. In some parts of the country, you can turn three corners and be back where you started. Around here, you turn three corners and you're hopelessly lost.

Seven minutes later, my GPS directs me to make a right turn onto Lark Street. *Your destination is on the right.* Of course, I don't know what house it is. But if I drive slowly, I should be able to figure it out. It was sort of an off-yellow color with light blue trim, just one story high, with a small but well-groomed front yard.

The houses on the street are all relatively small, single-family houses. I rent out a town house in Dorchester—surprisingly tiny given the steep rent, although it's two stories high. Dawn is far enough from the center of town that she probably pays less in rent than I do.

When I get about halfway down the street, I hit the brakes. There's a car parked in the driveway that looks exactly like the one I've seen Dawn climb into at the end of the day. A green Honda Civic.

It's the color of a turtle.

I turn my head to the right, and that's when I see it. The off-yellow house with the blue trim. Dawn's house.

I pull over outside her house. There are several windows in the front of the house, and all of them are dark. I don't see Dawn's silhouette in the window or any other indication that she might be home. But I also don't see any broken windows or signs that something terrible has happened.

I kill the engine and sit in my car for a moment, debating what to do. Dawn and I aren't exactly best friends. But I get the feeling Dawn doesn't have any real friends. All she's got is her elderly mother, who lives all the way up north of Boston. If something has happened to her, if she's hurt or sick, it could be days before anyone discovers what's wrong. And by then, it could be too late.

Help me.

Screw it. I'm getting out of the car.

I step out of my Hyundai, smoothing out the creases in my cream-colored skirt. Dawn always tells me how much she admires the way I dress. It's funny, because she always dresses in a very understated way. She has very delicate facial features—a button nose and giant brown eyes that take up half her face—as well as a trim figure, and if she wanted, she could be a knockout. But instead, she dresses in shapeless blouses and slacks that are at least a size too big for her. She keeps her brown hair hacked off about half an inch from her skull—too short to even be called a cute pixie cut. I've offered her some fashion advice, but she never seemed interested.

Honestly, if you weren't talking about turtles, it was hard to get Dawn to talk about much at all.

My red heels clack against the walkway as I make my way to the front door. I push my thumb against the door-bell, and chimes resonate inside the house. And then I wait.

No answer.

Not only is nobody answering, but I don't hear anything from inside the house. No footsteps. No vacuum drowning out the sound of the doorbell. Nothing. It's dead silent.

I ring the doorbell again, but it's no different the second time. It's obvious that nobody is going to answer the door.

I pull my phone out of my purse one more time, double-checking that Dawn never contacted me. She didn't. There's another text from Seth, but that's it.

The welcome mat below my feet is an image of two turtles swimming side by side, holding hands. Between their bodies is scrawled the word "welcome." I step off the mat and flip it over, hoping there might be a spare key underneath. No luck.

I check both ways down the block to see if anyone is watching me. Dawn's neighborhood seems pretty quiet. If something did happen here, there would be zero witnesses. I crane my neck and notice a path along the side of the house. I bet there's a back door.

I follow the path, which leads to Dawn's tiny backyard. I can see the back of her house as well as her screen door. This would probably look suspicious if anyone were watching me, but I don't think anyone is. Anyway, I'm not doing anything wrong—I'm just a concerned coworker. I don't exactly look like a burglar in my short skirt and red pumps.

I try the screen door, and it swings open. Then I put my hand on the doorknob to the back door. It feels cold in my palm, but it turns easily. The back door is unlocked.

I hesitate as I carefully push the back door open. It was one thing to go to Dawn's house and ring her doorbell. It's another thing entirely to enter her house without her permission. Everyone knows Dawn is a bit strange. What if she's sitting in the living room with a gun? Technically, I'm intruding. She could shoot me and she would be completely within her rights.

Then again, I can't imagine harmless little Dawn Schiff sitting in her living room with a sawed-off shotgun. And I can't shake the sense that she's in trouble. I have to check it out—she might need my help. And it's not like I could call the police. They're not going to come running over here because a grown woman won't open her door.

Please don't shoot me, Dawn.

"Dawn?" I call out as I enter her kitchen through the back. "Dawn, it's Natalie! From work?"

No answer.

Dawn's kitchen is extremely tidy. I'm not surprised exactly, but I wouldn't have been completely shocked to find out that Dawn was some kind of crazy hoarder with dirty dishes and old newspapers stacked up to the ceiling. I have to admit, Kim and I hypothesized about it a couple of times. But this kitchen is pretty normal looking. Could be anyone's kitchen. Well, except for the turtle salt and pepper shakers.

The kitchen itself seems normal, but there's something else disturbing about it.

There's a bottle of wine on the counter. Red wine, filled about halfway, still uncorked. There's also a wineglass on the counter, with a residue of red liquid at the bottom of the glass. And then there's a second glass. Except this one is shattered on the floor.

I may not be Dawn's best friend, but I know her well enough to know that she wouldn't leave a bottle of wine uncorked on her kitchen counter. And she definitely wouldn't leave broken glass on the floor.

I was right. Something terrible has happened here.

I walk slowly across the kitchen. As much as I want to find Dawn and help her, I'm scared there could be an intruder in the house. Well, *another* intruder. Whatever happened to Dawn, I don't want it to happen to me as well. I've got to be careful.

So that's why when I pass the block of knives on her kitchen counter, I pull one of them out. Better safe than sorry.

My fingers are bloodless, wrapped around the handle of the knife. I push open the door to the dark living room, and the first thing that hits me is a strange smell. It's not something rotting or anything like that. It's almost like…wet seaweed.

Before I can spend another second wondering about the strange smell, I catch sight of the giant tank filled with water. It's a fish tank, illuminated by a glow from within, but I don't see any fish inside. I lower my head to peer into the water.

It's a turtle.

An ordinary turtle, about the size of my hand, swimming around in this giant tank. Well, it's not so much swimming as much as sitting perched on a rock, its dark green shell glistening as it stares at me. I've never had any strong feelings toward turtles, one way or the other, but this turtle is unnerving me. I want to snap at it to stop staring. It's *rude*.

Turtles just don't have any manners, apparently.

"Dawn?" I call out again.

No answer. Where is she, dammit?

Next to the turtle tank, there's a large bookshelf. The room is dark, but I can still make out the contents. I always thought Dawn had a lot of turtles in her cubicle at work, but I was wrong. I didn't know what *a lot of turtles* meant until I saw this bookshelf.

Every single shelf is *bursting* with turtle figurines. Turtles, turtles, turtles. Glass, ceramic, marble, even stuffed turtles. Every single inch of the bookcase bears the likeness of a turtle, except for one bare space in the middle of the second-highest shelf.

Something about that bookcase makes my skin crawl.

I take a step back, but I nearly trip over an unfortunately placed ottoman. I look down—the ottoman has been overturned.

But I didn't knock it over. It was toppled over like that already.

That's when I notice the chair overturned, lying on the floor. I creep closer, squinting into the darkness. And then I see what's on the carpet.

And I scream.

CHAPTER 6

To: Vixed Employees
From: Natalie Farrell
Subject: Welcome party!

I hope everyone will give a wonderful welcome to our newest employee, Dawn Schiff! She's replacing Edgar Hines as our new accountant, so she has some big shoes to fill, but I can tell already that she will do an amazing job. I brought some refreshments to have in the break room at 3 as a welcome to the newest member of the Vixed family.

Please join us!
Natalie

To: Mia Hodge
From: Dawn Schiff
Subject: Re: Greetings

Dear Mia,

This week, I decorated my cubicle. I wanted to do something similar to what Natalie has because I love her sense of style. She has a plant growing in a pot in her cubicle, with pretty purple flowers, which I noticed her watering every day. I asked her about it yesterday, and she said it was an iris plant.

So yesterday, I went to the grocery store after work and I bought an iris plant just like Natalie's.

I know what you're thinking. You always said I shouldn't try to be like other, more popular girls. I should just be myself, yadda yadda yadda. But I didn't do exactly what Natalie did—I added my own unique touch. I decorated the plant with some of my turtles from home. I don't mean real turtles, of course. I have a bunch of glass turtles in different shapes and sizes and even colors, although it isn't really biologically accurate.

I put one of the turtles in the soil next to the flowering iris. Then I surrounded the pot with a few more turtles. I also have a turtle mouse pad that I brought in for myself—it's a photograph of a sea turtle swimming through the green-tinted ocean. Even though I still feel uncomfortable working in a new place, it made me feel better to have my turtles with me.

Natalie has made me feel welcome though. She has been so sweet. At the end of my first week, she threw a little welcome party for me in the break room with refreshments and everything! Well, the refreshments were just a bag of Doritos and a bottle of diet cola, but it was still very nice of her. I don't know if anyone has ever thrown me a party before in my entire life.

You always asked me why I never had birthday parties as a child or allowed you to make me one, and I was afraid to tell you. Well, here's my confession. When I turned five years old, my mother threw me a large birthday party in our house, inviting every child in our preschool class. But the children wouldn't stop playing with my stuff, and I started screaming, threw my beautiful vanilla frosted cake on the floor, and then locked myself in my bedroom and refused to come out. After that, I was too traumatized to ever want a party again, and my parents weren't excited to make me one.

I always preferred to have a private party with just you and me. Remember when we made that cake together, including our own buttercream frosting made entirely from scratch? Except we accidentally used double the butter and the buttercream frosting tasted like pure butter, and the cake was underbaked. We still ate it all though, and it was better than any party with a bunch of kids from school.

But Natalie's party was nice. Even though I dislike Doritos. And diet cola.

There's a café downstairs where a lot of people purchase their lunches, but I bring my lunch every day and store it in the refrigerator, although I strongly suspect nobody is cleaning it on a regular basis. I suggested to Seth that I could create a schedule for people to alternate cleaning days and post the schedule on the refrigerator door. He told me he would think about it. That was a week ago, and he hasn't given me an answer. Maybe I'll ask him about it again later today.

Today my lunch was white. Yes, I still prefer monochromatic meals. I can't explain why. I just feel uncomfortable when, say, I'm eating a sandwich that is mostly white and then there's this big hunk of green lettuce in it. Not to say I won't eat it, but I would prefer the sandwich was all one color. You're the only person in the world who didn't judge me for it. Remember how in the cafeteria at school, the other kids would play a game to try to squirt some ketchup or mustard onto my lunch to ruin the color integrity of it?

I've been eating lunch every day at approximately 11:40, give or take sixty seconds. I walk to the break room, retrieve my sandwich from the refrigerator, and then I fill up my mug with cold water from the filter. I was just sitting down to eat when Natalie and Kim came into the break room with their lunches (salads) in identical Tupperware containers.

Natalie and Kim spend a lot of time together. You don't have to ever worry about me becoming best friends with Natalie (as if anyone could ever replace you!), because Kim appears to have filled that role. Kim recently got engaged, which I know because Kim keeps coming over to Natalie's cubicle and then they talk about wedding planning for an hour or longer. Sometimes I consider joining in the conversation, but I don't know anything about wedding planning so I have little to offer. I wish they would ask my opinion on one of the dresses in the magazines Kim brings to show Natalie, but so far, they haven't. But today they asked if they could join me, and of course, I said yes.

In general, I prefer to eat by myself, but this was a good way to get to know Natalie better. And Kim as well. Maybe all three of us could be friends together. In school, it was always just you and me, and I know you said that was all we needed, but three people can be friends. That's allowed.

Kim asked me if I liked working here. I told them it was fine. I didn't want to tell them that the previous accountant left everything an indecipherable mess. I have had to sort through everything from scratch. But I don't even know that man, so it wouldn't be nice to talk about what a shockingly terrible job he did.

"I could never be an accountant," Natalie said. She flipped that silky blond hair over her shoulder, then she started talking about how bad she was at math, how she was always just barely passing her classes by the skin of her teeth.

I didn't want Natalie to get too down on herself, so I pointed out that Natalie is very good at sales. My mother always taught me that paying people compliments is a good way to make friends. I never used to listen to her, but now I realize she was probably right. And since I have a chance for a fresh start, why not take it?

And anyway, the compliment was true. I haven't been here long, but I already know Natalie is one of the top salespeople. The best at the company, according to the spreadsheets. She's extremely skilled at talking to people. I hear her on the phone sometimes, and I'll pause what I'm doing and just listen to her tap dance.

Kim started giggling and said, "Nat could sell ice at the North Pole. Especially to a *man*."

That comment resulted in Natalie and Kim

bursting into giggles. I guess they meant that Natalie is so attractive. There's a sales intern who is about 25 years old, and he always asks Natalie if he can get her something for lunch, but he never asks anyone else—and I'm fairly sure he doesn't make her pay for it. Kim is sort of pretty too, but she doesn't quite have the same indescribable quality as Natalie does.

Then Natalie paid *me* a compliment. "Cute mug," she said.

So guess which mug she was talking about? It's the one you gave me years ago, as a birthday gift. A lot of people will go into a store and buy the first thing they see—usually a candle—but you always put a lot of thought into every gift. This is the ceramic mug that is painted the color of the ocean, with the three-dimensional turtle swimming through it. Sometimes I like to run my fingers over the bump of the turtle shell. I can't even tell you how much I love that mug, and every time I drink from it, I think of you and get a happy feeling.

Natalie's words felt like a genuine compliment. Sometimes when people say nice things to me, it's clear they don't really mean it. Sometimes it almost feels like they're making fun of me. But Natalie meant it. For a moment, I was sitting at the cool table in high school.

So I thanked her. Then I asked the most import-ant question of all: "Do you like turtles?"

Natalie said she did. Then I explained that the turtle's shell is actually part of its skeleton. That it's a bit like a rib cage, which is why turtles can't be separated from their shells. Not without killing them. When I told her that, Natalie said, "Wow."

I felt so excited that Natalie and Kim were interested in learning more about turtles. You're the only one I've ever met who has been interested in hearing turtle facts, and that includes my parents. And honestly, there were times when I wasn't sure if even you wanted to hear about turtles. But me and Natalie and Kim ate together for the next 20 minutes, and I told them a lot of other interesting facts about turtles. They both listened to everything I had to say, and they even asked some questions that I of course was able to answer easily because I know so much about turtles.

There's a lot more I could have told them, but then Natalie said she had to get to a sales call, so they both had to leave. I'm already planning out some new interesting things about turtles that I can talk to them about tomorrow. I'll let you know how it goes.

Sincerely,
Dawn Schiff

To: Dawn Schiff
From: Mia Hodge
Subject: Re: Greetings

Yay for new friends! Speaking of turtles, I've got a present I'm sending you! It sounds like you're totally fitting in though. I knew you would!

XXO
Mia

CHAPTER 7

PRESENT DAY

NATALIE

I screamed for about a minute.

That's my estimate. Based on about how long it felt and also how much my throat feels scratchy right now. I screamed for a full minute, then I managed to get it together enough to dial 911 with shaking hands.

Needless to say, I got the hell out of that house.

Now the police are here. They are swarming around the house, dusting for fingerprints or whatever else policemen do at a crime scene. I don't want to know. I've been sitting in my car since they got here. I'm not supposed to leave, but I don't want to go anywhere near that house again.

I called Seth to let him know what was going on and that I wouldn't be back at work. He sounded rattled, but that's nothing compared to how I feel. I usually tell Kim everything, but I didn't want to tell her about this. She'd just treat it like interesting gossip, which would be disrespectful. So instead, I text Caleb. He'll say the right thing—I know it.

Sure enough, I get a text back right away:

Holy crap! Are you okay?
  Not really.

I'll be reliving what I saw in that living room until the day I die. All that blood...

Do you want me to come over there?

I've been trying so hard not to be a clingy girlfriend. Nothing is a bigger turnoff. But Caleb doesn't seem like the kind of guy who obsesses over something like that. And he *offered*. Plus, I want to see him. I want to bury my face in his chest. So I reply:

Yes please.

Just as I'm texting him the address, I am interrupted by the sound of tapping at the window of my car—there's a man at the driver's side window. He's wearing a dark gray suit and tie, and I remember him briefly introducing himself as a detective before I went to hide in the car. I roll down the window.

"Miss Farrell?" he says.

"Yes."

"I gotta talk to you. Can you get out of the car please?"

One of the uniformed police officers asked me a few questions before I ran out here. I suppose the detective has a bunch more questions. And maybe some answers, I'm hoping. Anyway, I don't have much of a choice, so I climb out of my car.

The detective is in his forties, tall and attractive in a craggy sort of way, with dark hair receding just enough to be noticeable. "Detective Santoro," he says.

I nod wordlessly.

"Sorry I gotta do this, Miss Farrell," he says.

The detective has a heavy Boston accent. As somebody who grew up in Massachusetts, it's a comfort to hear it. When he told me to get out of the car, he said "caah." And if we were eating lobster for some reason, it would be "lobstah." I don't have much of an accent myself, although Caleb claims he hears it. He says it's cute.

"It's okay," I manage. "Is Dawn... Did you...find her?"

He shakes his head slowly, and I let out a sigh of relief. When I saw the massive amount of blood on her carpet, I was certain she was lying somewhere in the house dead. "No sign of her. Just the blood."

"So maybe." I bite down on my lower lip. Too hard—I taste a hint of blood myself. "Maybe she hurt herself. Got a ride to the hospital."

Santoro nods. "Yeah, we're checking out that possibility. Calling all the ambulance companies and hospitals. So far though, we're not finding her."

I'm not surprised, but it's still a blow. "I see."

"So why did you come to Miss Schiff's house?"

"Well, she was late to work..." As I'm saying it, I see the skeptical look on his face, so I quickly add, "Also, she sent me this weird email yesterday, telling me she needed to talk to me about something important." He still doesn't seem convinced, so I add the clincher. "Plus her phone started ringing on her desk, and when I picked it up, it sounded like she was asking for help. Like she was in trouble."

"I see. Did you hear anyone else on the line?"

I shake my head. "No. Just her voice."

"Did anyone else hear the phone call?"

That's a strange thing to ask. What does it matter if somebody else heard the phone call? "No, just me."

"So you and Miss Schiff were friends then?"

A gust of November wind goes through my blouse and I shiver. "Yes. We were coworkers and...friends."

"Close friends?"

"Sort of." It's not true, but Dawn didn't really have any friends. I'd believe it if somebody told me I was her closest friend.

"Do you know if there was anybody who was threatening her? Anyone she was afraid of?"

"No. Nothing like that."

"Does she have a boyfriend?"

I almost laugh at how ridiculous the question is, but of course, he doesn't know Dawn. I can't envision her having a boyfriend. I can't envision her even kissing a man. I'm almost 100 percent certain she's a virgin, and she gives off the vibe that she isn't interested in ever *not* being a virgin anymore. Like the way she always wears these shapeless work outfits that look tailored for a man, with giant tortoiseshell glasses that are too big for her narrow face. Never even a scrap of makeup.

But I would never say any of that to a detective. "No. She didn't have a boyfriend."

Detective Santoro gives me a funny look. It takes me a second to realize why. "I mean, she *doesn't* have a boyfriend."

Oh God, I just referred to her in the past tense. Dawn is going to be okay. They're going to find her and she'll be fine. No past tense. Present tense, all the way.

But there was *so* much blood. How could she be okay if there was so much blood? And that phone call…

Help me.

"When was the last time you saw Miss Schiff?" he asks.

"Around five o'clock yesterday," I say. "When I left work."

"And she didn't show up for work this morning?" I nod, although he seems to be asking the question rhetorically. He already knows this is true. "So if something happened to her between five o'clock yesterday and this morning at…"

"A quarter to nine," I supply. "That's when she always shows up at work. Like clockwork."

"She's wicked reliable, eh?"

"Oh yes."

One corner of the detective's lips quirks up. "I like that. I'm the same way. It's good to be punctual."

I very much doubt this detective is anything like Dawn, but I'm not going to say that. He won't understand what she's like.

"So I have to ask you," he says, "where were you between five o'clock yesterday and this morning?"

My eyebrows shoot up so fast, my forehead gets whiplash. "Me?"

His smile is apologetic. "I have to ask."

I try not to be too offended by the question. Except I don't know what they think I did. Do they think I killed Dawn, made up a phony call where she asked for help, then went back to her house and "pretended" to find all that blood on the floor?

"I was with my boyfriend," I finally say. "His name is Caleb McCullough."

"All night?"

I wasn't with Caleb all night. We were together for part of the night, then he left my house. I open my mouth to tell him that, but a nagging voice in the back of my head stops me. My fingerprints are all over Dawn's house now. The detective keeps giving me a funny look, like he doesn't quite believe me.

And there's one other thing nagging at me.

"That's right," I say. "I was with Caleb the whole night."

There. That should wipe the suspicious look off Santoro's face.

"And this Caleb," he says, "does he know Dawn too?"

I lift a shoulder. "A little. He's been doing some part-time work for a company we work for. So he knows her, but barely."

"And that phone call this morning... You said it came to the phone on her desk?"

"That's right." I get a sick feeling in my stomach thinking of how terrified Dawn sounded on that call. I'm so glad I didn't ignore it like Seth told me to.

He rubs his chin thoughtfully. "We'll see what calls were placed to that number. Find out where the call was coming from."

Wherever Dawn is, I hope they can track her down based on that phone call. If she's being held captive, she must've managed for a few seconds.

Detective Santoro grills me with a few other questions about how I knew where Dawn lived, how I got into the house, and also about the broken glass on the floor of the kitchen. Even though I'm still feeling awful, I at least feel like the investigation is in capable hands.

This detective knows what he's doing—I can tell how serious he is based on the fact that his eyes didn't stray south of my face while we were talking. He's going to find Dawn, wherever she is.

I hope she's okay.

Just as he's finishing up and about to go into the house, a uniformed police officer comes out the front door. He makes a beeline straight for the detective.

"Detective," the police officer says. "We got into the computer in her bedroom."

Santoro rubs his chin. "Oh yeah?"

"Yeah. It was password-protected, but she had the password written on a Post-it note under her mouse pad."

Despite everything, I can't help but let out a little snort. That is *so* Dawn. So incredibly careful about everything, yet careless about other things. I bet her password was something like "password1."

But snorting was probably the wrong thing to do. Detective Santoro gives me a look like I'm being inappropriate, and he's probably right. But like I said, he doesn't know Dawn the way I do.

"All right," he says. "Let's see what's in there."

"Do you still need me?" I ask.

"Nah, you're good." He waves his hand. "But do you got a business card or something?"

I reach into my purse and pull out one of my business cards (or "cahds," as he said it). As I pass it to the detective, I notice he takes it only with the tips of his fingers. It strikes me as a little odd, but I try not to get too paranoid.

The detective and the policeman disappear into the

house, leaving me alone. Good—I can finally get the hell out of here. I turn around to walk back to my car just as the slightly beat-up green Ford pulls up in front of the house next door.

Caleb. Thank God.

I sprint over to him as briskly as my too-tight Louboutins will allow me. Caleb is getting out of his car, and I throw myself into his arms before he can even get the door closed. I bury my face in his chest, the tears gathering in my eyes. This is the worst day ever.

"Hey." His large hand strokes the back of my head. "It's okay, Nat. I'm here."

"Something terrible happened to her," I murmur into his shirt. I'm probably getting tearstains and mascara all over him, but he doesn't seem to care.

"Don't say that." He squeezes me to his chest. "I bet she'll turn up."

I pull my face away from him to stare up at him. Even in my heels, he's nearly a head taller than me. I've always liked tall guys. "What are you basing that on?"

"Um…"

"Because if you saw how much blood was in her living room, you wouldn't be saying that."

"Look, I don't know." He offers a helpless shrug. "I just think the best we can do is hope she's okay. You know?"

I feel guilty for snapping at him. He didn't deserve that after running out here for me. "I'm sorry. I'm just so shaken by everything."

"Yeah," he breathes. "I know. It's awful."

I rest my head back against his chest. His heart thumps reassuringly in my ear. We remain that way for a good two minutes—me pressed against him, him gently stroking my hair. More points for Caleb—he's kind to me during a tragic event. This is taking our relationship to the next level.

"Hey," I say.

"Yeah?"

"I need you to do me a favor."

"You need a ride home?"

I would love a ride home. But my car is here, and there's no way I'm going to leave it here. So I have no choice but to get back in there and drive back through the treacherous rush-hour traffic. "No, that's okay."

"So what do you need? Anything you want."

I tuck a strand of hair behind my ear as I pull away from him. "I need you to tell the police we were together all night last night."

Caleb stiffens. "What?"

"It's so stupid." I shake my head. "The police were asking me where I was last night. Like I need an alibi or something. As if I could have done something to Dawn! It's just a formality, I'm sure. I was there, so they had to ask me. So anyway, I told them we were together all night last night."

"But..." He scratches his chin. "We *weren't* together all night last night. I left around 9:30."

"Well, so what? We were together most of the night. That's good enough."

"So that's what I'll tell them. That we were together most of the night and I left at 9:30."

I narrow my eyes at him. "Is it that big a deal? I mean, you work with Dawn too. It helps you also to have an alibi."

61

His eyebrows scrunch together. "But it's a lie."

"It's a white lie. Neither of us did anything to hurt Dawn. So it will just confuse the investigation if we don't have an alibi."

"I don't know, Nat." He rubs the back of his neck. "I don't feel right lying to the police. Why is it so important that we have alibis? They're not going to think either of us did anything to hurt her."

I fold my arms across my chest. "Right, but I already told him we were together. So if you don't go along with it, I look like I'm lying."

"But you *were* lying."

There is a stubborn tilt to his jaw that's pissing me off. Caleb is a decent, honest guy. I always thought that was a *good* quality. Now I'm realizing it's not necessarily a positive thing.

"Caleb…" The tears that had started to dry up spring back to my eyes. "This has been an awful day. Look, they're probably not even going to ask you. But would it really be so awful to go along with my story?" Hesitation is in his eyes, and I squeeze his arm. "Please?"

After what feels like an interminable pause, his shoulders sag. "Fine. I guess it's not that big a deal."

I'm surprised by the rush of relief I feel when Caleb agrees to confirm my story. I mean, it's not like I would be a murder suspect or something. But given everything, it's better to have an alibi.

CHAPTER 8

To: Etsy Seller
From: Dawn Schiff
Subject: Problem with turtle figurine

Dear seller,

I recently purchased a product from your Etsy store advertised as a glass sea turtle figurine. Unfortunately, the product was not a sea turtle, and I would like a full refund.

Sincerely,
Dawn Schiff

To: Dawn Schiff
From: Etsy Seller
Subject: Re: Problem with turtle figurine

I'm so sorry to hear that, and we would like to try to make this right for you! What is the product you received?

To: Etsy Seller
From: Dawn Schiff
Subject: Re: Problem with turtle figurine

Dear seller,

As I stated, the product was advertised to be a glass sea turtle figurine. Unfortunately, the turtle I received was quite obviously a land turtle! Sea turtles have flippers instead of legs, and the two front flippers are generally longer than the two back flippers, but the turtle I received had all four appendages of approximately equal length, and their legs did not in any way resemble flippers. Also, on the turtle I received, the head was slightly more circular rather than rectangular, which would indicate a land turtle as well. I am terribly disappointed, as I was hoping for a sea turtle, and I clearly received a land turtle.

Sincerely,
Dawn Schiff

To: Dawn Schiff
From: Etsy Seller
Subject: Re: Problem with turtle figurine

Is this a joke?

To: Mia Hodge
From: Dawn Schiff
Subject: Re: Greetings

Dear Mia,

Yesterday on my drive home, I stopped off at a store that sells assorted little tchotchkes and unusual items. Ordinarily, I visit this store to see if they have anything turtle related. The old man who owns the store is aware of what I am looking out for, so when I stop in, he will always tell me right away if he has anything I would appreciate. Last time, I purchased a hinged box in the shape of a turtle—the shell opened up and one could put their trinkets inside, but I just put the box on my bookshelf, empty.

Yesterday, Ernie grinned at me with his yellow teeth and brought out a small turtle sculpture, which he assured me was hand-painted. The pattern on the shell was painted in gold, and the turtle was smiling, despite the fact that a real turtle lacks the ability to smile. It was a little expensive, but I had to have it.

Ernie found a little white box and he gift wrapped the turtle inside the box because I did not purchase the turtle for me. This morning, I brought the gift with me to work.

I'm not sure why, but Natalie and Kim haven't come to meet me for lunch again in the break room. For the last couple of weeks, they have been going out to lunch. And they haven't invited me along, perhaps because I always bring my lunch. But I still really like Natalie, and I'm hopeful the two of us can be friends. A thoughtful gift might help things along.

I waited for Natalie to arrive in the morning. I always get in at 8:45, but Natalie is liable to show up anytime between then and 10 o'clock. Once she didn't show up until noon, but I assume she was on a sales call. When she arrived at 9:13, she stopped at Kim's cubicle and the two of them talked for about 20 minutes. When she finally got to her cubicle, I jumped out of my seat to greet her. She smiled when she saw me and said hi.

Right away, I thrust the gift-wrapped box in her direction because I was so excited to give it to her. She was surprised by my gift. I could tell by how big her blue eyes got. She didn't seem to understand why I bought her a gift, so I just explained that I saw it and thought of her.

Natalie hesitated for a moment, but then she accepted the box from me. She sat down, and as she leaned forward to work on the wrapping paper, I caught a whiff of her shampoo. It smelled like flowers. You know how much I hate strong smells, but some- how Natalie's scent didn't bother me.

When she got the box open, she slowly pulled out the turtle. She held it in her hand for a moment without saying anything. Then when she finally did say something, she said, "Oh."

I also mentioned to her that I hadn't brought my lunch today. I suggested that I could come to lunch with her and Kim so I could tell them more about tur- tles. But Natalie insisted that she and Kim would just be talking about boring sales stuff.

I tried to tell her I didn't mind. I find the sales aspect of the company interesting. Not to say I could ever do what Natalie and Kim do. I can't imagine how they get on the phone and call companies or individuals and try to convince them to buy our products. I don't know how you convince somebody they need a capsule filled with vitamins to make their eyes healthier, especially when there is absolutely no data whatsoever to prove any of the products work better than a placebo. I expect if I tried, the person on the other line would hang up on me.

"Plus Kim has all this wedding stuff we need to talk about," she explained.

They've been talking nonstop about wedding planning. I overheard that the wedding is at the end of September, which Natalie said was "perfect." I didn't understand how Natalie could help so much since she's never been married before though. I pointed that inconsistency out to Natalie now.

Her lips pressed tightly together when I asked the question so that her lipstick was nearly invisible. "You don't have to have been a bride to know how to plan a wedding. I've helped a lot of friends with their weddings. And when I get married, they'll help me."

"*If* you get married," I corrected her.

She looked surprised when I said that. I always have to remind myself that Natalie is not an accountant like I am. She isn't facile with numbers, by her own admission. This was a great opportunity to educate her and earn her friendship. I explained in detail how the older you get, the chances of getting married decrease significantly. Because as more people in your own age group get married, the dating pool decreases, so your odds of finding somebody suitable to marry continue to go down. Of course, you could still marry somebody significantly younger, but most women, on average, seek men who are their own age or older. And of course, most men are seeking women younger than they are. So given her current single status, Natalie is likely to never get married.

"That's silly," she said to me when I finished explaining it all as simply as I could.

I pointed out that she doesn't currently have a boyfriend or a fiancé. So at her age, it seemed preposterous to think that she'd ever get married. That's when Natalie told me she had to get back to work.

I got the feeling I had upset Natalie, which didn't make sense because I was just telling her facts. If you had been there, you would have gotten it. You're logical like I am. Natalie doesn't think the way we do, but I'd still like to be her friend.

I tried telling her a few other interesting things about turtles. For example, there are turtles out there that weigh 2000 pounds and can be 8 feet long. Of course, that's not the kind you find in the pet store. An example would be the leatherback turtle, which is the largest sea turtle species. But she didn't seem that interested, believe it or not.

Eventually, I went back to my own cubicle. I was glad I gave Natalie a present, and it did seem like she liked it a lot, but I was surprised at how bad her manners were. Even I know that when somebody gives you a present, you're supposed to say thank you. I also suggested the turtle would look good next to her plant, but she didn't move it.

Do you have any ideas for better presents for Natalie? I just want to give her something she'd love, and you always come up with the best present ideas.

Sincerely,
Dawn Schiff

To: Dawn Schiff
From: Mia Hodge
Subject: Re: Greetings

I don't know Natalie, but honestly, I agree that she should have thanked you for that present! Just remember that not everyone is a nice person. If she isn't worth your time, you should stay away from her. Feel free to call me if you want to discuss this further.

XXO
Mia

CHAPTER 9

PRESENT DAY

NATALIE

I end up letting Caleb take me out to dinner. I don't quite feel like being alone or going home to my empty house, so we go to a chain restaurant and get some food. But we don't talk much. My thoughts keep going back to Dawn and what could have happened to her. I can't even articulate my worst fears.

When Caleb and I get out of the restaurant, the sun has dropped precipitously in the sky. In another ten or fifteen minutes, it will be dark. He squints up at the horizon. "Are you going to be okay getting home? You still seem a little shaky."

"Yes," I say, although it does make me a little nervous, given the afternoon I had.

He raises his eyebrows at me. "I know we both have our cars, but I could follow you if you want. Make sure you get home okay."

"That is so sweet." I lift my chin and pucker up, prompting him to kiss me. He grins and lowers his lips onto mine. "*You* are so sweet. But I'm fine. Really."

"Okay. But text me when you get home."

I squeeze his hand. I do wish I didn't have my car and could get a ride home in Caleb's Ford. But it seems silly to make him follow me home, especially since he lives in the opposite direction. And what are we going to do once we get to my place? Make out? I'm certainly not in the mood for that.

Still, I wish he were coming with me. Maybe I should have taken him up on his offer.

When I'm halfway home, my phone starts ringing. "Mom" is flashing on my car's phone display. I contemplate letting it go to voicemail, but I have a bad feeling I know why she's calling. If I don't answer, she'll just call back.

"Natalie!" My mother always sounds like she's shouting on the other line. She's never learned to regulate the volume of her voice on the phone. "I just heard the news on the television. They said a woman at your company went missing!"

"Yes." I don't mention the fact that I was the one who discovered that Dawn was missing. I don't think that information would go over well.

"Did you know her?"

"A little." Again, she doesn't need to know that Dawn occupied the cubicle immediately next to mine. That we shared a wall for nine months.

"God, how awful." She sniffles. "Is it safe to work over there? I don't like that neighborhood."

"Nothing happened at work. It happened at her house in Quincy."

"*What* happened? I thought she disappeared."

I bite down on the inside of my cheek. "Look, work is safe. I don't do anything unsafe."

"I know, but, honey, Daddy and I worry about you living all alone. I don't think it's safe for you to be in a house all by yourself."

"You wouldn't think that if I were a man."

"Exactly! It's not safe for a single woman." Her voice takes on a whiny tone that makes my skin crawl. "You need to get married, Natalie. Enough of this... whatever it is you're doing. Find a nice guy and settle down."

I grit my teeth. "What do you think I'm trying to do?"

"Well, you're not trying very hard! You're a beautiful girl. You could have any man you want. Just pick one of them!"

I start to explain that it's not so simple. But I have had this conversation with her hundreds if not thousands of times before. Possibly millions. She's never going to get it. I'm just wasting my breath.

Of course, I could tell her about Caleb. I can tell her that things have been going really well with him, and he just might be her son-in-law someday. He's cute and he's a good guy and he's good during a traumatic situation. But I don't want to get her hopes up. It's still early with Caleb, and truthfully, I don't feel like fielding a zillion questions about him.

"I have to go," I mumble.

"Where are you now?"

"I'm driving home."

"Will you call me when you get home?"

A vein pulses in my temple. When Caleb asked me to text him when I got home, it was sweet. When my mom asks for the same thing, it's annoying.

"Mom." I am on the verge of losing my temper. "I'm a

grown woman. I'm not going to call you every day when I get home from work. I'm fine. You have to trust me."

Before this can turn into an argument, I disconnect the call. Anyway, my house is on the next block.

Like Dawn, I rent out a small house. It's two stories with two small bedrooms and one bathroom and unfortunately no garage. I could have gotten an apartment like Caleb, but I like having the privacy of my own house. The rents aren't cheap in Dorchester, but it's worth it. Technically, Dorchester is part of Boston, but it was originally a separate town, and because it's so big, sometimes it feels separate from the rest of the city. When I'm driving from my house to the Back Bay or the South End, I usually say, "I'm going into Boston," even though I was technically in Boston to begin with.

Most people in my neighborhood are renting houses, and most of them are small like mine. My house is more of a cottage, constructed from brown bricks back in the early twentieth century, now slightly crumbling, with vines running along the sides of the walls. It's never been renovated, and you can tell. Whenever I turn a doorknob, it feels like it's about to come off in my hand, and the entire house has a total of about three power outlets. Yet it still costs a small fortune to rent.

During the day, my house looks quaint. But as I pull up on my quiet street, I can't help but compare it to the house I saw earlier today. The small house on a quiet street like mine, with all the lights out inside.

My stomach churns. I used to have a can of Mace that I carried in my purse. I needed it for a while, but that situation has thankfully ended, and at some point, I ditched the can of Mace. I did take a self-defense course a few years ago, but my skills are decidedly rusty, and also, there's nothing quite like a weapon.

I wish I had taken Caleb up on his offer to come home with me.

I climb out of my car, clutching my purse against my stomach. I hit the key fob, and the horn honks twice as the door locks click into place. The moon is absent from the sky tonight. My neighborhood looks so dark in the evening, with just a few dim streetlights dotting the sidewalk, especially since we set the clocks back last week.

As quickly as I can, I sprint down my walkway to the front door. My keys are still in my hand, and I fit the door key into the lock. I turn it to the right to unlock the door, but it doesn't turn. That's when I realize:

The door isn't locked.

I take a step back. Why isn't my front door locked? What the hell?

Okay, there's some possibility I forgot to lock the door this morning. Despite what my mother said, I live in a decent neighborhood. There aren't any break-ins around here. So yes, I do sometimes forget to lock the door behind me in the morning.

Did I forget this morning? Entirely possible.

I walk over to the window. I cup my hands over my eyes to peer inside. The inside of my house looks completely dark. I don't see any movement. No burglars. No murderers.

I can't very well call the police about this. *Hey, 911, my house is unlocked.* I could call Caleb, but I'm going to use up a lot of girlfriend points if I make him come all the way over here from his apartment just to walk me into my house for two minutes.

Screw it. I'm sure it's fine.

I twist the doorknob and push the door open, watching for signs of movement inside my house. It still looks completely dark. Silent.

"Hello?" I call out. It's the same thing I did when I was at Dawn's house. I try not to think about that.

I take a deep breath and step into the foyer. I hit the light switch.

Half of me is expecting to see some intruder in a black tracksuit and face mask standing in the middle of my living room. Instead, the living room is empty. It looks exactly the way I left it this morning.

My phone buzzes inside my purse, and I nearly jump out of my skin. I fumble around between a pack of Kleenex and my compact, and I pull out my phone. There's a blocked number on the screen, just like earlier at work. I swipe to answer.

"Hello?"

I wait to hear a string of foreign language or somebody asking me if I want to update my auto insurance, but instead, I hear only silence.

Or maybe breathing.

"Hello?" I say yet again.

Nothing.

I pull the phone away from my ear to disconnect the call, my heart pounding in my chest. I used to get calls like that all the time, sometimes with just silence, but sometimes with a string of threats on the other line. But I haven't gotten a call like that since…well, it's been several months. I doubt it's that same person—they have no reason to hate me anymore.

Although I did get that other blocked call during my podcast. Could it be from the same number?

Just as I'm starting to panic, a text message pops up on the screen. It's from Caleb, and the sight of it fills me with relief:

Make it home okay?

I step into the living room. I flick on a second light. The entire first floor of my house now is completely quiet. There's nobody here.

I'm fine. Thanks for checking.

I drop my keys on the table next to the front door and then plop down on the leather sofa in my living room. I need to chill out. What happened to Dawn is horrible, but it has nothing to do with me. Nobody is out to get me.

CHAPTER 10

I check the local news in the morning, hoping there will be a story about how Dawn turned up in, I don't know, a Dunkin Donuts or something drinking an iced Americano. And maybe all that blood was just a really bad cut from shaving her legs. But no such luck. The news reports that Dawn Schiff is still missing.

Still, I'm half hoping she'll be in her cubicle when I get to work, oblivious to the fact that the entire police department is searching for her. But no. Her cubicle is still empty.

I walk past her cubicle to reach my own. The first thing I see on my desk is that turtle figurine that appeared yesterday morning. After seeing that huge bookcase filled with turtles, the sight of yet another glassy-eyed animal makes me slightly ill.

Also, I distinctly remember that I took that turtle figurine and shoved it to the far corner of my desk so I wouldn't have to look at it. Yet somehow it's made its way to the center of my desk. Right in front of my keyboard.

Must have been the stupid janitors.

After I found all that blood in Dawn's house, it makes me rethink what that dark red material was on the turtle yesterday. Could that have been blood? Did someone put *a bloody turtle figurine* on my desk?

I snatch the turtle off my desk and stare at it. This time, it's clean at least. No blood or paint or whatever that was. But I still don't want it on my desk or anywhere near me. I don't want to see it ever again.

So I toss it into my garbage bin. There. At least that's one problem I can deal with.

"Oh my God, Natalie!" Kim's shrill voice rings out in my ear. "Can you believe it?"

"Yeah," I mumble. My temples are throbbing slightly. I don't feel like talking to Kim. "It's awful."

Kim's eyes are like saucers. "What did you see in her house when you went over there?"

"There was blood all over the floor." I drop my eyes. "Like, a lot of blood."

She clasps a hand over her mouth. "Wow. That's so terrifying. I hope she's okay."

I nod, knowing with every passing minute that they don't find her, it's less and less likely that she's okay.

Kim scratches at her nose with her left fourth finger, the one with the giant diamond on it. She developed that habit soon after her engagement. I thought maybe once she got married, she might stop flashing her giant rock in my face, but it's too ingrained. She can't help herself anymore. "Are you still going to do the race on Saturday?"

With everything going on, I had almost forgotten all about the 5K this weekend. I didn't even run this morning, even though I had been trying to go almost every day to stay in shape for Saturday.

But even so, canceling the race is off the table. I've raised a lot of money for the cerebral palsy foundation, and I can't just give up on all that because Dawn went missing.

"I'm sure we'll have more information by Saturday," I say. "I can't cancel though. If she's still missing, we can run in her honor. It might even end up being a good thing."

Kim frowns. "A good thing?"

I clear my throat. "I just mean there will be a lot of publicity around the race, and if Dawn is still missing, maybe it will help find her. You know?"

"Oh. Right."

"Anyway." I glance over at my computer. "I better get to work. If I can focus."

"By the way," Kim says, "Seth was looking for you a few minutes ago. He said to let you know he wanted to talk to you when you got in."

Great. What does my boss want from me? I'm not sure I want to know.

After Kim leaves, I plop down in my chair, not eager to run over to see Seth. I pull my compact out of my purse and check my reflection. I look even worse than yesterday. My eyes are slightly bloodshot, and there are purple circles underneath. I tried to cover them with concealer this morning, but I obviously didn't use enough. I had a lot of trouble sleeping last night, and when I did fall asleep, I tossed and turned.

I start to log on to my computer, but before I can boot up, my phone buzzes. I pull it out of my purse and look down at the screen. There's a message from Seth:

Please come to my office as soon as you get in.

I sigh. Looks like I'm taking a trip to my boss's office.

CHAPTER 11

Seth doesn't look any better than I do.

His dark hair is disheveled, and his shirt is a bit wrinkled, which is unusual for him. Seth is all about crisp white shirts. I was never sure if he took them out to be dry-cleaned or if his wife ironed them for him. Given the continued absence of his wedding band, the latter could explain why his shirt is wrinkled.

"Hey, Nat." His brown eyes are full of concern when he sees me. "Are you okay?"

"Fine," I croak out as I settle into the chair in front of his desk.

"Jesus, what a mess." He rakes his fingers through his hair, which makes it even messier. "I'm sorry I didn't take you seriously yesterday."

"It's okay. I can't blame you."

"I'm kind of surprised you didn't call out today," he says. "If you need the day off…"

I shake my head. "No, I'd rather work."

"You sure?"

"Absolutely. Better to keep my mind off it."

"Yeah. Yeah, that makes sense." He closes his eyes and rubs them with his fingertips. "I hope Dawn is okay."

I want to say something like, *I'm sure she is.* But that wouldn't be what I really think. So I keep my mouth shut.

"I spoke to a detective on the phone this morning," Seth adds. "Detective…Santoro? He said he's going to come by and interview everyone."

"Oh." I squirm in my seat. The last thing I want is to get grilled by that detective a second time. He was nice enough, but the thought of talking to him again makes a cold sweat break out on the back of my neck. "You know what? I think I might go home after all. I just…I feel like my head is spinning. And I hardly slept at all last night."

"Of course." Seth's eyes soften. "Take the day off. If you want, you can forward all your calls to my office."

My shoulders relax. "Thanks, Seth."

"Just stick around until the detective gets here, then you can head home."

The cold sweat returns. "What?"

Seth looks down at his Rolex. "It's no big deal. He should be here in thirty minutes. Maybe less. He said before ten."

"Yes, but…" I press my fingers into my left temple. "I have a splitting headache. And I already talked to that detective yesterday. So I'm sure he doesn't need to talk to me again."

"Actually, he specifically asked me if you would be there and said he needed to talk to you."

"Oh." Fantastic. "I guess I'll stay then."

I shift in my seat, wondering what else that detective could possibly want to ask me about. I already told him everything I know. It seems like a waste of time, but now that Seth has told me I have to stay, I don't have much of a choice. I can't walk out and claim ignorance.

Seth toys with a ballpoint pen on his desk. Once again, my eyes are drawn to the tan line from his missing wedding band. He follows my gaze to his ring finger. I look away, but it's too late.

"Melinda and I split up," he says.

"I'm so sorry to hear that."

He arches his right eyebrow. "Are you?"

Something catches in my throat. I'm not sure what to make of his tone of voice. He doesn't sound angry. More like…curious.

"I am," I say.

His eyebrow stays raised. "Are you still seeing Caleb?"

"Yes."

He nods. "He seems like a nice guy."

"He is."

"Good."

I still have that catch in my throat. I feel like I'm going to choke or something. "I better get back to my desk."

Seth nods and turns back to his computer screen. But I can feel his eyes on me as I leave the room.

CHAPTER 12

To: Seth Hoffman
From: Dawn Schiff
Subject: Refrigerator Cleaning Schedule

To Seth,

I have created a schedule for cleaning the refrigerator in the break room on a twice-weekly basis, with each employee assigned a designated date to clean. With your permission, I would like to post this schedule on the refrigerator. Also, I have attached an information sheet about common bacteria that grow at cold temperatures.

Sincerely,
Dawn Schiff

To: Seth Hoffman
From: Dawn Schiff
Subject: Refrigerator Cleaning Schedule Follow-Up

To Seth,

 Did you get my email about the refrigerator cleaning schedule? Please let me know ASAP!

Sincerely,
Dawn Schiff

To: Mia Hodge
From: Dawn Schiff
Subject: Re: Greetings

Dear Mia,

 I had a great day today. I came up with an idea that will save the company a ton of money. You're going to be so proud of me.

 I had considered talking to Seth about it privately, but he never seems interested in meeting with me. The only times I ever manage to catch him are when he comes to Natalie's cubicle to talk to her. I tried to talk to him last week, but he was on the phone. I waited in his doorway for him to get off, but then he pulled the phone away from his ear and said, "Jesus, Dawn, I'm talking to my wife. Can you come back another time?"

 So the meeting seemed like as good a time as any. The meeting was to talk about how sales are going with a new product that was just released by

Vixed. The product is called Collahealth. As far as I can tell, it's some sort of collagen product that is supposed to help your hair, skin, nails, and joints. At least that's what it says on the sales pamphlet, although once again, the research studies are noticeably lacking. Also, it's an advanced formula. I don't know what the non-advanced formula is, because this is the only formula they seem to have.

We all gathered in the conference room—Seth, his secretary, our sales team, our marketing team, and me. He sat at one end of the conference table, and Natalie sat next to him like she always did. It made sense, because she always seems to be a large part of these meetings.

Everybody kept their eyes on Seth expectantly while noshing on the croissants he always brings. Or at least his secretary brings them. Even though these meetings are largely useless, because we never really decide anything or figure anything out, he always tries his best. People find Seth likable, for the most part. There's nothing objectionable about him, I suppose, although he's not nearly as charming now that I've gotten to know him.

I've heard some of the female salespeople remarking that they think he's sexy. I'm not sure why they would be talking about that though, since he's married.

Seth was talking about how Natalie is "killing it" with her sales, which is true. He likes Natalie, but objectively, her sales numbers are superior to everyone else at the company. He joked around with her, asking her secret. And she just smiled and said it's a great product.

I wonder if Natalie uses collagen supplements. Her hair is very healthy and shiny, and her skin always has this immaculate glow, like she's an angel. And her nails are always perfect. Today they were painted dark purple, without a scratch or defect on them. They were the most perfect nails I had ever seen.

Remember that time when my mother dragged me to get a manicure? After five minutes, I left in a panic because the fumes were so toxic that I was scared to breathe. She was furious with me, saying I humiliated us both. These days, I keep my fingernails extremely short, like my hair.

"As for the rest of you," Seth continued, "most of you are not meeting quotas. I'm not going to point fingers, but we could be doing a lot better. A *lot* better. The Syracuse branch had twice as much profit as us this quarter, and they're in freaking *Syracuse*. What are we going to do about it?"

I was nearly sitting on my hands as people around the table spitballed ideas at him. My idea was so simple. But I wanted to wait a little bit, because at the first meeting, Seth told me I talked too often. He told me to "get control of yourself, Dawn. Jesus."

The ideas were pretty much what you would expect. They all involved a large amount of spending. My idea was the exact opposite of that. When I was satisfied nobody had anything brilliant to say, I raised my hand and waited for Seth to call on me. (Of course, then he got annoyed that I was raising my hand. He made a comment about how "this isn't school," which made everyone snicker.)

That's when I dropped the bombshell.

I'd been going over the numbers in detail for the last two weeks. And our sales are decent. I took the liberty of obtaining the expense report from Syracuse, which is a much more profitable branch, and that's where things really differ. Our expenses are *much* higher, as I told everyone at the meeting.

"Dorchester isn't Syracuse," Natalie spoke up. "Of course our expenses will be higher."

So I showed everyone the folder with all my numbers. The biggest expense is all the perks we give to customers. Food is a big one. On lunches alone, we have spent half of our expense budget. I found one lunch receipt that cost more than twenty-five cases of Collahealth! Twenty-five. Isn't that crazy?

Natalie was flustered, which I could tell by the way her long eyelashes fluttered. Her eyelashes are nearly twice as long as mine and much darker in color. Also, she doesn't hide them behind glasses the way I do. She started babbling about how she could make that money back easily and that it's an investment.

But it's not true, and I said as much. I have carefully collected data. I love numbers because numbers don't lie. And the numbers show that most of these lunches don't result in 25 sales or more. The stores usually agree to stock a small amount of the product to see if it sells. On average, they purchased one case, which is 16 bottles. So every lunch loses money for us.

When I finished talking, Seth was stroking his chin. He's always clean-shaven at the beginning of the day, but by the afternoon, he always has some hair on his jaw. As he stroked his chin, he kept saying, "Interesting, interesting."

Natalie wasn't convinced though. She started talking about how in the short term, the sales might not justify the expense, but in the long term, it does. Except that's just wrong. And I told her so.

"Well," she said, "maybe once you've made a sale, you'd be in a better position to weigh in."

I didn't understand what she meant by that. I had a good idea to save the company money. I could tell Seth thought so too. And anyway, how could I make a sale? I'm an accountant.

So I suppose it wasn't a complete success. Natalie didn't seem to agree with me, but that was only because she hasn't looked at the numbers. I tried to show her later, but she waved me off. Seth told me he was going to think about it though. I reminded him that he could save the company tens of thousands of dollars.

Of course, you're the first person I want to tell about what a great job I did! You're the only person who gets it. Even my parents didn't really care about any of my achievements. When I first moved out of their house, I would sometimes call to tell them about how things were going for me, but I don't do that much anymore. And then of course, that heart attack took my father, and now that he's gone, my mother has become even more critical of everything I do. You think she was bad before? She's much worse now.

For example, if I told her about the meeting, she would probably agree with Natalie. She would say that Natalie knows what she's talking about better than I do. So I should keep my mouth shut because nobody wants to listen to me anyway.

You're the only one who doesn't criticize me. When we were in high school, every day, my mother would pick on me. Why did I wear clothes that looked like they belonged to an old lady? Why did I always cut my hair so short? How come I never smiled? But when I showed up to school and saw you, you always had something nice to say about me. For example, when I got that turtle charm for my backpack, you were the first person to notice it and tell me how much you liked it. You never asked me why I never smiled, because when we were together, I actually felt like smiling.

I wish you would come to visit soon. I miss you.

Usually, I love being at home at night. I do live alone, but you know me—I appreciate quiet. There's nothing worse than too much noise. I live in a small two-bedroom, one-bathroom, single-story house in a quiet neighborhood in Quincy. Remember how much my mother hated my room when we were kids? Yet another thing she loved to pick on. She hated my turtle figurines and turtle posters. She thought I should put up posters of boy bands "like normal kids." But in my own house, I can do whatever I want. When you come here, I'll give you the grand tour.

For the most part, my furnishings are simple—a sofa purchased at a discount furniture store, a coffee table, a television. I have two bookcases, one of which is filled with books, and the other is filled with turtles. Turtle figurines, stuffed turtles—you name it. The centerpiece is a large ceramic turtle I purchased a couple of years ago that's about the size of a basketball. You don't have to worry about me being burglarized because if I had an intruder in my house, I could clock him on the head with that turtle and do some serious damage.

Also, I don't live *entirely* alone. I've got Junior. Well, her full name is Mia Junior. Yes, that's right, I named her after you! She is a Mississippi map turtle. Turtles make great pets, and you know I've always wanted one.

Every night, I feed Junior a few of her turtle pellets. That makes up most of her diet, although sometimes I'll purchase some dried crickets to provide her with a little variety. Three or four times a week, I'll add in some leafy greens. Junior isn't a big eater, but I want her to have a well-rounded diet. I can't wait for you to meet her. I think you two will really hit it off.

Sincerely,
Dawn Schiff

To: Dawn Schiff
From: Mia Hodge
Subject: Re: Greetings

I'm so proud of you for kicking butt at that meeting. George is excited for you too! Don't let yourself get intimidated. You are way better than that!

And don't worry—I will be there to visit you before you know it. Let me check my calendar and get back to you about some potential dates.

XXO
Mia

CHAPTER 13

PRESENT DAY

NATALIE

When I get back to my cubicle, my phone is ringing. I'm not in the mood to talk to anybody, but I do have a job to do, and maybe this will get my mind off everything going on. And when I recognize Carmen Salinas's number, I know it won't be an unpleasant call. Making a sale today would give me a lift.

"Natalie!" Carmen gushes when she hears my voice. "I heard about what happened at your company! About that woman who went missing. Are you all right?"

"I'm fine." I swallow a lump in my throat. "It's just been a long day."

"I can't imagine! Do they have any idea what happened to her?"

Despite everything, I almost laugh. Leave it to Carmen to call in search of gossip. But she's not going to hear any of it from me. "I'm afraid not."

"Oh my…" Carmen lets out a long sigh, and I can almost imagine her toying with the many strings and beads that she always wears around her neck. I've never seen that woman wearing less than five necklaces at a time. "I don't even work there, but the whole thing is making me stressed out. I can't even imagine how you must feel!"

"You should take a few capsules of LoStress," I tell her. "That product works miracles for anxiety. We've gotten nothing but great feedback."

"You know what, honey? I think we're fresh out. Do you think you could bring by a case of it later today?"

I can read Carmen's mind. She's hoping to pump me for more information about Dawn's disappearance later today, not that I expect to know anything more. Unfortunately, our stock is low at the moment, and LoStress is always a big seller. I've personally sold more of it than anyone else at the company. It makes me feel good that I'm helping people reduce their stress. How many people get to say that they truly help others at their jobs?

"I'm afraid I'll have to put in an order," I tell Carmen regretfully.

She's disappointed, and I'm worried she's going to tell me to forget about it, but then she surprises me by asking for two boxes. After we hang up, I enter the information into the computer, but just as I'm submitting the order, my attention is drawn to a commotion at the front of the office. I stand up, and over the edge of the cubicles, I can see Detective Santoro talking to Seth. They're shaking hands. I can't hear anything they're saying, which makes me uneasy. Especially when Seth points in the direction of my cubicle.

The detective waves to me. I wave back.

Then he's coming right toward me. I smooth out my hair and tuck a loose strand behind my ear. There's no reason to be nervous. I didn't do anything wrong. I'm sure the detective is just going to ask the exact same questions as yesterday, and then he'll move on to somebody else.

A few seconds later, Detective Santoro is approaching my cubicle. He smiles at me, and I have to admit, his smile disarms me. He doesn't seem upset or suspicious of me, and it also brings out a hint of dimples on both his cheeks. The detective is sexy in a swarthy sort of way.

"Miss Farrell, right?" he says.

I nod. "Yes. Detective Santoro?"

He beams at me. "You got a good memory."

"You have to have a good memory if you work in sales." It's true. Clients love it when you remember every detail they told you about their lives and their business. That's why I keep notes. "Have you found out anything about Dawn?"

The smile instantly vanishes from his face. "I'm afraid not. We're doing our best to find your friend. I promise you that."

"I appreciate that. Have you spoken to her mother?"

He nods grimly but doesn't elaborate. "I'm hoping I could ask you a few more questions, Miss Farrell. I'm trying to gather as much information as I can to find her."

"Of course. Anything I can do to help."

"Well, that's great." He jerks his head to the left. "Your boss said we could use the conference room. Do you mind?"

It's not like I have a choice. So I follow the detective to the conference room, all the while pushing away the sick feeling in my stomach.

CHAPTER 14

Miss Farrell, how close were you with Miss Schiff?"

Detective Santoro's eyes are trained on me as he asks me the question. His eyes are really dark. So dark, you can't tell the iris from the pupil. It somehow gives me the illusion that he can see into my soul. And if I were to lie, he would know it.

"Not very close," I admit.

"No?"

I shrug. "She works in the cubicle next to mine. We talk sometimes and we're friendly, but I wouldn't say we're great friends."

"Sure." The detective nods like he gets that. "You can't be friends with everyone, right?"

"Yes, exactly."

"But you did know where she lives."

I squirm in my conference chair. "I drove her home once, so I remembered her address. As I said, I have a good memory."

"And why did you go over to her house again?"

A muscle in my jaw twitches. "I told you this. She didn't show up for work yesterday morning, and I got that phone call…"

"Right. You said there was a phone call to Dawn's line at the office, and you heard her voice."

"That's right. Did you trace the calls that came to her number yesterday morning?"

"I did," he confirms. "And every single one of them was internal."

"Internal?"

"They all came from this office building."

Santoro looks unimpressed by this revelation, but it's enough to give me a sick feeling in the pit of my stomach. Dawn called here yesterday, begging for help. And the call came from *inside the office*.

Oh God.

For a moment, I'm too terrified to even speak. But Santoro doesn't seem at all concerned. That's because he didn't hear the way Dawn's voice sounded.

"So had you ever been to Miss Schiff's house before?" he asks.

"No. I just dropped her off that one time. I've never been inside." I wipe my sweaty palms on my skirt. "Why are you asking me all this? Why is it important?"

"Well, Miss Farrell, I'm just trying to understand some of the things we found in Miss Schiff's house."

"I…I don't follow."

Detective Santoro leans forward like he's about to tell me a secret. "So the thing is, we found your fingerprints on a knife at Miss Schiff's house."

I freeze. My fingerprints? "How do you have my fingerprints?"

"They were on the business card you gave me."

I feel violated. I offered him that business card of my own free will, and he used it to get my fingerprints.

But anyway, it's for nothing. The fingerprints are very easy to explain. "I grabbed a knife from the kitchen because I was scared there was an intruder. Then when I saw the blood, I dropped it on the floor. I told this to one of the police officers."

"Right." He nods. "We already knew that. But we found your fingerprints on another knife. One that was still in the knife block."

For a moment, I'm speechless. My fingerprints were on *two* knives? But it does make sense. "I didn't grab the first knife in the block. I think I checked a few of them to find one the right size."

I did, didn't I? I must have. Because how else could my fingerprints be on a second knife?

"Okay, that explains that." One corner of his lips curls up in a lopsided smile. "But how did your finger-prints get on the wineglass sitting on the counter in the kitchen?"

The question takes my breath away. My fingerprints were on that wineglass in the kitchen? How could that be?

I remember seeing the wineglass on the counter. And then the broken one on the floor. But I don't remember touching them. I grabbed the knife, maybe even touched a few of the knife handles, but I never touched the wineglass.

Did I?

I don't remember doing it, but if they found my fin-gerprints on the glass, I must have. It's the only explana-tion. And now that I think of it...

Yes, I definitely must have touched that glass.

"I touched the glass when I was in the kitchen," I say. "I moved it to the side. It...it looked like it might fall like the other one. I'm sorry. I didn't realize at the time that it was a crime scene."

Detective Santoro leans back in his chair again, considering my explanation. "So you never shared a glass of wine with Miss Schiff?"

"No." I lick my lips. "Look, Dawn was a nice person, but we weren't good friends."

"Why not?"

"She was...strange. It's hard to explain it exactly, but she was just a very strange person. If you met her, you would know what I mean."

"Yeah." He seems to be considering this. "You know, it's interesting..."

"What's interesting?"

"The way you keep referring to Miss Schiff in the past tense."

My mouth falls open. He's looking at me intently, obviously trying to get a reaction out of me. "I have an alibi for two nights ago," I remind him.

"An alibi," he repeats.

I should never have used that word. It makes me sound guilty. Innocent people don't need alibis. "I mean, I was with somebody."

"Right. You were with your boyfriend. I remember."

Except I wasn't really with Caleb. I'm counting on him to come through for me—I think he will. At the time, it seemed ridiculous to make up an alibi. But now I'm glad I did.

"So I got another question for you, Miss Farrell."

Santoro reaches into his jacket pocket, and I flinch, expecting him to pull out a pair of handcuffs. Of course, that's ridiculous. Why would he arrest me? Sure enough, he pulls out a photograph. "Could you take a look at this?"

He slides the photo across the conference table. I pick it up and stare at the familiar image. It's the bookcase at Dawn's house—the one that was filled with turtle figurines. Just the sight of it sends a shiver down my spine.

"Do you recognize this?" he asks me.

I cringe. "Yes. It was in Dawn's living room."

"Notice anything strange about it?"

He's got to be pulling my leg. Do I notice anything strange about a bookcase filled with *statues of turtles*? Is there anything *not* strange about it? "Um…"

The detective taps on the center of the photo. "Right there. There's something missing."

He's pointing at the gap I remember seeing in the bookcase when I was at Dawn's house. The bookcase was so full, but there was that empty space right in the middle. I had assumed it was a decorating choice.

"It was like that when I got there," I say. "You think there was something there?"

"The pattern of dust made it look like something was removed recently."

I shake my head. "I'm sorry, I can't help you."

"You sure?"

He levels his dark, dark eyes at me. My hands are sweaty again, even though I've wiped them on my skirt two times since I've been in here. "I'm sure."

He doesn't drop his eyes. He keeps staring at me like

he's waiting for me to break and tell him everything. But I *have* told him everything.

"One more thing," he says in a low, almost conspiratorial voice. "We found an email Dawn sent to you two days ago asking to meet about something important." He pauses in a meaningful way. "What did she want to meet about?"

"I don't know. We never had a chance to talk."

"No? You sure about that?"

I never genuinely believed that Santoro truly thought I could be a suspect until this moment. But when my eyes finally meet his gaze, I realize he knows something. Something damning.

"I wish we *had* talked." I fight to keep my voice steady. "Maybe it would have kept her alive."

He doesn't have an answer for that. I keep my hands under the table because I don't want him to see how much they're shaking.

I glance over at the door to the conference room. "So are we done here?"

"Yes." The detective's eyes never leave mine. "We're done. For now."

CHAPTER 15

To: Seth Hoffman
From: Dawn Schiff
Subject: My Helpful Suggestion Idea

To Seth,

I was wondering if you've given more thought to implementing my suggestion about eliminating business lunches.

Sincerely,
Dawn Schiff

To: Seth Hoffman
From: Dawn Schiff
Subject: Helpful Suggestion Idea Follow-up

To Seth,

I previously was inquiring about the business expenses. I'm attaching a proposal that would show how limiting expenses would save our company a large amount of money. Natalie alone accounts for at least half the expense budget.

Sincerely,
Dawn Schiff

To: Seth Hoffman
From: Dawn Schiff
Subject: Helpful Suggestion Idea Second Follow-up

To Seth,

Did you receive my previously emailed proposal?

Sincerely,
Dawn Schiff

To: Seth Hoffman
From: Dawn Schiff
Subject: Helpful Suggestion Idea Third Follow-up

To Seth,

Did you receive my previous email about whether you received my previously emailed proposal?

Sincerely,
Dawn Schiff

To: Dawn Schiff
From: Seth Hoffman
Subject: Re: Helpful Suggestion Idea Third Follow-up

Yes, I got it. Decided to go in another direction.

To: Mia Hodge
From: Dawn Schiff
Subject: Re: Greetings

Dear Mia,

So today I did something I probably shouldn't have.

This morning, I knocked on the door to Seth's office. He was doing something on his computer, and when I showed up at his door, he didn't smile.

I wasn't sure how to take that. A lot of the time, I have trouble reading facial expressions. Other people seem to know when another person is angry or sad or happy just based on their face. I have no idea how they do that. If somebody is smiling, I assume they're happy, but beyond that, I am at a loss. You're the only person whose expression I can read. Well, and my mother, but that's an easy one because she's always annoyed with me.

So I thought there was a chance Seth wasn't happy with me. I had sent him a few emails recently about my ideas to save the company money, and he only replied with one sentence or not at all. So I figured it was better to speak with him face-to-face. Except then the first thing he said when I walked in was, "What is it now?"

I don't know why he said that. It's not like I bother him a lot.

I sat down in one of the wooden chairs in front of his desk. He was looking at me now, so I went forward and explained once again why it would be wise to implement my plan. While I spoke, he kept running his hand through his hair, which is thinning just a little bit at the top. Not too bad though, for a man his age. He keeps a photo on his desk of his family, and every time I'm in his office, I look at it. It's Seth and a woman—his wife, I assume. His wife is about his age and sort of plain looking with brown hair and a round face, but she seems like she might be a nice person. She seems like the kind of person we could have been friends with.

When I finally finished talking, he shrugged. It was the same as his email responses. He didn't even give me a *reason*. So I asked him. Why? Why can't we limit spending?

Again, he didn't have a good answer. "Why don't you let me worry about that, Dawn?" That's what he said to me.

So I said back, "It's just a very poor managerial decision."

Maybe I shouldn't have said that. But you always tell me to stand up for myself. For once, I decided to do it.

Seth didn't like me saying that. He wasn't smiling. In fact, he was definitely frowning. "Good thing you're not the manager then," he finally said.

It was the wrong thing to say. I shouldn't have told him that he made a bad decision. He did make a bad decision, but he did not want to hear that. Some people only want to be told that they're right.

My legs felt a little wobbly as I walked out of Seth's office. I didn't need to scrutinize his expression to know that he was angry with me. And worse, he wasn't going to take my suggestion. I gave him advice that could save the company, and he just blew it off. For no reason.

Anyway, that was when my day went from bad to worse.

I decided to get a cup of coffee before returning to work. I don't like to waste a lot of time in the morning, but everybody else does it, so why not? There's a coffee machine in the break room, and there's a tub full of those little coffee pods. Seth probably wastes a fortune on those, but I'm sure he does not want to hear my advice on that.

I selected a French roast and set it brewing in the coffee machine. I reached into the cupboard to grab my turtle mug, but then I got a big surprise.

My mug was lying on the shelf above the sink, in five pieces.

I almost cried when I saw it. I couldn't help myself. You bought me that mug! It's one of my most prized possessions. I've brought it with me to every job I ever had!

I retrieved the pieces from the shelf. At first, I thought I could attempt to reassemble them, but it was too badly broken. In addition to the five pieces it had been shattered into, other shards were missing. The mug was unusable.

That's when I noticed Natalie was standing at the entrance to the break room. Watching me. I had partially reassembled my mug, but when I released it, it fell apart immediately. One of the pieces dropped to the floor and broke in three.

"Oh no!" Natalie cried. "Your mug! How awful."

There was a lump in my throat, but I swallowed

it down. I didn't want Natalie to see me crying over a broken cup. I didn't want her to think I was a loser who would cry over a mug. Even the raised part with the turtle was broken in half.

"What a bummer," she sighed. "You know what I bet happened? I bet you left it on the edge of the shelf, and then when somebody was reaching for their own mug, it just tipped right off."

That didn't sound right. I'm careful to never leave my mug close to the edge of the shelf for that very reason. In fact, I remember telling Natalie that when she was putting her mug back too close to the edge. I warned her that sort of thing could happen. I told her she should try not to be so careless.

But I supposed she was right. Obviously, my mug had fallen and broken, so somebody must have knocked it over.

"Next time," she said, "you should try not to be so careless."

With those words, she turned on her red high heels and walked out of the break room. I picked up the pieces of my mug and stashed them in my purse to take home with me. I tried to put them back together tonight, but it just wasn't the same. I ended up having to throw them away.

I know it's impossible, but is there any way you could let me know where you purchased the mug? I know it was years and years ago, but I feel lost without it. I'm counting on you.

Sincerely,
Dawn Schiff

To: Dawn Schiff
From: Mia Hodge
Subject: Re: Greetings

Oh no, that's awful! I'm going to find you another mug ASAP. My brother is visiting at the moment though, and he's dragging me to every tourist attraction. Maybe he can help me look for another mug. He sends his love, by the way. I know you always had a bit of a crush on him, wink wink.

XXO
Mia

To: Mia Hodge
From: Dawn Schiff
Subject: Re: Greetings

Dear Mia,

I hardly remember your brother, and I assure you that I did not have any sort of romantic infatuation with him. But if you feel he would be of assistance in finding another turtle mug, feel free to take him with you.

Sincerely,
Dawn Schiff

CHAPTER 16

NATALIE

I don't end up leaving work after all. I *can't*. It would be worse to sit at home, wondering what was going on here. Wondering what everybody was saying to that detective.

I have a view of the conference room if I stand up inside my cubicle. It seems like Santoro is interviewing every single person who works at the company. I just had the honor of being first. And the only one whose fingerprints are all over Dawn's house.

Seth was second. Like me, he didn't seem thrilled about the idea of being interviewed by the police. He spent a long time with them. Definitely more than half an hour. I wonder if Santoro asked him about me.

I don't know why Santoro is so suspicious of me. I was just being a good coworker, checking up on Dawn when I was worried about her. If I did something to her, I would have gotten far away from her house. How could he possibly suspect me? And what does he think she wanted to talk to me about?

He can't possibly know about…

No, I'm being paranoid.

Usually, I eat lunch with Kim, but I'm too anxious today. I just grab a bag of chips from the vending machine downstairs and eat it in my cubicle. I make a few sales calls to take my mind off everything, but every twenty minutes or so, I stand up to see what's going on in the conference room.

It's just after lunch when Caleb sits down with the detective.

I didn't even know Caleb was going to be at the office today. He usually doesn't come in on Wednesdays. But there he is, sitting across from Detective Santoro. He looks nervous—his left leg keeps bouncing on the floor. Twice he scratches at his head until his hair sticks up.

Caleb hardly knew Dawn. So it's unlikely the detective is spending a lot of time asking him about her. I have to assume the questions being fired at him are all about me.

Yesterday, he agreed to tell the detective we were together all night the previous night. But he wasn't happy about it. If I had known he would be interviewed today, I would have checked in with him again and made sure we were still on the same page. Caleb is too honest. I can imagine him cracking and telling the detective the truth—we were together that night, but not the *whole* night.

I check my watch. How long has he been in there? For God's sake, what could they be talking about for so long?

Finally (finally!) Caleb emerges from the conference room. As soon as he gets out, his eyes meet mine across the room. He doesn't look away, which I consider a good sign. I raise my eyebrows at him, and he comes over to me. I nearly yank him by the arm into my cubicle.

"What were you talking about all that time?" I'm trying to sound casual, but my voice comes out screechy.

"Actually," he says, "he asked me a lot about *you*."

My legs wobble beneath me. I had been worried about something like that, but I had tried to convince myself I was just being paranoid. Apparently not. "Like what?"

"I don't know. A bunch of questions."

Ugh, Caleb is such a *guy*. So aggravating. "Like *what*?"

He shrugs. "Just if you and Dawn were friends and if Dawn ever talked to me about you. It was strange."

"Did he ask you about Monday night?"

"Yes."

My chest feels heavy. "And what did you tell him?"

"I…I told him we were together the whole night."

I can't help myself—I throw my arms around his shoulders. "Thank you."

"Yeah, but…" He pulls away, his cheeks pink. "I don't feel great about this, Nat."

"It's a white lie."

He drops his voice several notches. "How exactly is lying to the police about our whereabouts a 'white lie'?"

I grit my teeth. "So…what? You think I killed Dawn or something?"

"No, of course not!" Then he hesitates. "But…when we said we were going to meet, you said you had to do something else that night. Remember?"

I stare at him blankly. "What?"

"I remember you said that. When I said you should come over, you said there was something else you had to do that night. What was it?"

My cheeks get so hot that I'm sure my face is bright

red. "I just had to drop off a couple of cases of Collahealth at a vitamin store. Are you serious? You really think I had something to do with what happened to her?"

"No. Sorry, I just…"

"Look, you're just saving us both some grief. I mean, between the two of us, you're much more physically capable of hurting Dawn, and you're getting an alibi out of this too. So *you're welcome*."

Caleb takes a step back, his face dark. "But *I* don't have a motive."

"And I do?"

He averts his eyes. "Fine. Whatever. Anyway, it's done."

I've been going about this wrong. I'm starting to antagonize my boyfriend, who is already feeling ambivalent about this whole thing. I need to tone it down. And make him remember what a great time we have together.

"Listen." I run a finger up the thin fabric of his dress shirt. "Why don't you come over to my house again tonight? I'll cook you some dinner."

He looks down at his watch. "I can't. I came here because Seth told me I needed to talk to the detective, but I've got to get out to Newton right now, and I'll be stuck there till late. This took a lot longer than I thought it would."

"Oh. Maybe tomorrow then?"

"Yeah, maybe." He sounds distracted. "I'll text you, okay?"

It's hard to hide my disappointment. It's hard not to notice that Caleb isn't looking at me anymore like he's lucky to be with me. He looks like he wants to take off. I had really thought Caleb could be the one—somebody who might stick around for the long term. I thought I had found a great guy. And now that great guy is slipping through my fingers.

But before I can get too worked up over it, he grabs my shoulders and plants a kiss on my lips.

"I've got to go," he says. "I'll see you later, Nat."

I watch him walk away, his shoulder slumped. I still can't tell if I've blown it or not.

CHAPTER 17

When I left the house this morning, I double- and triple-checked to make sure I locked my front door. And sure enough, it's still locked when I get home.

The first thing I do when I walk in my front door is flick on all the lights. It's wicked dark outside. It feels like it's the middle of the night, when it's actually only like five thirty.

I hate having roommates, but this week I've been feeling increasingly uncomfortable about living alone. After all, Dawn lived alone, and look what happened to her. Well, we don't actually know what happened to her. But nothing good. I found a bunch of blood on her floor, and nobody can find her anywhere. Whatever the outcome, it doesn't look good for Dawn. I still can't stop thinking about the way she sounded during that phone call.

Help me.

My phone rings inside my purse. I fumble for it,

my fingers crossed that it's Caleb, having changed his mind about dinner. Or maybe it's Kim. But instead, it's a blocked number.

Just like when I got home yesterday.

Months ago, I was getting a lot of calls like this. Blocked numbers, hanging up on me or hissing threats in my ears. Except the difference is that back then, I knew who was responsible for the calls, and that person has no reason to bother me anymore. It seems even less likely to be related to Dawn's disappearance—it's probably just another one of those stupid spam calls. I shouldn't even answer it, but before I can stop myself, I swipe on the screen to take the call.

"Hello?"

It's the same as yesterday. No sales pitch. No strange foreign languages. Just silence.

My fingertips squeeze the phone. "Who is this?"

No response.

After waiting another beat, I press the red button to end the call. I look around my empty house, which is so quiet, I can hear myself breathing. I kick off my red heels and walk over to the coffee table. I grab the remote and flip on the television.

There. Now it's not so quiet.

Except I have unwittingly tuned in to the evening news. The top local story is about the disappearance of Dawn Schiff. The camera is panning in on her little yellow house, then a shot of the four-story building where we work. Then it skips to a shot of Detective Santoro.

"We have not yet located Dawn Schiff." His dark eyes flash under the lights of the camera. "But we have identified a person of interest in her disappearance."

A person of interest? What does *that* mean? But he doesn't elaborate.

"We feel confident that we'll be able to find out what happened to Miss Schiff," Santoro continues.

Am I the person of interest? Would I know if I were a person of interest? Do they tell you stuff like that?

I grab the remote and change the channel. It's *Wheel of Fortune*. Somebody is buying a vowel.

I pick up my phone from where I dropped it on the sofa next to me. I stare at the screen, which is black. The truth is, there's only one person I want to talk to right now.

But I shouldn't. I really, really shouldn't.

Then again, making stupid decisions is my specialty.

Hey. Could you come over?

I send the text message before I can overthink it. It's a mistake. I know it's a mistake. But…well, I've already done it.

Barely thirty seconds later, a text appears on my screen:

When?
    How about now?

I watch the three bubbles hovering on the screen. A few seconds later, the reply pops up:

I'll be there in fifteen minutes.

CHAPTER 18

FIVE MONTHS EARLIER

To: Melinda Hoffman
From: Seth Hoffman
Subject: Tonight

I'll be home late tonight. Eat without me. I'll grab dinner for myself on the way home.

To: Seth Hoffman
From: Melinda Hoffman
Subject: Re: Tonight

Again??? How late are we talking? I wouldn't mind eating on the late side...

To: Melinda Hoffman
From: Seth Hoffman
Subject: Re: Tonight

It's really busy here. Completely swamped. Probably won't be till after ten. Eat without me. Really sorry, will make it up to you.

To: Seth Hoffman
From: Melinda Hoffman
Subject: Re: Tonight

But promise you'll be home on time tomorrow, okay?

To: Melinda Hoffman
From: Seth Hoffman
Subject: Re: Tonight

I promise. Love you.

To: Mia Hodge
From: Dawn Schiff
Subject: Re: Greetings

Dear Mia,

I had the most terrifying experience this morning.

When I got to my cubicle this morning at 8:45 a.m., there was already a woman standing in the middle of the small square space. She had on a black trench coat, and her stringy brown hair was pulled into a bun that had come partially unraveled. Natalie sometimes wears messy buns, but hers are stylishly messy. This woman just looked disheveled. Like she slept in the street.

The scariest thing was the glint in her eyes. I might not be skilled at reading facial expressions, but it was clear this woman was furious. She looked so frightening that I took a step back. She accosted me and started asking all these questions about whose cubicle it was, and it sounded like she was looking for Natalie, so I pointed her in the direction of Natalie's cubicle.

Of course, it occurred to me right after that this woman might mean Natalie harm, and perhaps it was unwise to tell her where Natalie's cubicle was. But it was too late.

The woman pushed past me, jostling my shoulder. I swiveled my head to watch her march into Natalie's small space, still unoccupied. The woman dug something out of her purse as I studied her facial features—she looked familiar. I had seen this woman somewhere before. I was sure of it.

Finally, the woman retrieved a folded sheet of paper from her purse. After her hesitation, she placed the paper on Natalie's desk and dropped the turtle figurine on top of it so it wouldn't fly away.

"Make sure Natalie gets that note," she instructed me.

I nodded, afraid to refuse the woman. And just as she was marching off, I realized why she looked familiar. I recognized her from a photograph. The one on Seth's desk.

She was Seth's wife.

I looked around the office. Natalie was nowhere in sight. She rarely showed up before nine, so it would be a while before she came in and discovered the note from Seth's wife. I wondered what it said.

You know I am not the sort of person who usually snoops. I find it detestable, to be honest. But I thought it was important that I investigated what the note said. What if it said that there was a bomb in the building? If I didn't look at that note, everyone might be killed. It would be irresponsible of me not to look at the note.

I took one last peek around to make sure nobody was watching me. Then I slipped into Natalie's cubicle, right next to mine. I took the note out from under the turtle and carefully unfolded it.

The note was written in red ink. Scribbled, really. The handwriting was messy but large enough that it was easy to read what it said:

If you touch my husband again, I will kill you.

I stood there for a moment, reading and rereading the message. *If you touch my husband again, I will kill you.* The message was written by Seth's wife. That means her husband was...Seth. So she was telling Natalie that if she touched Seth, she would kill her.

No, actually, she said that if Natalie touched Seth *again,* she would kill her.

I was still working it all out when I felt a searing gaze boring into me. I ripped my eyes away from the note. Natalie was standing at the entrance to her cubicle, her arms folded across her chest. I could tell by the way the corners of her lips were turning down that she was not happy with me.

I was so embarrassed that she caught me. You know I don't usually snoop, but after something like that...well, I couldn't help myself. I started stammering out an apology, explaining my concerns about a possible bomb threat, but even to my own ears, it sounded incredibly inadequate. I should not have read the note. It was an inexcusable invasion of her privacy.

Thankfully, Natalie didn't press the issue further. She plucked the note out of my hands, and I watched the way all the color drained from her face as she read those 10 words.

"Shit," she muttered under her breath, which seemed like a very reasonable response given the circumstances.

But at least now her ire was directed at the other woman and not me. I figured this was a good opportunity to make up for my transgression, so I asked if there was anything I could do.

"You can mind your own damn business from now on, okay?" was what she said.

I told her I would, but she kept pressing me. She said I couldn't tell another soul about this. And that if I did, she would make sure I was sorry. Really and truly sorry.

I was so freaked out, I took a step back and bumped into her desk. My fingers knocked into the turtle figurine, and it went toppling to the ground. Much like my mug, it shattered into several pieces on the floor.

Of course, then she yelled at me for how clumsy I was and said I should clean up the pieces of the figurine that I had so thoughtfully purchased as a gift—now destroyed beyond repair. To be fair, I was the one who knocked into it, so it was reasonable for me to clean it up. While I was cleaning, one of the shards sliced into my finger, but I ignored it, even when a drop of blood trickled out. I dumped the pieces of the turtle into her garbage pail.

I offered to buy her another one but she told me not to bother.

I kept my promise to Natalie for the rest of the day. I didn't tell a soul about that note on her desk. Not that there was anyone I could tell. It wasn't like I had a friend that I shared gossip with. I would have had to go out of my way to tell anyone.

But even though I kept my mouth shut, that didn't mean I didn't think about it. The whole day, I couldn't stop thinking about it.

Natalie and Seth.

Now that I know the truth, it makes so much sense. He's always smiling at her and talking about how great she is. And he *always* has his hand on her arm or shoulder. I thought he was just friendly, but he never touched me that way. Or anyone else. Just Natalie. And why *wouldn't* he like Natalie? She's beautiful and she's nice and she's smart and everybody likes her.

No wonder he didn't like my idea about getting rid of lunches. Natalie has him wrapped around her finger. He can't say no to her.

But after thinking about it all day, I don't feel too bad about the whole thing. I had been upset that Seth didn't like my idea, but it turns out his rejecting the idea had nothing to do with whether he liked it or not. And now Natalie and I share a secret.

Maybe we can be friends after all. After all, there's nothing that binds two people like a shared secret.

Sincerely,
Dawn Schiff

CHAPTER 19

NATALIE

The headlights appear in my front window. I glance outside just in time to see the silver Audi pulling up right behind my own car. I pull my compact out of my purse and do one last check. Not that it matters so much, but it's almost an instinct at this point.

And then the doorbell rings.

I dash over to the door in my stocking feet. I don't check the peephole or ask who it is. I know who it is. I open my lock and my deadbolt and throw open the door.

Seth Hoffman, my boss, is standing on my doorstep. His shirt is even more wrinkled than it was this morning, and he's got a five-o'clock shadow on his chin. He's always clean-shaven in the morning, but he grows hair fast.

"Hey," he says.

"Hey," I say.

Now that we have dispensed with the small talk, Seth steps forward and grabs me, smashing his lips against mine. He kicks the door closed behind him, and a second later, we're ripping each other's clothes off.

God, I really, really missed this. I'm crazy about Caleb, but I don't think anyone has ever driven me wild the way my married boss does. Even though I knew it was the dumbest thing I could do, I found myself falling for him hard. But I was the one who ended it, because I was pretty sure Melinda was going to slit my throat if it kept up, and also, I was becoming increasingly convinced he would never, ever leave her.

I was wrong about that one.

As Seth and I collapse together onto the sofa, his lips still on mine, I feel almost dizzy with excitement. This must be the way a drug addict feels when they get a snort of cocaine after being off it for four long months.

Seth pulls his lips away for a moment. "So what happened to Caleb, huh?"

"Still in the picture."

"Is he?"

"Yes. This is a one-off. Okay?"

He doesn't even have to think about it. "Okay."

Then he goes back to kissing me. I missed this so damn much.

Over an hour later, we're both on the sofa together, our bodies still intertwined, naked and sweaty and *happy*. I *really* needed that. I didn't even realize how much. It wasn't cheating, exactly. Caleb and I haven't even slept together yet. You can't cheat on somebody if you're not sleeping with them. And anyway, this was a one-off with an old flame. It doesn't even count.

"Jesus," Seth murmurs into my hair. "You're unbelievable, Natalie."

"You're not so bad yourself."

He laughs. "It's you. You bring it out in me."

"Sure I do."

"It's true." He lifts his head to look at me. "That's why Melinda and I split up, you know. Because of you."

"You didn't tell her that, did you?"

"No," he says in a way that makes me not quite believe him.

I don't like the idea of Melinda thinking it's my fault her marriage fell apart. When she found out about me and Seth, she didn't take it well that her husband was sleeping with his employee, who also happened to be fifteen years younger than she was. There were threatening calls and notes—the calls would rouse me from sleep at two in the morning, a female voice hissing in my ear that I was a "husband-stealing whore." Even when I blocked her number, she'd find a way to call. Once, I saw her tan Lexus parked across the street from my house late in the evening, and I almost had a heart attack.

That's when I got the can of Mace and started keeping it in my purse at all times. I considered a restraining order, but it turned out that breaking up with Seth ended the harassment almost instantly.

"I love you, Nat." He squeezes my body close to his as he says the words. "I don't think I even realized how much until you broke it off. I'm so crazy about you."

"Hmm. Your timing is kind of bad on that."

"I know." He sighs. "I screwed up. I wanted to do the right thing, but I didn't know what the right thing was. I haven't loved Melinda in years. Even before you came around, we were like two strangers living in the same house. Maybe it would have been different if we had kids, but she couldn't and...I don't know."

Seth told me about Melinda's heartbreaking infertility issues. And about how she never forgave him for refusing to adopt.

"Anyway," he says. "By the end, I could barely stand being around her. And that wasn't fair to either of us."

I pull away from him and prop myself up on my elbow. "You know I'm dating someone else now."

"I know."

"And you've been separated from Melinda for...?"

"Two weeks."

"Oh God," I groan. "Seriously, Seth. I think it's better if we stay friends."

His eyes shoot down to my naked breasts and he wags his eyebrows. "Friends?"

"I told you, this was a one-off!"

He slides his hand down my thigh as he grins at me. "How about a two-off?"

I want to tell him no. I should definitely tell him no. I've got a boyfriend who I like a lot. And he is two weeks separated from his wife of twelve years. He is still *married*. There are so many reasons not to do this.

But then again, he's already here. So why not?

CHAPTER 20

FOUR MONTHS EARLIER

To: Natalie Farrell
From: Kimberly Healey
Subject: DS

Do you think she's a virgin?

To: Kimberly Healey
From: Natalie Farrell
Subject: Re: DS

Omg obviously! Can you imagine that woman ever having sex?

To: Natalie Farrell
From: Kimberly Healey
Subject: Re: DS

You never know...

To: Kimberly Healey
From: Natalie Farrell
Subject: Re: DS

Literally the only way Dawn has ever had sex is if she did it with a turtle.

To: Natalie Farrell
From: Kimberly Healey
Subject: Re: DS

Omg, you are HILARIOUS. Can't you just imagine?????

To: Kimberly Healey
From: Natalie Farrell
Subject: Re: DS

Totally. Can't you just picture her stroking that hard shell? Talking about how big and green it is and how sexy the turtle is because it's, like, a sea turtle instead of a land turtle.

To: Natalie Farrell
From: Kimberly Healey
Subject: Re: DS

I dare you to ask her if she's ever had sex!

To: Kimberly Healey
From: Natalie Farrell
Subject: Re: DS

With a turtle or just in general?

To: Natalie Farrell
From: Kimberly Healey
Subject: Re: DS

ROFL!!!!!

To: Natalie Farrell
From: Zelda Morris
Subject: Your terrible product

Natalie,

I'm writing to express my outrage with Vixed and your horrible products. I started taking Collahealth two months ago to get a boost to my energy level and because you stated it would make my skin and hair shinier. Well, this was the start of a nightmare I wish I could wake up from.

Three weeks after starting my daily regimen of Collahealth, I woke up with the room spinning. I managed to make it to the bathroom, but I had to hold on to the wall. Additionally, my fingers and feet were tingling. I thought I had the flu, and I stupidly continued taking your product, hoping it would help me get over it faster.

Unfortunately, the opposite happened. I became dizzy all the time to the point where I couldn't drive. My hands and feet tingled and burned, which kept me awake at night. And a few days after the symptoms started, my hair started falling out of my scalp in large clumps.

You gave me your card, so I called you to tell you about my symptoms. You assured me that not only was Collahealth not responsible for my symptoms, but it was likely a vitamin deficiency causing the problem and I should DOUBLE my dose. Stupidly, I listened to you.

Over the next several weeks, my symptoms got progressively worse. I couldn't feel my feet anymore, and I started falling. I needed a cane just to walk around my living room. I have always had excellent vision, but now my eyes became blurry and I started seeing double.

My doctor was initially baffled, but when I showed him a list of ingredients, he was horrified. He says your product is responsible for all my symptoms. I haven't taken it in nearly a month, and I'm still not better. My life is ruined because of Collahealth and the lies you told me about your product. I honestly don't know how you can sleep at night!

Expect to hear from my lawyer.

Sincerely,
Zelda Morris

To: Mia Hodge
From: Dawn Schiff
Subject: Re: Greetings

Dear Mia,

This morning, I did something I shouldn't have done. I answered Natalie's phone.

This was not a decision I took lightly. Natalie was already in the office by then. I saw her waltz in around 9:15, but then shortly after, she disappeared. At about 10 o'clock, her phone rang. Eventually, it went to voicemail. But then it rang again. And again. It was making it hard to focus on my work.

I looked for her first. I really did. I got up and checked up and down the hallway. But when I couldn't find her, I had no choice. Just so there would be no confusion, I answered the phone: "Natalie Farrell's desk."

The woman on the other line started telling me the craziest story ever. She said that Natalie sold her a vitamin A cream, which was making her skin peel off. Peel off! She said her face was red and looked like it had been burned. Then she started sobbing that she looked like a zombie. She kept saying it over and over. "I look like a zombie! I look like a zombie!" It was terrible.

She wanted to talk to Natalie right away, but I explained she wasn't available. I took down a message on one of a stack of Post-it notes on Natalie's desk and scribbled down the woman's phone number, even though I suspect she has already left half a dozen phone messages.

The woman sobbed to me for a few more minutes about her zombie skin, then I finally managed to get her off the phone. My hands were shaking after I hung up. You know how I hate dealing with intense situations like that. I'm not good at customer service. That's why I became an accountant.

I took the sticky note with the woman's information on it and started looking for Natalie. I wasn't surprised when I found her in the break room with Kim, poring over the pages of a bridal magazine while sipping on a cup of coffee. I replaced my beloved turtle mug with a plain white one that I picked up at the drugstore. I wrote my name on the bottom in permanent marker.

Natalie looked up from the pages of the bridal magazine when she saw me. I wonder if Natalie ever uses that vitamin A cream, because her skin is so bright and glowing. She could easily get a job modeling for skin care products. Maybe that's why she is so good at selling them.

"Dawn!" she said. "I was hoping you would come by."

In the time since I found out that Natalie was sleeping with Seth, she has not been very nice to me. It's odd, because you would think she would want to butter me up to ensure my silence. But she doesn't seem overly concerned that I'll divulge her secret. Or else she knows that I'm going to keep my mouth shut either way.

She was playing with one of her earrings, and that's when I noticed the way it sparkled. Diamonds. It had to be fake though. They don't pay us that much here. "Kim and I were wondering..." Kim nudged her, and Natalie nudged her back. "Are you a virgin, Dawn?"

Kim dissolved into giggles, but Natalie kept a straight face, even as I felt the skin on my cheeks start to burn. The sad part is that this wasn't the first time someone has asked me that exact question. I mumbled something, and the two of them kept giggling. Finally, Kim smacked Natalie on the arm and said, "Cut it out. You're so mean." Natalie just shrugged and said I didn't have to answer if I didn't want to.

I know this is something you and I haven't talked about in a while. I didn't want to make you feel guilty for being so happy with George, and I genuinely think the two of you will spend the rest of your lives together. But I'm never, ever going to have that kind of relationship. The truth is, yes, I'm a virgin. I still haven't even ever had a boyfriend. I've never even been on a date that wasn't sprung on me by my mother without my knowledge or consent. And none of those have led to second dates.

The truth is, I haven't even kissed a boy.

The closest I came was that game of spin the bottle in fifth grade at that horrible birthday party we went to at Jenny Horan's house. I had been so surprised and pleased when Jenny invited us—you were the one who figured out it was because her mother had forced her to invite the entire class. You refused to participate when the group of kids in Jenny's basement gathered in a circle to play the game—I should have done the same.

And then when Ned O'Keefe spun the bottle in my direction, I saw the look of disgust on his face.

Before he could protest that he didn't want to kiss me, I ran away and hid in the closet for the rest of the party. I refused to come out, even when you knocked on the door and begged me. I stayed in the closet until my mother arrived to pick me up.

Finally, Kim said to leave me alone, that I wasn't interested in stuff like that. I was desperate to change the subject by then, so I told Natalie about the phone message. I handed her the sticky note, and when she saw it, she rolled her eyes and crumbled it up. I tried to explain about the zombie skin, but Natalie just shook her head.

"She's just overreacting," she told me. "This woman is crazy. The only people who use these products are nut jobs."

I was surprised to hear her say that, because I assumed she must use the products herself. But when I asked her about her use of Vixed products, she and Kim burst out laughing simultaneously. I didn't know what that meant exactly. I wasn't making a joke.

Then Natalie got up and told Kim something about page 16 in the magazine and how the dress would be perfect for her. I thought that was the end of our interaction, but then she turned to look at me. I don't know what it is about her, but whenever she pays me attention, it always makes me feel special. I crave it.

"Dawn," Natalie said, "don't answer my phone again. *Ever*. Got it?"

That wasn't what I expected her to say. This was yet another moment in my life when I desperately wished I had a shell that I could vanish into. Turtles have it so good. Even though I love them, there are times I feel jealous of them. But of course, I told her I wouldn't touch her phone again. *Ever*.

Natalie brushed past me out of the break room, leaving behind the faint flowery scent of her perfume. Despite everything, I still love her perfume. I wonder if I could find a bottle of it. Do you think if I started wearing the same scent, she might like me better?

Sincerely,
Dawn Schiff

To: Dawn Schiff
From: Mia Hodge
Subject: Re: Greetings

OMG do NOT buy perfume to impress that woman! She is NOT worth your time! Stay away from her! I repeat: stay far away from Natalie!

Also, I'm sad that you felt you couldn't tell me your feelings about your love life. Dawn, you are a wonderful person. I am 100 percent sure that someday there is going to be a man who will understand how completely amazing and intelligent and beautiful you are. And every day, he is going to thank his lucky stars just for being with you. I promise you, you will find someone who feels that way. I hope you believe me.

XXO
Mia

CHAPTER 21

NATALIE

I feel *good* this morning.

Seth and I had a really nice night together. After round two, we ordered in Chinese food, then watched TV together on the couch. Back when he was still with Melinda, there was always a sense of urgency. He could never stay too late, because she would get suspicious. I liked more laid-back Seth, who was happy to cuddle up with me on the couch indefinitely.

I did send him packing before midnight. Even though we had already slept together, I felt like it would be a betrayal to Caleb for him to spend the night. Well, *more* of a betrayal. I recognize what I did last night doesn't exactly make me girlfriend of the year. But it's been a stressful couple of days, and Caleb was acting distant yesterday when I needed him the most. He lost a lot of boyfriend points for the way he acted yesterday.

Anyway, I got a great night of sleep after the activities of the evening. I woke up bright and early this morning, downed a cup of coffee, and now I am doing my morning run. My blond hair is pulled back into a ponytail, my Spotify playlist is blasting pop hits in my earbuds, and I've got on a T-shirt and leggings. When I left my house, it was a brisk forty-degree November morning, and I was freezing when my feet first hit the pavement, but now it feels perfect.

I'm glad to see that taking a break for a few days hasn't affected my stamina. The 5K is in only two days, and it would be embarrassing if I wasn't one of the front runners, considering I'm the one who organized it.

The endorphins are flowing through my bloodstream. I could climb a tree or even a mountain. I feel the best I felt in days.

That is, until I see Detective Santoro leaning against a gray Volvo parked in front of my house.

Before I went to bed last night, I checked a local news site on my phone to see if there were any updates about Dawn. The most recent article mentioned that the police were still looking for her. It didn't seem like the police had made much progress. Dawn was still hopelessly missing as of last night.

And if the detective is here to see me, it doesn't seem likely that Dawn has turned up alive and well.

I stop short, not sure what to do. For a moment, I consider doing an about-face and putting in another mile or two. But that won't do me much good. The detective doesn't look like he's planning on going anywhere until he talks to me. And it's not like I can go to work in my T-shirt and leggings, covered in a layer of sweat.

And anyway, I think he sees me.

Sure enough, the detective straightens up and waves at me. I grimace, wishing I didn't have to talk to him in my sweaty running clothes. Well, I wish I didn't have to talk to him at all, but my attire doesn't make the situation better.

"Miss Farrell!" He waves again. "You got a minute?"

I don't find his Boston accent even slightly endearing anymore.

I walk the last half a block to my house. Detective Santoro looks me up and down with his shrewd dark eyes. "Get in a nice run?"

"Yes."

He squints up at the sky. "Nice weather for it. And it's supposed to be a nice day when you've got that race on Saturday."

Of course, he knows all about my agenda for the week. "It's not exactly a race. It's more like a fun run for charity."

He nods like he couldn't possibly care less. "Would you mind if we went inside?"

"Did you find Dawn yet?"

He doesn't answer me but instead jerks his head in the direction of my front door. "I just have a few more questions, if you don't mind."

I should agree. I have nothing to hide. Yet I find my jaw clenching. I didn't do anything wrong, and it's like this detective has it out for me. It's not *fair*. "I'm afraid I've told you everything I know."

"So it should be real quick then."

Santoro's black eyes are leveled at me, and it's unnerving. I squirm in my sneakers, wishing I could hit the shower before having a conversation with him. I've got pit stains, after all. But it seems like I don't have much of a choice in the matter.

"Fine," I say. "But I have to get to work soon."

"This won't take long," he says. "If you want, I'll write you a note."

I bristle at the idea of this man writing me a note, like I'm some teenager and he is my dad excusing me from school. I don't dignify his offer with a response. Instead, I start up the walkway to my front door. I unlock the door, and he comes in behind me.

Santoro lingers in my foyer. "Mind if we sit down?"

"Actually, I do mind." I fold my arms across my chest. "Like I said, I don't have a lot of time. So what do you need to know?"

He gives me a look like he is surprised by my nerve, but I don't back down. I'm not going to let this detective push me around.

"So I just want to get more of a sense of your relationship with Dawn," he says.

My right eyelid twitches. "I told you, we were coworkers. We were friendly but not really friends. Is that all?"

"What do you mean by 'friendly'?"

I stare at him. "I mean we said hello to each other every day. I gave her a ride home once when she needed it. Occasionally we ate lunch together. But that's about it."

"Okay, I get it." He nods. "And was there ever a situation where you fought with Dawn?"

"No," I say firmly. "Never."

"Did you ever make fun of her?"

"Make fun of her?" I repeat. "What am I—in grade school?"

"Well," he says thoughtfully, "from what I hear, Dawn was kind of odd. When people are different, it might be natural to poke fun at them."

"Well, I never did."

"Never?"

"No!"

"So you never told anyone that you thought Dawn lost her virginity to a turtle?"

My jaw drops. "I... It... Who *told* you that?"

He lifts one of his dark eyebrows. "A few people, actually."

"Shit," I mutter under my breath. "Okay, look... I mean, yes, I might have said that. As a joke. I didn't say it to *Dawn*. I just...I was making a joke. You know, because she liked turtles so much. I didn't do it to hurt her feelings." I dig my fingernails into the palm of my hand. "It doesn't make me a terrible person because I made one joke."

"Of course not." But there's something in his voice that makes me think he believes otherwise. "So are there other jokes you made about Dawn?"

"No. I mean, I don't remember any."

"Did you invite her to office parties?"

I blink at him. "Yes, of course I did."

"Because several people said you deliberately kept her from going to workday parties."

"I did no such thing!" I burst out. "I always sent out an email to the entire office. I wouldn't exclude Dawn on purpose."

"Did she come to the parties?"

"No, but that's not my fault, is it?" I plant my hands on my hips. "Was I supposed to give her an engraved invitation?" I glare at him. "What are you accusing me of, exactly?"

He cocks his head to the side. "Several of your coworkers felt you were bullying Dawn Schiff."

This time, my jaw feels like it's about to become unhinged. "Bullying Dawn? Are you serious? Who said that?"

"I'm not at liberty to say. But it wasn't just one person."

"They're lying." I can feel a fleck of saliva fly out of my mouth as I spit out the words. "I never bullied Dawn. We're not in *school*. What does that even mean?"

He frowns. "It means that there was a pattern of cruelty to her perpetrated by you."

"A pattern of cruelty?" I can't believe my ears. "Because I made a *joke* about her?"

"Because you excluded her from company events. You kept her out of meetings. You damaged her personal property…"

"I…*what*?" My head is spinning. "I never did anything like that. I was nice to her. Nicer than she deserved."

"Nicer than she deserved? What does that mean?"

I immediately regret my choice of words. "I just mean Dawn was strange. People didn't like her. But I tried to be nice to her, okay? Maybe I made a couple of jokes about her behind her back, but so did everyone else. I never *bullied* her."

Santoro gives me a look that makes me think he doesn't believe one word I'm saying. I wonder who told him these terrible things about me. Probably somebody who's jealous of my sales record.

"Just because Dawn was different," he says, "you didn't have to be cruel to her."

"I wasn't!" Tears spring to my eyes, and I struggle to keep them from rising to the surface. "Ask my boss. Seth Hoffman. He'll tell you I was nice to her."

Santoro's eyebrows shoot up to his hairline. "Seth Hoffman? You mean your married boss who you were sleeping with?"

Okay, now I feel like I'm about to keel over from a heart attack. How does he know about that? I get that he's a detective, but it seems out of the scope of the investigation into the disappearance of a completely unrelated person. "Did Seth tell you that?"

"No. He only said nice things about you."

"So who told you I was sleeping with him?"

He hesitates a split second. "Dawn wrote about it to a friend in emails we found in her computer."

Oh God.

Yes, Dawn knew about me and Seth. It wasn't like I confided in her. She happened to witness Seth's wife leaving me a threatening note. But she was nice about it. She promised not to tell anyone. God knows who this "friend" is that she told about my exploits. I didn't even realize she had any friends to blab to.

And it makes me wonder what else she wrote about me.

But what's the difference? So what if Dawn wrote a few things about me in a couple of stupid emails? She certainly had a unique view of the world, and it doesn't mean anything she said was true. None of this is real *evidence* of anything.

"This is harassment, Detective." I grit my teeth. "I've got to get to work. And we don't even know anything bad really happened to Dawn. She probably just took off on a trip without telling anyone."

A deep crease forms between his eyebrows. "No. She didn't."

"Well, how do you know?"

"Because," he says, "we found Dawn's body early this morning."

CHAPTER 22

My legs almost give out from under me. I reach for the banister of my stairwell, but it's not enough. I sink onto the first step. My head is spinning, and for a moment, I have to put it between my legs.

We found Dawn's body early this morning.

No. It couldn't be.

"She…" I gulp. "She's dead?"

"Yes."

I didn't realize until this moment that I had believed Dawn was still alive. Even though I saw that blood on the floor in her apartment, I still truly thought she had to be okay.

But she's not okay. She'll never be okay again. Now she will spend the rest of eternity buried in the ground. There will be a funeral, where we will talk about how much we miss Dawn. About what a great person she was, about how she was taken from us far, far too early.

"What happened to her?" I manage.

He hesitates for a moment, as if he's not sure he wants to tell me. "She was beaten to death with a blunt object. She died of head trauma."

I let out an anguished cry. That sounds like an absolutely horrible way to die. Beaten to death. Poor Dawn. Even though she was strange, there was an innocence about her that made her seem almost like a child sometimes. Who would do something like that to her?

I lift my eyes again to look up at the detective. He thinks *I* am the one who did this to her. He thinks I somehow beat her to death with a blunt object. As if I could do such a thing.

I mean, physically I suppose I could. Dawn was such a small person. She could not have weighed more than one hundred pounds dripping wet. And I am admittedly in pretty good physical condition. He just caught me going for a run. So I suppose it isn't out of the question that I *theoretically* could have done it to her.

But *why*? Why would he think I did it?

"This is terrible." My voice trembles as a tear rolls down my cheek. "I…I can't believe it."

"It's a terrible thing," he agrees. "So you see why we want the person responsible for doing this to her to be brought to justice."

I swipe at my eyes with the back of my hand. "Yes. Yes, of course."

"So would you mind if I took a look around your house?"

I stare at him. "Around my house? Why would you—"

"Like I said. We just want the person responsible for doing this to her to be brought to justice."

"I…" My mouth feels almost too dry to get out any words. I have to clear my throat. "I have an alibi for that night. I told you that already."

"Right." He nods. "Right, the boyfriend. I forgot."

"Right," I say tightly.

"Unless…"

"Unless *what*? I have an alibi."

He shrugs. "Well, unless both of you killed her together."

I don't even have the words to respond to that one. But something is tugging at the back of my head. I should get a lawyer. I need to get a lawyer before this gets out of control. I need a lawyer before something happens that I can't undo.

But doesn't that look guilty? Why should I shell out a bunch of money for a lawyer? I didn't do anything, for God's sake!

"I have to go to work now, Detective." I'm struggling to keep my composure. "So if you don't have any other questions, I really need to go."

He shoves his hands into his jacket pockets. "Okay, we'll talk more later then."

No. No way. "I hope you find whoever did this to Dawn," I say.

"Believe me, Miss Farrell," he says. "We will."

CHAPTER 23

FOUR MONTHS EARLIER

To: Mia Hodge
From: Dawn Schiff
Subject: Re: Greetings

Dear Mia,

First of all, I want to say thank you for those lovely flowers you sent. You're the only person in the world who remembers that tulips are the one flower that doesn't irritate my sinuses. It brightened my day when they showed up. Especially after the terrible week I've been having.

So you know how much I pride myself on being prompt. In school, I never got even one tardy slip—you used to get them all the time! Sorry, I don't mean to make you feel bad about your tardiness, but it's just a fact. When somebody tells me to be somewhere at a specific time, you can bet I'm going to show up there on time. No excuses. In fact, I'm usually a few minutes early.

There's nothing worse than being late.

So you can imagine how embarrassed I was when I walked into a meeting in the conference room this afternoon and saw that the meeting had already commenced. I checked my watch, but I wasn't late. The meeting was supposed to start at two, and it was a few minutes before two. Yet everyone was seated at the conference table, most of the croissants had been eaten, and Seth was in the middle of a sentence.

"Gee, thanks for joining us, Dawn," Seth said.

As I replied, "You're welcome," a few people snickered. I didn't understand what was so funny though. The polite thing to do when somebody thanks you is to say you're welcome. You learn that in kindergarten. Except I wasn't sure why Seth thanked me in the first place, because about 60 seconds later, he ended the meeting and everybody left. I looked down at my watch again, feeling even more confused. Especially when Seth asked me in an irritated voice why I was an hour late to the meeting.

I tried to explain that I was not late. That the meeting started at 2 o'clock, and it was now 2 o'clock. Except then Seth tried to insist that the meeting started at one, which I know is not true, but it was hard to argue when everyone was in the room before me and the meeting clearly had come to a close.

Then Seth brought up the fact that I didn't show up to a meeting yesterday, even though that meeting had been canceled. Except Seth told me it wasn't canceled, and everyone was there but me.

I didn't know what to say. I just stood there, my knees wobbly. This wasn't like me. I always show up on time to meetings. And I would never not show up when I'm supposed to. There was definitely an email saying the meeting yesterday was canceled. I got it first thing in the morning in my inbox.

From Natalie.

Natalie, as the senior salesperson, is often the one to send out emails about the sales meetings. She was the one who sent out the email yesterday saying that the meeting was canceled. And she was the one who emailed me to say that the meeting was at 2:00 p.m. today.

I explained all this to Seth. He did not look like he believed me. He folded his arms across his chest and just kept shaking his head. In his eyes, Natalie can do no wrong.

"Why on earth would she do that?" he finally asked.

I wish I had an answer to that. Even now, I'm racking my brain. What did I do to make Natalie hate me so much? I know sometimes I do things to people that get them upset and I don't realize I even did it. Obviously, I did something like that to Natalie. I wish I could take back whatever it was. I just want to be her friend.

Then Seth told me that whatever is going on between me and Natalie, I have to find a way to work it out. Those were his words to me. *Work it out, Dawn.*

Except how? Natalie doesn't like me. I don't know how to change that. I don't even understand why she doesn't like me. It's not like I told anyone her secret. Well, I did tell you, but you're not going to tell anybody about it.

Maybe she's angry with me because I knocked

into her turtle figurine and it broke. Maybe I should buy her a new one. Except somehow I don't think that's it. She seemed mad at me before that happened.

I get so frustrated sometimes. Why is it so hard for me to make friends? It's so easy for other people. When I watch Natalie and Kim engaging in a conversation together, they have this great rapport, and I get so jealous. I keep trying, but it never works. You know this isn't the first time someone has hated me for no reason. It's happened more times than I can count.

I want to fix it. I've got to find a way to fix it. I'm smart. I can figure this out somehow if I think hard enough. If you have any ideas though, I'd love to hear them.

Sincerely,
Dawn Schiff

CHAPTER 24

PRESENT DAY

NATALIE

As soon as Detective Santoro leaves, I scour the internet for information about Dawn.

It's breaking news. Only a couple of stories have popped up, and those have minimal information. She was discovered in a patch of woods in Cohasset—another town about a twenty-minute drive down the South Shore—partially buried in the dirt. There's little other information available, although I bet more will surface as the day goes on.

I consider calling out sick from work, but I finally decide it's better to go in. After all, people at work might have more information than I do. And the truth is I want some answers.

How could that detective think I was bullying Dawn? How could anyone think that? I'm not that kind of person. I was *nice* to her. I even tried to be her friend, for what it was worth.

But obviously, I must've done something to make

people think I was bullying her. *Multiple* people told him that. And Dawn herself wrote about it in a bunch of emails to a friend. Which has made me a suspect in her murder.

I can't believe she thought that about me. And I'd really like to know who else said that about me. And who was this *friend*? I'm shocked to discover Dawn had a friend she felt close enough with to be telling them her intimate secrets.

Apparently though, I wasn't the worst of her problems. Someone else hated her. Someone else hated her enough to beat her to death with a blunt object.

What if it was the alleged friend? The one she was emailing about me. God knows, Dawn had a tendency to get on people's nerves. Maybe her friend couldn't take it anymore and decided to…

God, I can't stop thinking about what someone did to her.

When I get to the office, I head straight to my cubicle. I need to stop thinking about this and lose myself in my work. What happened to Dawn is horrible, but it isn't my fault. And thanks to my wonderful boyfriend, who from now on I will be completely exclusive with, I have an alibi. So Detective Santoro can think whatever he wants—I'm untouchable.

Except when I get to my cubicle, I stop short.

Two days ago, I came to work and there was a turtle figurine on my desk. Yesterday, I threw it in the garbage. I remember doing it. I didn't want to look at that thing ever again.

Yet now it's somehow back on my desk.

I am as terrified as anyone could possibly be of a

turtle figurine that's three inches long. I threw that damn thing in the garbage, and yet somehow, against all reason, it's *back*. I can't stop staring at it, with its black glassy eyes and shiny green shell.

What. The. Hell.

Okay, I need to calm down. Maybe the janitors did it. Maybe they saw the turtle in my garbage when they were emptying it and assumed it had fallen in there by mistake. And they thought they were saving it for me.

It's possible.

Anyway, I am getting rid of this thing once and for all. There aren't going to be any janitor mishaps this time.

I snatch the turtle from my desk. I clutch it in my right hand as the little arms and legs dig into my palm. And I march over to the break room, where I toss it directly in the communal trash. And by "toss," I mean that I hurl it in there with all my might, so that it makes a loud thump as it hits the bottom of the trash barrel. By lunchtime, that turtle will be buried in garbage.

I'll never see it again.

I'm nearly back to my cubicle when the phone on my desk starts ringing. Usually, I screen calls. But I'm off my game right now, so I snatch up the phone without thinking. A deep voice booms in my ear, "Is this Natalie Farrell?"

"Yes." I hate being on the phone without knowing who I'm speaking to when I start the call. The caller ID shows a blocked number. My heart sinks—not again. "Who is this?"

"It's Dave Fulton. From the Vitamin Hut."

"Oh, right." I let out a sigh of relief. I made a sale to Fulton about a month ago. He was a little reluctant to sample our products in his small store, but after we had a nice long lunch together, I managed to change his mind and he purchased five boxes' worth. "How can I help you, Mr. Fulton?"

"Look, Natalie." His voice has a rough edge. Like the detective, his Boston accent is heavy. "Nobody is buying Collahealth. Nobody wants it. And the few sales I made, they returned it. They said it doesn't work. Except for one woman, who said it gave her some crazy side effects like her feet started tingling."

"Yes, but it takes two to three months to see a response," I explain. "Did you tell them that?"

"You said two to three weeks."

"No, two to three *months*. That's how long it takes to build up the collagen levels."

"Whatever," he grumbles. "The point is, I can't move this crap. And I can't deal with people coming in complaining about side effects."

"There are no side effects. Studies have shown that Collahealth is perfectly safe."

"That's not the point. I want a refund. I've got three boxes I haven't even opened yet."

"I'm so sorry, Mr. Fulton. Vixed does not allow refunds."

There's a long silence on the other line. "What the hell are you talking about, Natalie? You told me I could get a refund if the product didn't sell."

"You must have misunderstood," I say in my most apologetic voice. "Vixed products have a limited shelf life, and we couldn't possibly allow refunds."

"Are you serious? This shit is expensive. You're saying I'm stuck with three boxes of your crap that I can't sell?"

Fulton's voice is getting louder. I imagine the veins bulging out on his thick neck, his eyes popping in their sockets.

"I'm *so* sorry," I say. God, it's too early for this. "It's just that this is the company policy. I don't make the rules. They do. If it were up to me, I would give you a refund."

"But you told me I could get a refund! That's the whole reason I bought them!"

"I…I don't know what to say. I'm very sorry."

Fulton is breathing hard on the other line. Now I imagine smoke coming out of his hairy ears. "I want to talk to your manager."

"Of course," I say. "Just hold on one moment."

I press the hold button and put down the phone. I look down at my nails—there's an uneven edge on my left index finger. I dig around in my purse until I locate my nail file. I file down the uneven edge. I blow off the dust from my fingernail. Fixing my nails always makes me feel better.

I push my newly filed nail against the hold button and pick up the phone. "Mr. Fulton?"

"Yeah?"

"I'm so sorry." I sigh. "I just checked with my manager, and he's on another call, but he told me to let you know that we can't make any exceptions to our policy. I'm afraid we can't offer you a refund."

Again, there's silence on the other line. "You lied to me."

"Excuse me?"

"You lied to me," he spits out. "You told me I could get a refund on your crappy product, and that's the only

154

reason I bought it. And also because you stuck your tits in my face."

"Mr. Fulton—"

"You're a lying bitch," he hisses. "And I hope your piece of shit company goes out of business."

With those words, there's a loud click on the other line. Dave Fulton has hung up on me.

I stare at the dead line in my hand, slightly shaken by the whole encounter. But seriously, this is a business. And you don't get to be the company's top salesperson by handing out refunds.

Ordinarily, I would've shrugged off a call like this. Most people like our products, but there are always going to be some people who don't. And it's not like I care about some dinky little store tucked away in Cambridge. He'll go out of business before we do.

But today, his words leave me shaken.

You're a lying bitch.

That is not true. I told him our refund policy. It's not my fault that he was too distracted by my breasts to listen carefully. I'm not a lying bitch. I'm doing what I have to do to sell our product. I'm doing my *job*.

It's not my fault.

CHAPTER 25

After I take a few deep breaths, I head back to the break room to grab some coffee. Kim has arrived as well, cupping a mug of coffee in her hand while she scrolls through the screen on her phone with her other hand. She usually spends the first hour of the workday in the break room. And she also goes in there three or four more times during the day. I'd estimate in a given week, Kim only does maybe one or two hours of real work.

I've tried to give Kim some tips to improve her sales, but she's not that interested. Honestly, sometimes I think she's trying to get fired. It will give her an excuse to stay home and let her rich husband pamper her.

"Hey, Nat!" Her eyes flick up at me. I notice the skin on her forehead is starting to peel a bit from the sunburn she got on her honeymoon. "Did you hear they found Dawn? Or at least what's left of her."

I grimace at her remark. It's not quite a joke, but it feels very inappropriate. "I heard."

Kim blinks up at me. "Who could have done that to her? I mean, we all sort of wanted to strangle her sometimes, but who would actually do something like that? It's so awful."

"Yeah." I slide into the seat next to hers. "Listen, Kim, did you talk to that detective yesterday?"

"Oh right." She takes a sip of coffee. "He was kind of hot, wasn't he?"

I crinkle my nose. If I ever might have found Santoro attractive, I certainly don't anymore. "Not really."

"He seems like he knows what he's doing." She opens another little cup of cream and dumps it into her coffee. Kim likes her coffee light brown. "I bet he'll catch whoever did this. Make sure they spend the rest of their life in prison."

For some reason, her remark makes me very uneasy. "Right."

"God, who do you think could have done it?"

I was reading this morning about what generally happens when a young woman is murdered the way Dawn was. In cases like this, the husband or boyfriend is often the culprit. But Dawn didn't have any significant others in her life. Unless her turtle murdered her.

"Maybe it was a burglar," I say.

But that doesn't feel quite right. Aside from whatever was in that gap in her bookcase, it sounds like nothing was missing from Dawn's house. And if she startled a burglar and he killed her, why would he hide the body? It doesn't make any sense.

Nothing about this makes any sense.

"So." I clear my throat. "What did you talk to the detective about yesterday?"

She shrugs and looks down at something on her phone. "I don't know. He had a bunch of questions about her."

"Did you tell the detective I was bullying her?"

I used to always know when Kim was lying because her face would turn pink. Unfortunately, her new suntan has made that difficult. "I don't know. Why?"

I want to shake her. "Kim, *did you tell him I was bullying Dawn*?"

Finally, she sighs. "I mean, you kind of were."

"No, I wasn't!"

She gives me a look. "It's not like I blame you. Dawn was so strange. She was obsessed with those turtles. Who is obsessed with *turtles*? Turtles are so *boring*. You know what would be better than turtles? *Anything*."

I can't help but think about the turtle I found on my desk the last three days. Or that live one I found crawling around the tank in Dawn's house. Or the bookcase brimming with turtles. She has no idea how creepy turtles can be.

"I wasn't bullying her," I insist. "I would never do that."

"You said that thing about how she lost her virginity to a turtle."

"Oh my God, that was a *joke*." I cringe. "It wasn't a big deal. Everyone made jokes like that about her. If I was bullying her, so were the rest of you."

"Whatever, Nat."

"Listen to me, Kim," I say through my teeth. "You need to stop lying about me to the detective, okay? Because this looks *really* bad for me."

"I just told him what really happened."

"Oh, is that what you did?" I raise my eyebrows. "Well, maybe I should tell your new husband what *really happened* the night of your bachelorette party. About that guy at the bar who you—"

"Natalie!" Kim reaches out and grasps my hand across the table with lightning speed. "You *promised* you wouldn't tell anyone—"

"And I won't." I level my eyes at her. "But you need to stop making me look bad. Okay? This is a goddamn murder investigation now. It's no joke."

For a moment, Kim looks like she's about to burst into tears. "Okay, I'm sorry. I didn't think it was a big deal. So you messed with Dawn a little bit. We all did."

"Right," I say. "We all did."

I give Kim one last long look. I feel confident that she's going to keep her mouth shut—she does not want her husband to know what she did that night. Lucky for me, I had the foresight to take a lot of photos the night of the bachelorette party.

Unfortunately, I have worse problems than Kim.

CHAPTER 26

I eat lunch again at my desk. I'm usually a very social person, but all anyone is talking about is Dawn's murder, and it's starting to make me physically ill. Also, I hate the idea that several people in the office thought that I was bullying Dawn. I still don't understand how anyone could have said that. If anything, I was the only one who tried to be nice to her!

While I am taking a bite of my turkey sandwich, a text message pops up on my phone. It's from Caleb.

Can we talk?

No good conversation has ever started with those three words. If he had something good to tell me, he would just go out and tell me. He wouldn't preface it by asking if it was okay to talk. This is a prebreakup text.

I scoop my phone off my desk and stare at the screen. I don't want to break up with Caleb. Despite my little lapse in judgment last night, I still think he's the perfect boyfriend. If anything, I want to move things forward. Before this week, I would have said he adored me. That he was stupidly infatuated with me.

What if he knows about Seth? What if he came to my house last night and saw his car parked out front? That would give him ample reason to initiate a breakup conversation.

I'm glad he didn't hear the detective's comment about how he and I could have killed Dawn together. That's beyond ridiculous. We certainly didn't kill her together. We weren't even actually together that night. But of course, I couldn't tell the detective *that*.

I can't take it anymore. I have to talk to Caleb.

I click on Caleb's number from my list of recent calls. I feel a tiny bit of relief when he doesn't sound outright angry when he answers the phone.

"Hey, Nat," he says.

"Hey."

"I heard about Dawn," he says quietly. "Are...are you okay?"

My eyes fill with tears. "Not really. I...I can't stop thinking about it. What happened to her..."

"I know."

"She was *beaten to death*, Caleb. Can you imagine?"

"I know. It's awful." There is an interminable silence on the other line. "Listen, I just wanted to say that I'm sorry about yesterday. I was kind of a jerk to you."

"Oh." That was the last thing I expected him to say. "Well, it's okay. I mean, it was a stressful day."

"It *was*." His voice sounds a little scratchy, like he didn't get enough sleep. "I've never been grilled by a

161

detective before. And that guy was *rough*. He just kept pushing me, trying to get me to crack."

"But you didn't."

"I didn't," he confirms. "Look, I do think it would be better to just tell the truth, but I get why he made you feel like you needed an alibi. And geez, it's obvious you couldn't have done this."

Maybe it's obvious to him. But the detective doesn't seem to feel the same way.

"So anyway," he says, "I'm sorry I freaked out. Do you forgive me?"

Only if you forgive me for sleeping with another guy last night. But no, probably better not to bring that up. He never needs to know about it. And like I said, it was a one-off. Seth knows that.

"Do you want to come over tonight?" I ask. I hate the idea of coming home to my empty house again.

He groans. "I wish I could, but I'm going to be at work late today. I don't even know how late. How about tomorrow?"

"Okay." I wish he were coming tonight, but as long as I'm going to see him soon. "And maybe this time you really can spend the night."

He sounds shocked. "Really?"

"Why not?"

"I…I just assumed with all the stuff going on with your friend, you wouldn't want to…"

"Dawn wasn't really my friend," I say slowly. "I mean, she was my coworker. I liked her. But we weren't friends."

"Oh," he says.

Did I say something wrong? Is it really so inappropriate

162

to have my boyfriend over after a coworker *who I hardly even knew* was murdered?

"Also," I say, "the 5K is on Saturday. You're still running, aren't you?"

Again, he sounds surprised. "That's still on?"

Despite everything, I feel a jolt of irritation. "We raised a lot of money for charity, Caleb. I can't just cancel it."

"Well, okay."

"I mean, this is for *kids with cerebral palsy*. It's not like I'm throwing a sweet sixteen party."

"No, I get it," he says. "I, uh…I guess I'll be there then."

I had imagined Caleb and me running together the whole way. He has longer legs, but I've been training harder than he has. He runs on the treadmill at the gym, but he hasn't specifically been training for this. I'll hold my own.

But I don't know what's going to end up happening with the 5K now. Dawn's murder has changed everything. I don't want to ruin everything we've worked for though. Maybe I need to put a new spin on things.

CHAPTER 27

THREE MONTHS EARLIER

To: Vixed Employees
From: Natalie Farrell
Subject: Bridal shower!!!!

This Friday afternoon at three, we are going to have a bridal shower to celebrate Kim's upcoming nuptials! Gifts are allowed and encouraged, and there is no spending limit! After all, Kim will only be getting married once. (We hope!) We are also going to do this potluck style so please let me know what yummy treats you will be bringing so we don't all bring the same thing!

To: Vixed Employees
From: Dawn Schiff
Subject: Re: Bridal shower!!!!

I'm so excited! I'll be bringing my famous turtle cupcakes. Sometimes with respect to desserts, "turtle" refers to candy made with pecans and caramel dipped in chocolate, but these will be actual turtle cupcakes! The inside will be chocolate, and while I won't be giving away all my secrets, trust me when I say these cupcakes will very much resemble turtles. I'm so excited to share them with you!

Sincerely,
Dawn Schiff

To: Vixed Employees
From: Natalie Farrell
Subject: Re: Bridal shower!!!!

For God's sake, Dawn, you don't need to always hit "reply all" on emails!!! I will let you know if anyone else claims cupcakes.

To: Mia Hodge
From: Dawn Schiff
Subject: Re: Greetings

Dear Mia,

This morning, I came to work with a tray of a dozen cupcakes. Natalie never got back to me about whether it was okay for me to bring them, but I figured you can never have too many cupcakes. I made chocolate, because we all know everybody loves chocolate. But I did use vanilla frosting, because I was able to add blue food coloring to make the icing look like the ocean, and then added green gummies to turn them into turtle cupcakes. I worked so hard on them. I'm attaching a photo so you can see how beautiful they were.

The bridal shower was at three o'clock in the conference room. Natalie spent most of the day preparing for it. Every time I looked up, she was in the conference room decorating. I thought about asking if I could help, but I didn't want to annoy her. So I kept my distance.

At three o'clock, my coworkers started filtering into the conference room with trays of food. I ran to the break room to grab my cupcakes, which I stashed on the bottom shelf of the refrigerator.

Except the cupcakes weren't there.

I was sure I put them in the refrigerator. I did it as soon as I came in, so the cupcakes would stay fresh. I checked every shelf, although the tray was bulky enough that it didn't seem like it would get lost in the refrigerator. Then I started checking the cabinets above the sink, wondering if somebody stashed the cupcakes up there.

After about five minutes of searching, I was starting to panic. My heart was racing as I rummaged through all the drawers and cabinets in the break room. I had been so excited to show everyone my cupcakes. What could have happened to them?

But then it hit me. Somebody probably saw the cupcakes and brought them over to the conference room, assuming they were for the shower.

The bridal shower had been going on for about fifteen minutes at this point. I rinsed off my hands and headed to the conference room to join the others. I could see almost everyone in the office was participating. This was an excellent opportunity to get to talk to my coworkers in a low-pressure environment.

Natalie was by the conference table, talking to Seth, who was munching on a tray of food. Seth had a smile playing on his lips, the same way he always did when he was talking to Natalie. I never figured out if he knew about his wife showing up at work and leaving that threatening note for Natalie. I did think about telling him, but I decided to take your advice and keep out of it.

But today I watched the two of them for a moment from outside the conference room. It was weird but I could almost imagine him leaning forward and pressing his lips against hers, running his fingers through her long, silky hair. It's not hard to see why he likes her.

I grabbed the handle of the conference room door. Instantly, Natalie jerked her head up. She abandoned Seth and sprinted across the room to the door to greet me. But she didn't look happy to see me. She started asking a million questions about what I was doing there, even though I was on the email where she invited the entire company.

Then she pointed out that it was a potluck and I hadn't brought anything. I was still hoping the turtle cupcakes had migrated to the party on their own, so I let her know that I was the creator of the turtle cupcakes. But when I said that, she acted like she didn't know what I was talking about. "There are no turtle cupcakes in here," she kept saying. Then she accused me of lying about having brought them.

"Please don't tell lies, Dawn," she said. "It's so unattractive."

When she said the word "unattractive," she made

a pointed gesture at my outfit. Unlike Natalie, I usually wear slacks to work. Skirts make me uncomfortable. And I don't wear fitted blouses like she does either—ones that strain at the bosom—although to be fair, I don't have much to show off in that department. My mother always used to say I have the figure of a prepubescent boy.

I kept insisting I made 12 chocolate cupcakes, but Natalie would not step aside to let me into the bridal shower. Finally, she said she didn't understand why I was here in the first place because I'm not even friends with Kim. When I pointed out that she invited me, she just shook her head.

"I sent that to everyone, but I assumed people realized they shouldn't come if they weren't friends with Kim—that's just common sense," she told me.

Except when I looked over Natalie's shoulder, it seemed like every single person in the company was in that conference room. It wasn't just friends of Kim. It was *everyone*. Everyone but me.

Before I could point that out, Natalie closed the door in my face and went back to talking to Seth.

I didn't know what to do after that. I could have gone back to doing work in the otherwise empty office, but I couldn't focus. I had thought this party would be an opportunity for me to finally get to know some of my coworkers. Maybe even make a friend. Obviously, I recognize I'll never have another friend like you. I've abandoned that foolish notion. But since we're living at different ends of the country, I'd love it if there was somebody I could have lunch with from time to time at least.

Finally, I opted to go back to the break room. I definitely brought the cupcakes to work this morning. I was sure that if I could find them and bring them to the conference room, Natalie would let me into the party. She *had* to. Everyone would want to try those cupcakes. Who wouldn't like turtle cupcakes?

So while everybody else was at the party, I went back to the break room alone. I checked the refrigerator one last time and then went through all the drawers and cabinets systematically. It was only on a whim that I pushed my foot on the pedal to open up the garbage bin.

And that's when I found my cupcakes. Smooshed together in a big messy pile at the bottom of the trash.

All my hard work was in the garbage. Nobody had the opportunity to see them or taste them. I spent hours on those cupcakes. For nothing.

You always used to tell me never to give other people the satisfaction of seeing me cry. If I was ever on the brink, you would tell me how awesome I am and that I need to be strong.

But it was easy not to cry when you were right here with me. It's a lot harder when you're alone. But you're right. No matter what, you can't let anyone know they've gotten to you. Because that's when they win.

So I went back to my cubicle with my chin held high. I wouldn't give them the satisfaction. You would have been proud of me.

Sincerely,
Dawn Schiff

To: Dawn Schiff
From: Mia Hodge
Subject: Re: Greetings

OMG Dawn!!!! This Natalie person has crossed a line! You need to go to HR and report her. I'm serious.

To: Mia Hodge
From: Dawn Schiff
Subject: Re: Greetings

Dear Mia,

I understand why you would say that, but I would rather not go to HR. I will just make another batch of cupcakes and keep them in my cubicle for the next party. Besides, the head of HR loves Natalie.

Sincerely,
Dawn Schiff

CHAPTER 28

NATALIE

I've got another interview in the late afternoon to promote the 5K, this one for a local radio station. My head isn't entirely in the game, but it'll be a good distraction. I've been doing sales calls all morning and haven't made one sale. But I can do an interview in my sleep. I've been told that I have a nice speaking voice. Someone once told me I should do voice-overs.

I was supposed to get a call from Rita Duke at four, but when it's a quarter past and I still haven't gotten the call, I find her number in my address book. Maybe I got the time wrong. Although I've got it written on my calendar. I don't usually make mistakes like that.

After several rings, I'm certain the call will go to voicemail, but then Rita picks up. "Natalie?"

"Hi, Rita!" I chirp into the phone. "Weren't we supposed to record the interview at two? Did I get it wrong?"

"No." She's quiet for a moment. "I guess I just

assumed you didn't want to do it anymore since your coworker…" She drops her voice several notches. "You know, was killed."

I'm not surprised she knows about Dawn. It's been all over the news today, since her body turned up. "Actually, I thought we could talk about that during the interview. We're raising money for cerebral palsy, but now we're also going to be running in Dawn's honor."

She's quiet for so long that I almost think she's hung up. Finally, she says, "Really? Do you think that's in good taste?"

"In good taste? What are you talking about? Dawn was brutally murdered, and the killer is still out there. This will draw more awareness—maybe it will lead to finding the bastard who did this to her."

"Natalie, do you know what everybody is saying on the internet?"

I get a horrible sinking feeling in my stomach. "What?"

"Your company is trending." Rita says it like it's a *big deal*. "Everybody is saying that Dawn was severely bullied by the staff who work there. It's all over the place."

I grab my phone and bring up my Twitter feed. "What should I search for?"

"Hashtag VixedBullies."

Oh God.

"It's not true," I say to Rita. "It's just a horrible rumor. You know how these things get started."

"Uh-huh…"

"I liked Dawn." My voice sounds almost whiny, but I can't help it. "She and I were friends. Good friends. If anything, I protected her from other people bullying

172

her. She was *different*, you know? But I liked that about her. I liked that she was different."

"I get it," Rita says, "but I just feel like the climate is wrong right now. I can't take the side of the enemy, you know?"

"I'm not the enemy!" I want to pound my fists on my desk. "I'm the one who found out she was missing in the first place!"

"Yeah, I saw a post mentioning that." Rita coughs. "It was hashtag suspicious."

I'm too stunned to speak. It takes a second for my voice to come back to me. "You know, I have an alibi for the night she disappeared."

"I'm sure you do," Rita says vaguely. "Look, I just don't think it's a good idea to do this interview right now. But I hope it all works out for you, Natalie."

"Gosh, thanks, Rita. I appreciate your support."

Before she can respond, I hang up the phone. That was unbelievable. Rita has been interviewing me every single year since I started doing the 5K. I thought we were friends. I can't believe she would hang me out to dry like that after just a hint of a rumor.

Now that I'm off the phone, I have to see what Rita was talking about. I bring up my Twitter feed, and I type in the hashtag.

Oh no. This is worse than I thought.

CHAPTER 29

We are trending. In 280 characters or less, everybody on the internet is sharing stories about workplace bullying and how awful it is that poor Dawn was tormented the way she was. Even though it's almost physically painful, I scan through the litany of horrible comments about my company and the people who work there. It's almost too awful to read. People as a whole can be terrible. Mob mentality and all.

> The people who work at that company should all go to jail. #VixedBullies
>
> Child bullies grow up to be adult bullies. #justice-fordawn #VixedBullies
>
> I took Collahealth and it was the most useless supplement I have ever tried. Basically sugar pills. Did nothing. #VixedSucks
>
> You're lucky it did nothing. It made my hair fall out. #VixedSucks

Oh my God, Collahealth does *not* make your hair fall out. That is a complete lie. Yes, it doesn't work for everyone. But for the people who do have benefits, the effects can be amazing. I mean, I don't take Collahealth personally. My collagen is already fine. But I've read the literature on it, and it's a really good product.

After a while, I'm just searching for my name. For the most part, whoever leaked the story about Dawn has kept my name out of it. Thank God. But a few people have chosen to criticize me as an employee of Vixed.

Natalie from Vixed is the worst lying snake you will ever meet. She will say anything to get you to buy their crap. #VixedSucks

It's hard not to take it personally.

"Nat?"

Seth is standing over me, hovering at the entrance to my cubicle, wearing his trench coat. I was so absorbed in looking at my Twitter feed that I didn't even see him approach. His eyebrows are scrunched together.

"Hi," I mumble.

"You okay, Nat?"

I drag my gaze away from my phone. "We're getting trashed on the internet, you know."

"I know." He seems unperturbed, given that his name got mentioned quite a bit as well. *Manager Seth Hoffman did nothing to stop the bullying.* "You should stop looking at it."

"How can I?" Even as I'm talking to him, I'm looking back down again to read the next comment. There's a new one popping up every few seconds.

"It's easy." He reaches out and snatches my phone off

175

the desk. "Just stop. It's not going to help find who did this to Dawn."

"Hey!"

"It's for your own good, Nat."

"Everyone thinks I bullied Dawn. That I'm a terrible person."

"That's bullshit." Seth says the words so vehemently, I almost want to hug him. Even Kim seemed to believe that I had been bullying Dawn, and she's my best friend. "You were *nice* to Dawn. You didn't do anything wrong. These people on the internet are just speculating. They're just looking for somebody to blame. They don't know you like I do."

I tug at a lock of my hair. "Aren't you freaking out though? Corporate is not going to be happy about this."

"It's fine. They know it's just a rumor and it will blow over. What happened to Dawn is terrible, but it wasn't our fault."

"What if they fire you?"

He grins crookedly. "Then my income drops precipitously, which will be great for my divorce proceedings. Relax, Nat. This is going to be okay."

"Give me back my phone."

"I'm going to walk you to your car, then I'll give it back to you."

Seth seems intent on holding my phone hostage, so I snatch my jacket off the back of my chair and wrap it around myself. There's a chance he could be right. I'm pretty sure nothing good can come from reading these posts. It is what it is.

At least nobody has called me a murderer. So there's that.

I follow Seth down the hall to the elevators. He's still got my phone shoved into his own coat pocket. I still don't understand all the hate directed at us. We didn't bully Dawn, although God knows, we could have, because she blatantly disregarded so many social conventions. But we were nice to her—I mean, *mostly*. Were there a few times I got irritated and snapped at her? Sure, I'm only human. But I really did try to be patient with her in general. I even made an effort to include her in work events. Like even though she wasn't friends with Kim and was sometimes outright rude to her, I made a point of inviting her to the bridal shower we threw for her—even though she didn't end up coming.

And even if we did bully her, what does that have to do with her murder, for God's sake? Do they think we bullied her to death?

"You're still thinking about it," he notes.

"I can't help it!" I tug at my pantyhose, which rip slightly under my fingernail. Damn it. "I'm not used to people hating me." Well, except for his wife. But even she seems to have lost interest in harassing me.

"Nobody hates you, Nat." His light brown eyes meet mine across the elevator. "I sure don't."

I look away from him. This is not going to lead to anything good.

The sun has already gone down when we get out of the building. The weather is brisk and it's almost drizzling. November just started, and it's promising to be a wet, cold month. Soon it will start snowing. Saturday is supposed to be nice at least.

Seth stands close to me as we walk through the parking lot in the direction of my car. I notice he's parked only a few spots away from mine. A few times as we walk, his shoulder brushes against mine. I don't comment on that.

When we reach my car, I turn to look at him. "Can I have my phone back now?"

He fishes into his pocket and pulls it out for me. As I take it from him, my fingers brush against his. I can't help but notice how close he is standing to me.

"So," he says.

My hair is starting to curl in the cold mist. "So."

He leans to kiss me. He gets within about an inch of my lips, but then I come to my senses. I press my palm firmly against his chest, pushing him away.

"No, Seth," I say. "I can't."

"Come on," he pleads with me. "Just a one-off."

"Last night was the one-off," I remind him. "If we do it again, it's not a one-off. Then it's just cheating. And I don't want to cheat on Caleb. He's a good guy."

"So break up with him. Be with me instead."

I can see in his eyes that he's serious. He wants me to dump Caleb and go out with him instead. He must be out of his mind. Yes, last night was amazing and he is wicked sexy. But he's a mess. His personal life is a disaster. And my own head is still spinning after everything that's happened this week. I just can't do this.

"I'm sorry," I say.

Before he can start declaring his love for me again like last night, I grab my keys out of my purse and get into my car. Seth backs away to let me get out of the spot, but he doesn't get into his own car. Even as I'm driving out of the parking lot, he's watching me.

CHAPTER 30

TWO MONTHS EARLIER

To: Rhonda Schiff
From: Dawn Schiff
Subject: Advice

Dear Mother,

What is the best way to get a coworker to like you better? Do you have any strategies I could use?

Sincerely,
Dawn

To: Dawn Schiff
From: Rhonda Schiff
Subject: Re: Advice

Who are we talking about? A man?

To: Rhonda Schiff
From: Dawn Schiff
Subject: Re: Advice

Dear Mother,
    No, this coworker is a woman.

Sincerely,
Dawn

To: Dawn Schiff
From: Rhonda Schiff
Subject: Re: Advice

Who cares if some woman likes you? It's probably a lost cause, so don't even bother. Anyway, you need a man. You're not getting any younger. Also, I'm going to need a little extra money this month. About $2,000 should cover it, but more would be better. The car broke down.

To: Rhonda Schiff
From: Dawn Schiff
Subject: Re: Advice

Dear Mother,
    I'm sorry, but I can't. My rent is higher in Quincy, and I don't have much extra. I could send $1,000 more this month, but that is the maximum.

Sincerely,
Dawn

To: Dawn Schiff
From: Rhonda Schiff
Subject: Re: Advice

You really can't afford an extra two thousand dollars after all I put up with from you? Constantly calling me and whining about how you have no friends. I wish I had a dollar for every hour I listened to you going on and on about those goddamn turtles. You can't even give your own mother a little extra money one month?

To: Rhonda Schiff
From: Dawn Schiff
Subject: Re: Advice

Dear Mother,
    I'm afraid I can't. I apologize.

Sincerely,
Dawn

To: Dawn Schiff
From: Rhonda Schiff
Subject: Re: Advice

Well, I can't believe how ungrateful you are. Don't bother asking me for any advice ever again.

To: Mia Hodge
From: Dawn Schiff
Subject: Re: Greetings

Dear Mia,

I must be desperate because I emailed my mother to get her advice. Not that your advice hasn't been great, but I need to try something different.

I've tried smiling more at Natalie and being as nice as I possibly can, but it's not working. I don't know for sure she's the one who threw out my turtle cupcakes, but I have a strong suspicion. And even if she didn't do it and it was all a terrible accident, she was still mean to me when I tried to come to the party.

She has also given me misinformation about two other meetings. I've now gotten in the habit of calling Seth's secretary, just to make sure I don't miss them.

I considered trying to talk to Seth again, but he won't do anything. Even if I had evidence that she threw out my cupcakes, he would simply tell me to deal with it myself. Or worse, he would take *her* side.

I've got to do something about this. I've got to turn Natalie from enemy to friend.

Unfortunately, emailing my mother for advice was a big mistake. I hadn't emailed her in months, and I haven't called her in even longer. When I first moved out of my parents' house up in Beverly, I used to call home once a week. I always dreaded it though. Right before the call, my stomach would twist up in knots and I wouldn't even be able to eat anything. You know how my mother can be, and she's a million times worse now.

Even emailing my mother made me nervous—so nervous, I could barely eat dinner. Tonight's color was yellow. I made yellow Spanish rice with corn mixed in. But mostly I pushed it around my plate.

Anyway, she didn't have any helpful advice. Not only that, but she started pressuring me to give her more money. Did I tell you that I've been sending my mother checks every month? Just enough to help her get by now that my father is gone. She didn't ask me to start doing it, but if I'm ever late, she does call me up and ask me when the check is coming.

I couldn't tell her that I'm making less money at Vixed than at my last job. I never even told her why I left that job.

My mother didn't like hearing I couldn't give her any extra money though. That's when I decided not to contact her again.

Instead, I looked on the internet for ideas.

I found an article listing ways to get people to like you. Some of the stuff was obvious. *Be empathetic.* Well, of course. *Make them feel good.* Naturally. *Smile.* I knew that one.

There were a lot of tips about body language. Besides smiling, the article recommended tilting your head toward the other person. The science behind this is that evolutionarily, tilting your head exposes your carotid artery so you're letting the other person know that you aren't looking for a fight. You can also touch the other person to establish a bond.

They also mentioned eye contact. You know I'm terrible at eye contact. I don't know why, but it makes me incredibly uncomfortable. Sometimes I force myself to look at the person's nose, but meeting their eyes is virtually impossible for me. You're the only person I can ever make eye contact with.

The article suggested asking the other person about herself and trying to find things that interest them. I could do that with Natalie. I know she likes turtles like I do, so we could talk about that, but I suspect there are other things she likes that we can talk about as well. The article also mentioned flattery. That would be an easy one since Natalie has so many good qualities.

After reading through the article, my neck felt tense and uncomfortable. I'll do what I need to do to try to get Natalie to like me back, but none of those suggestions in the article are things that come easily to me. It will be a lot of effort.

My life would be so much easier if I were a turtle. Junior doesn't have to worry about mean girls at work. I could be alone all the time and hide in my shell whenever I want.

Honestly, if I didn't have you to talk to, I don't know what I would do. Do you think I might be able to come out to visit you and George in Palo Alto soon? Spending a week away from here will make all the difference. Please let me know when a good time to visit would be!

Sincerely,
Dawn Schiff

To: Dawn Schiff
From: Mia Hodge
Subject: Re: Greetings

We would absolutely love to have you, but my work is insanely busy right now, and George's parents are flying out this weekend. It may not be the best time. Could we talk about it in a few weeks? I would love to see you!

Also, I shouldn't have to tell you this, but don't give your mother any more money! And for God's sake, don't ask her for advice!

XXO
Mia

CHAPTER 31

PRESENT DAY

NATALIE

The sky is completely black when I get back home.

I park out on the street in front of my house, and once again, I'm relieved to discover that I managed to lock the door this morning. I step into my empty house and commence with my new ritual of flipping on every single light switch when I walk into the living room.

I wonder what Dawn was doing when the intruder came into her house. Was she first getting home from work and they startled her as she was coming in the door? Or was she sitting on her sofa, a plate on her lap, enjoying a quiet dinner while she watched TV, when somebody came up from behind her and…

God, maybe I should have let Seth come over after all.

I plop down on my sofa and turn on the television. It turns out to be a massive mistake, because every channel is talking about Dawn. They keep flashing that ID photo of Dawn on the screen, the one where she doesn't even have a hint of a smile and her tortoiseshell glasses take up half of her face. A lot of people have terrible ID photos, but Dawn's is particularly awful.

Mine is actually pretty good. I happened to be having a very good hair day.

"Dawn Schiff was found partially buried in an undisclosed location," the reporter on the screen tells the camera. "The cause of death was reported to be head trauma. Police say she was brutally beaten with a blunt object to the point where most of her teeth had been knocked out. Her glasses were found shattered on the ground beside her."

I imagine Dawn's tortoiseshell glasses lying in the dirt, stained with her own blood—the lenses cracked, the frame destroyed. My stomach turns.

Oh God. I need to turn this off. I need another distraction. Something that has nothing to do with Dawn or her brutal murder.

Maybe I'll do my laundry.

One of the best things about my house is that I have my own washer and dryer. Before this, I lived in an apartment, and I had to stuff my laundry into a basket every week and throw it in the trunk of my car, then drive to the local laundromat. And then I would just have to freaking *wait* there while my laundry spun around for an hour in the washer. If you went at the wrong time, the competition could be brutal. The whole process was inhuman.

Now all I have to do is grab my laundry hamper and drag it to the washer and dryer at the end of the hallway. There's never a line, and I can remain in the comfort of my own home while my clothes are being cleaned. Of course, I still have to send out a bunch of my stuff to get dry-cleaned, but most of my clothing comes out pretty well on the gentle cycle.

I haven't done my laundry in about two weeks, so the hamper is fairly full of clothing. Still, I'm surprised by how heavy it feels as I lug it down the hall to the washer. Is it usually this heavy? It's just clothing inside, but it feels like it's full of rocks.

I throw open the washing machine and add the cup of detergent. Then I sift through my hamper, pulling out the colored laundry. I always separate my whites and my colors. I don't want my white blouses to turn pink.

As I reach into the depths of the laundry basket, my fingers hit something unfamiliar near the bottom of the basket. Something that definitely isn't clothing. It feels smooth and kind of cold.

What the hell *is* that?

I push away my clothing to get a better look. There's something green and shiny at the bottom of my laundry hamper. I catch a glimpse of the overhead lights reflected on its shiny surface. It's some kind of ceramic pot or globe, about the size of a basketball.

I reach in with both hands to pull it out so I can get a closer look. When my fingers close around the object, it feels like a piece of glazed pottery. It's heavy too. No wonder the laundry hamper was so hard to carry.

I grunt with the effort of pulling it out of the hamper. In the dim light of the hallway, it's hard to tell what I'm holding until I get it all the way out. But when I see what it is, I almost throw up.

It's a ceramic turtle.

And it's covered in blood.

CHAPTER 32

Oh God oh God oh God oh God…

Why is there a freaking bloody turtle in my laundry hamper?

Police say she was brutally beaten with a blunt object.

I think back to the bookshelf in Dawn's house. The bookcase filled with turtle figurines. And then, of course, there was a gap in one of the shelves. Where something was missing. The detective even asked me about the missing object.

Something roughly the size and shape of this ceramic turtle.

Oh God.

There's dark red material caked into the shell of the turtle. My first assumption was that it was blood, and I can't think of any reason to think otherwise. If this came from Dawn's house, and there was blood all over her floor, it stands to reason that the missing turtle from her bookcase would have blood on it.

That part makes sense. What doesn't make sense is *why is this thing in my laundry hamper?*

This is bad. Detective Santoro already thinks I've done something terrible to Dawn. How am I supposed to explain why I have this turtle in my house? I can't come up with anything that makes sense. Someone put it here. But who would do that?

Police say she was brutally beaten with a blunt object.

Of course, the answer is obvious. Whoever killed Dawn smashed this ceramic turtle over her head, and then they brought it to my house and planted it here. To frame me.

It makes perfect sense to me. But I'm not so sure Santoro will be convinced.

I need help. I don't know what to do.

It surprises me that the only person I want to call right now is Seth. Caleb is my boyfriend, but he was already freaking out about having to lie for me. I get the feeling if I asked Seth to fudge an alibi, he wouldn't have any qualms about doing it. I told him to get lost earlier, but the truth is, I trust him. He cares about me. He was the only person today who didn't seem to think I was some coldhearted bully. And even though it's not entirely convenient, he loves me. I believe him when he says that.

If I tell him about the turtle and explain that I don't know how it got there, he'll believe me. He'll help me.

Just as I'm about to go back into the living room to retrieve my phone, the doorbell rings. The ceramic turtle slides out of my fingers and topples to the floor. The impact causes it to crack, splintering loose a triangle of bloody ceramic turtle.

Crap.

For about five seconds, I stand there in my hallway, not sure what to do. I don't want to deal with whoever is at the door. Hopefully, whoever it is will go away.

And then the doorbell rings again.

I stuff the pieces of the turtle back into the laundry hamper. I push it all the way down to the bottom and cover it up with clothing. My hands are sweaty but don't have any blood on them at least.

I swear, if this is somebody selling Tupperware or dictionaries or the word of God, I'm going to lose it.

It's only when I get close to the front door that the single flashing red and blue light outside my window become visible. It's an unmarked police car.

Oh no.

CHAPTER 33

TWO MONTHS EARLIER

To: Caleb McCullough
From: Natalie Farrell
Subject: Need help pleeeeeeease!!!!

So I hear you are the new computer expert. I'm having this weird bug on my machine, like a virus or something, and I'm freaking out!!! I was wondering if you could help me fix it? I would be soooo grateful!

To: Natalie Farrell
From: Caleb McCullough
Subject: Re: Need help pleeeeeeease!!!!

Sure. I just need to finish this mock-up of the sales portal for Seth that he said he needs ASAP, but I'll be there as soon as it's done.

To: Caleb McCullough
From: Natalie Farrell
Subject: Re: Need help pleeeeeeease!!!!

Seth always says he needs everything ASAP. Please come help me!!! My computer keeps popping up all these crazy windows. It's going to start showing me porn soon! Please save me! I promise I will definitely make it worth your while!

To: Natalie Farrell
From: Caleb McCullough
Subject: Re: Need help pleeeeeeease!!!!

I'll be right there.

To: Mia Hodge
From: Dawn Schiff
Subject: Re: Greetings

Dear Mia,

This morning, I found Natalie in the break room. Kim was away on her honeymoon, so she was with the new guy, Caleb, and she had a stack of booster sheets in front of her. Over the last couple of months, Natalie has been organizing a 5K run for charity. She does this every year, apparently.

I watched at the doorway to the break room for a moment. Caleb was hired a couple of months ago to help out with the company's website, which Seth is hoping will become a larger source of sales. Caleb works part-time, so he's only here a couple of days a week, but I've been noticing him hanging around with Natalie a lot during that time. From my perch at the doorway, I could see the way he was looking at her. It was the same way Seth looked at her.

And then Natalie reached out and touched his hand. I wonder if she likes him. Caleb is attractive—tall and lean with nice teeth—although I wouldn't go so far as to say he's handsome. But when he smiled at Natalie, it transformed his face into the kind that would turn heads.

When they looked up, I could tell Caleb didn't know who I was. Natalie finally cued him in and told him that I'm Dawn, "the one who has, like, five billion turtles on her desk." When she said that, he seemed to know who I was and said hi in a nice but disinterested kind of way.

Before Caleb left, Natalie bugged him to make sure he would be running at the race. He smiled and told her of course he would. It was obvious he liked her, but that's not surprising because everyone likes Natalie. Everything is so easy for her—all she has to do is smile at an attractive man, and that's all it takes. Caleb is smitten.

As soon as Caleb left the room, the smile dropped entirely off Natalie's face. That meant she wasn't happy with me. I knew that much.

But I took it as a challenge. I thought back to all the websites I read about befriending people and said, "Hi, Natalie," because one of the websites said that using somebody's name when you talk to them makes them like you better. Then I asked if she wanted me to participate in the 5K.

She said it was fine, that they already had enough people. I didn't understand that. Why wouldn't Natalie want me to run? Every person running is more money for her charity. Not that I am a great runner, but I could have spent the month training. 5K isn't very far.

The website said paying someone a genuine compliment makes them like you better. There were so many compliments I could've paid Natalie at that moment—I was spoiled for choices—so I said, "I like your necklace, Natalie."

Her fingers flew to her neck. It *was* a very pretty necklace. Understated and studded with diamonds around the delicate curve of her throat. But instead of taking it as a compliment, she snapped at me, "What are you saying? Are you saying you don't think I can afford a necklace like this?"

I didn't understand why she was so upset, so I reassured her that I wasn't implying anything and that I was simply complimenting her necklace. And I tried to use her first name as many times as I could when I said it. Then I told her she would definitely find some-one to marry her, because it seemed like she didn't like it when I told her the truth about that.

Natalie said, "Gee, thanks." Although to be honest, it didn't sound like a sincere thanks.

The website mentioned that reaching out and making a physical connection can be helpful. That was something I hoped I wouldn't have to do. Physically touching people is very difficult for me. I never had to do any of this stupid stuff with you. We just connected and were friends. You never cared if we hugged or even touched each other.

But I was willing to do whatever it took if it meant winning Natalie over. So I reached out and put my hand on her shoulder.

She didn't react the way I thought she would though. She jerked her arm away like I had just touched her with a burning hot poker. And then all of a sudden, she was sticking her finger in my face and hissing, "Don't you *ever* touch me. Don't you dare lay one finger on me. You hear me?"

Natalie's face was bright red now. She definitely wasn't smiling. I'm bad at reading expressions, but this one was easy.

I sputtered an apology but she didn't say anything. Her shoulder jostled mine as she pushed past me and left the break room. For a good minute after she left, I just stood there, my legs too shaky to carry me out of the room.

I don't know what I did wrong. I keep thinking about it, but I can't figure it out. I was so nice to her. I used her name. I gave her several compliments. Nothing worked.

I don't know what to do, Mia. Please help me.

Sincerely,
Dawn Schiff

CHAPTER 34

PRESENT DAY

NATALIE

No no no no… The police can*not* be at my front door. I freeze about five paces from the front door. I don't know what to do. I can't answer the door for a police officer when I have a murder weapon in my laundry hamper. What if they ask to look around? I'll be so screwed.

But they can't just come in without asking. I can always say no. Unless they have a warrant…

No. They can't possibly have a warrant. I haven't even done anything wrong!

While I am working myself into a panic at the door, the doorbell rings a third time. At this point, I have to answer. Whoever is at the front door probably heard my footsteps. I'm making things worse by not answering.

My hands are shaking so badly, it takes a few tries for me to turn the locks. I throw open the front door and there he is. Detective Santoro. My new freaking best friend.

I wonder if it's time to get a lawyer. It seems like such a guilty move, and I can't afford it, but I don't want to be one of those stupid people who didn't lawyer up at the right time and then regrets it.

"Miss Farrell." His face bears that grim smile I've come to hate. "Can I have a moment of your time?"

"I'm sort of busy," I say tightly. "Haven't we already talked twice now? I've told you everything I know."

"I just have a few more questions, Miss Farrell. It won't take long."

I hug my chest so he can't see how much my hands are trembling. "I'd rather not. I have nothing else to say."

"We could talk down at the station if you'd prefer."

Oh God, no. That's much worse. "Fine. Go ahead."

"Can I come in?"

Am I going to invite a police officer into my house when I have what is almost certainly a murder weapon hidden in my laundry hamper? I think not. "I'd rather you didn't."

"It's just…" He glances over his shoulder. "It's cold out. I'm letting all the heat out of your house. And also, you look cold."

"I'm fine."

"You're shaking."

He's not wrong. But the reason I'm shaking has nothing to do with the cold. And I'm worried he might know that. "What are your questions, Detective?"

But he doesn't ask them right away. Instead, he looks past me, into my house. He's craning his neck to see inside. "Is it just you living here?"

"Just me."

"Wow," he says. "That's a big place. Must be expensive."

"It's not that bad."

"Oh yeah? I was trying to get a place in Dorchester, but everything was so pricey. Ended up renting the second floor of a house in Weymouth."

I take a peek at Santoro's left hand. No ring. Married to his job, probably. "Maybe you didn't look hard enough."

"So what kind of money do you make at Vixed?"

"Excuse me?"

"Your boss wouldn't tell me how much you make. I'm just wondering."

I hug myself tighter, now actually feeling the cold. I do sort of wish we could do this inside, but I don't dare. "Detective, what does this have to do with Dawn?"

"I was just thinking…" He scratches at the five-o'clock shadow on his chin. "Dawn was the accountant at your company. So if any shenanigans were going on with the payroll, maybe she found out about it. And that would give you a pretty damn good reason for wanting to get rid of her."

My throat is suddenly dry. "*What?*"

"It's just a thought." He blinks innocently. "Did Dawn ever come to you about any concerns like that?"

"*No.*"

"Huh." He raises his eyebrows. "So you were saying you didn't meet with Dawn on Monday night about the money she found missing from the Vixed account?"

"Oh my God, *no!*" I have to grab on to the door-frame to keep my legs from collapsing beneath me. "Why would you think that?"

"She sent you an email on Monday afternoon, didn't she? Asking to meet with you?"

I can't deny that. I already told him about Dawn's

email, plus I'm sure there's a record of it if they were able to get into her computer. "Yes."

"So what did you discuss when you met?"

"Nothing!" My hands are shaking so badly, I have to clutch them to my chest. I'm surprised my legs are even able to hold me up anymore. "I never met with her."

One of his thick eyebrows arches up. "No?"

"No! I didn't!" I have to struggle to keep my composure. "I didn't steal money from my company, Detective. And I certainly never had a conversation with Dawn about it on Monday night! I was with my boyfriend the entire night."

"Yeah, so you say."

"It's the *truth*. You spoke to Caleb. He told you we were together."

"Yes, that's what he told me."

"Do you really think the two of us plotted to kill her together?"

"No. I don't really think that."

My left eyelid twitches. "So why the hell are you bothering me then?"

Detective Santoro looks like he's considering my question. He purses his lips, thinking it over. "Here's the thing, Miss Farrell," he finally says. "In my line of work, people tell me a lot of things. And a lot of those things aren't true. So I've gotten pretty good at knowing when someone is blowing smoke up my ass."

I just stand there, staring at him.

"If you got your boyfriend to lie to me," he says, "I'll figure it out eventually. It's what I'm good at. It's what I do." He pauses. "So it'll be easier on you if you tell me the truth."

The truth? I can't tell him the truth. I can't tell him that I have no alibi for most of the night Dawn was killed. I can't tell him that I pressured my boyfriend into lying for me. And I sure as hell can't tell him about that bloody turtle in my laundry hamper. The only way I'm not walking out of here in handcuffs is if I keep my fool mouth shut.

"I've told you the truth," I say. "I didn't steal from my company. And I didn't see Dawn on Monday night."

He stands on my front porch for about ten more seconds, but it feels like ten hours. The whole time, his black eyes bore into me. A lesser person might have cracked. But I keep my mouth shut.

"Have it your way, Miss Farrell," he says.

I watch him walk over to his car, get inside, and drive away. As his taillights fade into the distance, I release a breath. I've been spared. For now. He's got nothing on me.

As long as I get rid of that turtle in my laundry hamper.

CHAPTER 35

I can't go anywhere right away. There's a chance Santoro could be keeping an eye on my house, and I don't want to risk him seeing me doing anything suspicious. And what I'm about to do is going to be very suspicious. But I can't take any chances.

So I force myself to eat some dinner. I boil some spaghetti on the stove, but I'm so distracted that I forgot all about it. The water boils all the way down, so the spaghetti is half-burned and stuck to the pot. It doesn't matter though. I don't have any appetite.

About four hours later, I get back in my car.

One nice thing about living on the South Shore is the number of beaches we have out here. I'm only about ten minutes away from the Quincy line, and there are a ton of beaches to choose from. During the summer, I'll grab my reclining chair and towel, and I'll try to get out to the beach every single weekend.

I don't need my GPS to get to Wollaston Beach.

It's my favorite beach, and I've been to that one dozens of times, even just this past summer. I love the way the grains of sand feel under my feet, I love the way the ocean water licks my ankles, and I love the way the sun beats down on me while I lie on my beach towel. I love the array of little shops lining the beach, all selling delicious but incredibly unhealthy fried seafood that you can smell from down the block. Fried clams are just the best.

Unfortunately, the beach in November isn't quite as much fun. But the good news is it will be empty.

I spend the entire drive trying to figure out who would have put that murder weapon in my laundry hamper. I'm racking my brain. Because it's obvious that whoever put it there was hoping the police might find it and pin the disappearance on me.

And then there were all those fingerprints they found in Dawn's house. I had convinced myself that I must've touched more items than I thought in her kitchen, but now I'm not so sure anymore. It strikes me that if I wasn't the one who went to check on Dawn and reported her missing, those fingerprints would have looked a lot more suspicious. It seems like somebody is trying to make it look like I'm responsible for what happened to my coworker.

The question is, who would do something like that?

I don't have any enemies. Everybody likes me. Okay, there are a few disgruntled customers. But nobody is angry enough over a few boxes of vitamins to murder somebody and then frame me for it. That's pretty diabolical.

I suppose Melinda Hoffman isn't too fond of me. She may even blame me for breaking up her marriage. But aside from that one-off, which happened *after* Dawn's disappearance, I hadn't gone near Seth in months. It seems crazy she would hate me enough to frame me for murder. That is just too far.

As for *how* they did it, that part is easy. My door was unlocked when I came back from Dawn's house. I'm careless about stuff like that. It would be easy for just about anyone to walk right in and bury the ceramic turtle in my laundry hamper.

At this point, I'm starting to seriously wonder if I need to hire a lawyer, but I can't imagine how I'll afford something like that. When Seth's wife was threatening me and I was looking into taking legal action against her, the hourly rate of all the local lawyers made me realize being threatened by your boyfriend's wife isn't *that* bad. I'm innocent, so why do I need a lawyer anyway? Lawyers are for guilty people.

During the summer, it's impossible to find a decent parking spot at the beach—every single one of the spots lining the coast is taken by families eager to enjoy a nice refreshing swim and a day in the sand. But on a cold night in November, the parking lot is barren. It's so quiet here, I'm pretty sure I would know if there was a car following me. But mine is the only vehicle in sight.

It was nippy during the day, and now that the sun is down, it's *really* cold. Below forty degrees, for sure. And because of the mist in the air all day, when I take my sneakers off in the sand, the grains feel wet and uncomfortable under my bare feet. But I don't want to get sand in my shoes, so I have no choice but to carry them.

Seth was always reluctant to go anywhere in public with me, because he was too scared of getting caught, so a beach trip wasn't in the cards for us. Then Caleb and I started dating in the middle of September, and it wasn't beach weather by then—the summers are short in New England. I fantasized about bringing him to the beach next year. I wanted him to see me in a teeny tiny bikini. I wanted us to playfully splash each other in the waves.

If I don't get rid of what's in my shoulder bag, I'll be wearing an orange jumpsuit by next summer.

Before I left the house, I stood on my back porch and smashed the ceramic turtle into pieces. I figured it would be challenging to get rid of a basketball-shaped object, and this way, if the pieces wash up, nobody will know what they are. So I've got about a dozen shards of pottery stuffed into my shoulder bag with "Save the Whales" emblazoned on the front.

I walk through the beach up to the edge of the water. The tide hasn't come in yet, so I have to go out pretty far. I keep walking until the sand squishes beneath my toes, and then the water kisses my feet. The water feels freezing, but I guess it's not technically freezing, because if it were, it would have turned to ice.

When I was a little kid, my father used to take me to the lake, and he would show me how to skim rocks. You had to throw them at just the right angle and they would bounce on the water. I pick out a piece of pottery from my bag and I throw it the same way I used to throw those rocks when I was a kid. It doesn't bounce, but it goes pretty far.

Five minutes later, my shoulder bag is empty. I over-turn it, just to be sure, and shake the pieces out onto the water. At this point, even if somebody saw me here, the evidence is out to sea. Nobody could identify those pieces of pottery. And the dried blood will be washed away by the water.

I'm safe.

I trek back to my car, clutching my shoulder bag with my right hand and my sneakers with my left. I left my purse in my car, and just as I wrench the door open, my phone starts ringing. Who could it be? Is it Caleb calling to wish me good night? Is it the detective, with "just a few more questions"?

I fish my phone out of my purse. It's a blocked number.

Great. Not again.

"What?" I bark into the phone. "What is it?"

No answer.

"I know who you are," I spit into the phone, even though I absolutely do not know. But if I say it confidently enough, they might wonder. "I know that you're messing with me. And it better stop *right now.*"

I wait for some sort of response. A protest. Even laughter. But there's nothing. Only silence.

"I'm calling the police. I'm telling them all about you. All about what you did to Dawn."

Silence.

"Answer me, damn it!" The veins bulge in my neck. "Say something, you piece of shit!"

I want to hurl my phone across the beach, but that probably wouldn't do me any good. Instead, I jab my thumb into the red button to end the call. It's utterly unsatisfying.

I climb into the driver's seat, my body buzzing with frustration. Somebody is toying with me. And the thought occurs to me that maybe the ceramic turtle isn't the only thing planted in my house. Maybe there's something else I haven't found yet. Just about anything could be in my house, tucked away.

And I would never know.

CHAPTER 36

ONE MONTH EARLIER

To: Vixed Employees
From: Kimberly Healey
Subject: Ketchup

Okay, so two days ago, the bottle of ketchup I keep in the fridge was half full and today it was gone! The bottle was CLEARLY labeled with my name. If you want to use ketchup, I suggest you BRING YOUR OWN. I don't steal anyone else's food, so please do me the same respect and don't steal mine!!!!!

Kim

To: Vixed Employees
From: Dawn Schiff
Subject: Re: Ketchup

I am extremely sorry that your ketchup went missing.

Today was a green food day for me and yesterday was a white food day, so clearly I could not be responsible for the missing condiment as it would have destroyed the integrity of the meal. However, I wish to point out that if we created a schedule for refrigerator cleaning and maintenance, we could ensure that the contents of the fridge are protected and also disposed of in a timely manner.

Sincerely,
Dawn Schiff

To: Mia Hodge
From: Dawn Schiff
Subject: Re: Greetings

Dear Mia,

Today has been the worst day since I came to work at Vixed.

I need to talk to someone about it, or I fear my brain will explode. And I need to remember this day, so if I am ever tempted to be friendly to Natalie, I'll have a reminder of what she's capable of. And I'll know to stay far away from that woman.

My desk and my cubicle are carefully arranged and decorated. I'm a clean person, so I maintain everything in a very organized fashion. I don't have any photographs arranged in my workspace, but my main decorative elements are the plant I got (the iris) which is blooming beautifully and barely bothers my allergies, then the glass turtles surrounding it, one ceramic turtle, and then a stuffed turtle with big anime eyes. In total, there are 10 turtles of various sizes. It comforts me to keep all those turtles in my work-space. They don't get in the way. And even though when Seth sees them, he always says, "Jesus," it's not that big a deal.

So I can't comprehend why she did this to me.

When I came to work this morning, the first thing I noticed was that my plant was toppled. There was dirt scattered all over my workstation. But that was fine. I don't even like plants that much, although I was annoyed I would have to clean up the mess.

But then I noticed the turtles.

The glass ones were all smashed to bits. The arms and legs were in pieces on my desk and the floor. The ceramic one was broken into three large chunks. They were all destroyed. Unsalvageable.

I could have possibly convinced myself that it was an accident on the part of the janitorial staff. Perhaps they were cleaning my desk and got overzealous, although the extent of destruction hinted that it was purposeful. Still, I was willing to try to believe it.

But then I saw my stuffed turtle.

It was lying on its back, overturned onto its shell. A slit had been cut down the center of its belly. And there was a red liquid leaking out.

Like blood.

When I saw that, I screamed.

Everyone came running. Within a few seconds, the entire office had gathered around my cubicle to observe the gruesome crime scene. My heart was slamming in my chest and tears were gathering in my eyes. The only thing that kept me holding it together was your voice in my ear. *Don't give them the satisfaction of letting them see you cry.*

Don't...

Nobody was as horrified as I was. A few people were snickering and one person called out, "Look! There's fake blood on the turtle! That's so cool!"

I started shouting at them then. I screamed at everyone that these were my turtles and this was NOT cool. I didn't stop screaming until I heard Natalie's voice telling me to calm down.

"It's just some toy turtles," she said. "You had too many of them anyway. It was an eyesore."

She was never at work this early, but somehow today she got in before I did. The whole time I worked here, I was trying to be friends with Natalie. But I don't want to be her friend anymore. I want to scratch her eyes out. Except my fingernails are too scrawny. She would have a much easier time scratching out *my* eyes with her long red nails.

I heard Seth's voice through the crowd, and people parted to let him come through. I was glad he was coming. I had already told him multiple times about what Natalie was doing to me, and he never listened. He kept telling me to work it out on my own. But now he would see with his own eyes what she was capable of, and he would be forced to take action.

"Jesus," Seth said when he saw my desk. "Dawn, you've got to get this cleaned up."

I couldn't believe it. Seth thought that *I* did this to my own turtles? I told him in no uncertain terms that my desk had been vandalized, except he still didn't seem that upset about the whole thing. He acted like it was a silly prank—no big deal. Finally, I said I wanted to talk to him in private, in his office. He wasn't happy about it, but he agreed.

The crowd parted again to give us room to walk away. I was glad to get away from my cubicle. I didn't know how I would ever be able to go back there again.

As I passed Natalie's cubicle on the way down the hall, I noticed she had put her trash bin right by the entrance. I glanced down and I saw an empty bottle of ketchup inside—the same one Kim complained was missing yesterday. She threw out the evidence in plain sight, right where I was sure to see it.

She wanted me to know it was her.

I was barely keeping it together by the time I got to Seth's office. But I had to maintain my composure so he would take me seriously. He would write me off as crazy if I was a sobbing mess. As it was, he seemed more put out that I wanted to talk to him, even though the real issue was that one of his employees was targeting me.

"Natalie did this," I told him, even before he sat down in his leather chair.

He just shook his head. He didn't believe it, even as I laid out the evidence. The way Natalie had been lying about times of meetings, how she threw out my cupcakes, and then the bottle of ketchup in the trash bin. Seth was unimpressed.

"Maybe she was eating something with ketchup," he said.

I was so frustrated. I wasn't going to let him do this to me—not again. I explained again about how she's been targeting me. That she hates me. That she *wanted* me to see that ketchup so I would know she was the one who did it. Except he just kept saying that it couldn't be her and that I was being paranoid. He kept insisting it was probably the janitors.

"Why won't you believe me?" I demanded to know. "Is it because you're sleeping with her? Is that why you always give her preference?"

Seth did not like me saying that. His mouth fell open and a bright red color crept into his cheeks. I had been trying to keep my mouth shut about the whole thing, but it was too frustrating. I had to say something.

Seth started babbling on and on, trying to cover the fact that I was absolutely right. He pointed at the photo on his desk, of himself with the plain-faced middle-aged woman, explaining how he's married and so of course he wouldn't sleep with Natalie. And then he reminded me she's dating Caleb. By the time he finished, his whole face was scarlet, and he looked at me like he was expecting me to take it back.

But I didn't take it back. I mean, it's true.

So then he said, "I'm your boss. You shouldn't speak to me this way. It's really inappropriate."

I was sure the next words out of his mouth would be, "You're fired." I was waiting for it. I've been fired from every job I've ever had. I was fired once on my first day of work. It was in college and I got a job at a shoe store. I was trying to help a customer and I got so overwhelmed with all the shoe choices and their demands, I ended up locking myself in the storeroom and crying.

But Seth didn't fire me. He just turned away from me, toward his computer screen, and he didn't look at me as he told me to go back to my desk and clean up the mess. He said I should work things out with Natalie, and he didn't want to hear about it anymore. "I've got a business to run," he said.

I could have stayed and demanded justice, but that would've been pointless. Seth wasn't going to do anything. Whether or not he's still sleeping with Natalie, he obviously likes her a lot. Much more than me. After all, nobody likes me.

I know, I know—you like me. But it's not enough. Not while you're not here. If you were here, maybe I could deal with this. But you're not.

So I got up and went back to my cubicle. The crowd had dispersed, leaving behind the turtle crime scene. I was the one who had to clean it up. I had to dispose of the plant and all the pieces of my beloved turtle figurines.

But before I cleaned it up, I took a photograph. I'm pasting it below so you can see what that woman is capable of.

Sincerely,
Dawn Schiff

To: Dawn Schiff
From: Mia Hodge
Subject: Re: Greetings

My mouth is hanging open. I can't believe someone would do that to you. You can't let her get away with it.

I repeat:

YOU CAN'T LET HER GET AWAY WITH THIS.

CHAPTER 37

PRESENT DAY

NATALIE

When I drag myself into work the next morning, I can barely keep my eyes open.

As soon as I got home from the beach, I practically ripped my house apart, looking for something else that could incriminate me. I didn't even know what I was looking for. A bloody glove? A wood chipper with a dismembered leg sticking out of it? Whatever it was, I didn't find it. My house was clean.

But I still couldn't sleep. I tossed and turned in bed, intermittently looking at the clock. At three in the morning, I gave up and watched television for a while, then finally fell asleep on the couch. All in all, I got a few hours of sleep, broken up into twenty-minute chunks. I kept waking up in a cold sweat, my whole body trembling.

Needless to say, I didn't go running first thing in the morning.

On the bright side, Detective Santoro didn't greet me at my front door this morning. Maybe he's finally decided I didn't have anything to do with Dawn's murder. Maybe he decided to believe my alibi. Except I doubt it.

On my way to my cubicle, I pass Greg Lowsky at the copy machine. Greg comes in once or twice a month to install updates on our computers or troubleshoot any tech issues. He may even know more than Caleb does when it comes to computer stuff. Unlike the rest of us, he usually shows up in jeans and a T-shirt. And there's usually a math or computer-related joke on his T-shirt—one I almost never get. Today his T-shirt reads, "No, I will not fix your computer." It strikes me as a strange T-shirt for a person to wear when he is literally here to fix our computers.

Greg is nowhere near as cute as Caleb is. He's short with a bushy beard and sort of reminds me of one of the creatures from *Lord of the Rings* or some other nerdy movie I never saw. And he's almost as strange as Dawn. He once hinted that he wanted to take me to lunch, and I found a kind way to turn him down. But he still half-heartedly flirts with me whenever he comes in, even though it will never go anywhere.

"Hey, Natalie," he says. "What's up?"

I wonder how much Greg knows about all the drama with Dawn. He wasn't here on the day when Santoro was grilling everyone. And as far as I know, the detective hasn't been back. Even the Vixed bullying hashtag has died down. People on the internet lose interest quickly.

"Not much," I say carefully. "I'm sure you heard about Dawn…"

"Oh yeah." Greg looks down at his hands. "That's awful. I hope they figure out who did it to her. It's crazy how you can just be in your own house and somebody can come and…well, you know."

"Yeah."

"I hope you're staying safe, Natalie."

He has no idea. But suddenly, a brilliant thought occurs to me. "Actually, I was wondering if there's something you could help me with."

"Of course!" His face lights up. "Anything for you, Natalie."

I reach for my purse slung on my shoulder and pull out my phone. "Do you know how to figure out who's been calling from a blocked number?"

"Sure. There's an app called TrackCall that will reveal any blocked numbers."

"Oh." That makes sense. There's an app for everything. "Can I use that now to find out the number of someone who called me last night?"

"Probably not. I think the app has to be installed when they make the call."

Damn. I was hoping to figure out who used the blocked number to call me the last three nights. It's hard to believe those calls aren't somehow linked to this whole thing. And even if they aren't, I'd like to know who's harassing me.

"I'm sure if somebody is bothering you, they'll call again." He frowns. "If you're worried, I'd be happy to escort you home after work today. I don't have any plans."

"No, that's okay."

"I don't mind."

Well, I do. Even if I didn't have plans with Caleb, I wouldn't want to encourage him. "I better not." I wink at him. "I don't want to make Julia jealous."

Greg's eyes widen. "Julia? Jealous?"

"Oh my God, yes." I lower my voice. "She told me she thinks you're really cute."

Julia is one of our secretaries who sits near the front entrance, and she is so far out of Greg's league, it's not even funny. He should know that, but the way he puffs out his chest makes it clear he thinks he might have a shot.

Greg kindly offers to install the app himself without insisting on escorting me anywhere again, and he even shows me how to use it. After I feel confident that I can figure out the phone number of the blocked caller, I leave Greg at the copy machine and continue on the way to my cubicle. Dawn's cubicle is still empty, like it's been all week.

It's so horrible. No, Dawn wasn't my favorite person in the entire world, but she was sweet. There was something innocent about her, like a child. I can't bear the thought of her being tortured at the hands of some pervert and then beaten to death.

I step past her cubicle and into my own. I start to drop my purse on the desk when something gets my attention. Something that makes my heart skip a beat.

The tiny turtle figurine. It's back on my desk.

No. It can't be. It *can't* be. I threw it out. *Twice.* I didn't just throw it out, but I brought it all the way to the garbage in the break room. There's absolutely no way a janitor could have thought I mistakenly threw it away and brought it back to my desk. It was a stretch last time, and now it's an impossibility.

Somebody put this turtle on my desk on purpose.

"Natalie."

Who would do that? Who would torture me this way? It couldn't be some random person on the street. It would have to be somebody who works at this office who has access to my desk. Or at least somebody who has a way to get a key to the office.

"*Natalie.*"

I'm vaguely aware of a sharp voice calling out my name. I turn my head, and Seth is standing behind me, a few feet away. There's a dark look in his eyes.

"Natalie," he says flatly. "I need to talk to you."

"Does it have to be now?" I look back at the turtle, then back at him. "Because I—"

"Yes. *Now.*"

I can tell from the look on Seth's face that he's not messing around. What now? I can't deal with any customer complaints right now. I've got much worse concerns.

"In my office," he adds.

"Fine," I say. "Let's go."

CHAPTER 38

ONE WEEK EARLIER

To: Mia Hodge
From: Dawn Schiff
Subject: Re: Greetings

Dear Mia,

I have discovered something very unsettling and I need your advice on how to deal with it:

There's money missing from the company.

It's a good amount. Enough that whoever has that money could go on a nice holiday with it. But not so much that Seth would notice without somebody digging around.

I missed the discrepancy up until now because it happened *last* year. The accountant who preceded me either didn't notice it himself or else decided not to say anything about it.

Something else is fairly clear to me.

All the account discrepancies are around sales

that Natalie made. Not tiny sales, like a few boxes of product. But large sales to huge companies, where a few thousand dollars could potentially get overlooked.

After I noticed it in last year's records, I went back and checked the year before. Once again, money was missing. Approximately the same amount.

I spent the better part of the afternoon today trying to figure out what to do about it. Of course, the obvious thing to do is go straight to Seth. Part of my job is to catch things like this, and he has a right to know that somebody is stealing from his branch. But at the same time, this is a very serious charge. Like, *jail* serious. Natalie could get arrested for the amount of money she has stolen.

Despite everything she's done to me, I don't want her to go to jail. I don't know how things became so contentious between us, but I don't want anything bad to happen to her. I've even forgiven her for what she did to my turtles. Maybe she was having a bad day.

After spending the whole afternoon mulling it over, I arrived at a conclusion. I should go to Natalie first. I'll tell her what I found. I'll explain to her that she needs to return the money, or else I have no choice but to turn her in.

I've been trying so hard to get Natalie to like me, and this might do the trick. I'm sure she'll appreciate me giving her a heads-up instead of going straight to Seth. After all, that's what friends do.

Sincerely,
Dawn Schiff

To: Dawn Schiff
From: Mia Hodge
Subject: Re: Greetings

Why are you giving this woman any chances???? You need to go straight to your boss and let him know she's been stealing from the company! Promise me you will talk to your boss!!!! DO NOT LET HER GET AWAY WITH THIS!!!!!!!

CHAPTER 39

PRESENT DAY

NATALIE

Seth doesn't say a word to me or give me any indication of what's wrong as I march behind him to his office. Seth is the only employee at this branch who gets his own office. It used to bother me, but since I spend a lot of time out of the office, I try not to get too upset about working in a cube. But eventually, I'll have to relocate to another company where I can get a decent workspace.

"Sit," Seth says in a clipped tone.

He shuts the door behind me. He always used to shut the door like that when we were about to fool around, and like Pavlov's dogs, I find myself getting a little turned on, despite everything. It's completely inappropriate, given how my world is crumbling around me right now, but Seth just really does it for me. Too bad the circumstances didn't work out between us.

I settle down into one of the chairs in front of his desk. "What's going on?"

Seth sits in his own leather chair. His hands are

clasped into fists. "That detective paid me a visit this morning."

"Oh."

"Oh?" His eyebrows shoot up. "Is that all you have to say?"

I shake my head. I don't know what he's all worked up about. *He's* not the one lying about my alibi.

"Is there anything you want to tell me, Natalie?"

Seth always calls me Nat. The fact that he's repeatedly calling me Natalie makes me think he's pissed off at me. That and the way his face is red and his knuckles are white.

"No…"

He slams his palms flat on the desk. "Santoro said you stole money from the company. Dawn knew all about it, apparently."

All the air seems to leave my body. I open my mouth, but no words come out. "I didn't…" I manage.

"Dawn wrote all about it in an email," he continues like I hadn't spoken. "She was about to confront you about it. About the money you stole from me."

"No," I breathe. "I didn't steal anything—"

"That huge house you have in Boston." He shakes his head. "I never understood how you were able to afford it. Or all those fancy labels on your clothing… those insanely expensive shoes…"

"Seth…"

"I always noticed how flirty you were with the last accountant we had," he muses. "Now I finally get it. And of course, it explains why you were so nice to *me*."

"Seth!" My eyes bulge out. "You can't possibly think that I would ever—"

His eyes are filled with rage. "I know what you're like, Natalie. I've seen you bullshit customers. I've seen the way you do whatever you have to do to get what you want. I just...I never thought..." He heaves a breath. "I never thought you'd mess with *me* to get what you want."

"Because I wouldn't!" I cry. "Seth, please..."

He holds up his hand. "I don't want to hear it. You're on unpaid suspension. Since we don't have an accountant right now, I'll go through the accounts myself today. Figure out how much you ripped us off for."

"I didn't rip you off!" My eyes are swimming with tears. I've managed not to cry through this whole ordeal, but I've never seen Seth look at me this way. He's always been kind to me—I could always count on that. "I swear to you, I wouldn't do that."

"Yeah, right." He turns away from me, his eyes focused on his computer screen. "We're done here. Get your stuff and go."

"Seth..."

"*Now*, Natalie," he says through his teeth. "Or do I need to call security?"

I know Seth really well. We were seeing each other for over a year before I called it quits. There's nothing I can say to change his mind. He is pissed off at me. And on top of that, he's hurt. He thinks I played him. He believes every word the detective told him.

This is far from over.

CHAPTER 40

As I'm coming out of Seth's office, Kim runs over to me. Her eyes are wide and curious. She grabs my arm to slow me down on my trajectory back to my cubicle.

"What happened in there?" she asks me. "Seth came around asking for you earlier, and he looked *really* upset."

I want to spit at her that it's none of her damn business. Kim used to be my best friend in this office, but our power dynamic has changed over the years. When she started here, we were both single. We used to go out to bars together and meet guys. We had fun together.

Then Kim met the guy she ended up marrying. He wasn't exactly handsome, but he was wealthy and offered her the life she always wanted. The second she got engaged, everything was all about her upcoming wedding—the honeymoon, the giant house he was *building* for her, and all the perfect children they were going to have. I started to feel like Kim's loser friend.

It didn't help that she knew about me and Seth and

was super judgmental. Yes, I know it's not a wise personal or career move to sleep with your boss. It wasn't like I planned it out. You can't control who you fall in love with.

Still, Kim is my friend. It's not her fault that she's gotten her life together faster than I have. And she was right—it *was* really stupid to sleep with Seth. It's blown up in my face more than once.

"It's fine," I mumble. "I'm just going to work from home for a bit."

"Why?"

I forgot how nosy Kim can be. She's also a gossip. I'm sure as hell not going to tell her I got suspended for allegedly stealing from the company. "It's been a stressful few days. He's giving me some flex time."

Yes, unpaid flex time while he's investigating me for embezzlement.

She frowns. "Is the race still on?"

"Of course it is," I snap at her. "I've spent the last three months organizing it. Do you think I'm going to just cancel it on one day's notice?"

"Yes, but—"

"You're coming tomorrow, aren't you?" It occurs to me suddenly that with everything going on, people might not show up for the 5K. In terms of the charity, it doesn't matter. I already have the donations. But I've got a local news crew coming, and it will look horrible if I'm the only one who shows up. "You're going to be there, right?"

"Um…" Kim chews on her thumbnail. "I'm just not sure if it's a good idea right now. With everything going on…"

I close my fingers around her arm. "Kim, you've got to come. I need people to show up to this. You can't leave me hanging."

"Nat…" She squirms. "You're hurting my arm."

I release my grip, my cheeks burning. "Please. You need to come."

I don't mention those pictures from her bachelorette party. She knows I've got them.

She finally nods. "Okay, I'll be there. You can count on me."

My shoulders relax slightly. Kim will be there, and Caleb will show up. So that's at least three of us. And I'm sure at least a handful of other people from the office will come. Greg Lowsky will surely make an appearance, even if he can't finish the race.

"And maybe they'll find Dawn's killer by then?" Kim says.

I don't know a lot of things for sure, but I know they're not going to find Dawn's killer by tomorrow morning.

CHAPTER 41

Ordinarily, I would love having an unexpected day off. I might go for a run or go to my favorite massage place in Quincy. Or maybe get a manicure. Something about getting a manicure always lifts my spirits.

I don't feel much in the mood for a manicure right now. Detective Santoro would probably use it against me. *She's able to afford a manicure. She's obviously embezzling money.*

God, haven't they ever heard of Groupon?

So instead, after taking care of a few quick errands, I spend the entire day on my couch, listlessly flipping between the channels. I mostly end up watching reruns of old sitcoms I've already seen a dozen times before. I'm just killing time before Caleb comes by after work. He'll make me feel better.

In the late afternoon, my phone rings. My first thought is that it's Caleb, maybe on his way over early. But then when I look down, "Mom" is flashing on the screen. Great.

But I don't have anything better to do, so I snatch up the phone. "Hello?"

"Natalie!" Again, she's shouting into the phone at the top of her lungs. I only hope she's not in public. "I heard they found that girl from your company! That she's dead!"

"Yeah," I mutter. "I know."

"Do you know what the newspapers are saying?" she says. I'm not sure I want to know, but she's definitely going to tell me. "They're saying people at your company *bullied* her. Did you bully her, Natalie?"

"No! My God, Mom…"

"You should be kind to people who aren't as popular as you are, Natalie." Even though I'm thirty, my mother still loves to lecture me. "Even though she's not as pretty as you are or as well-liked, you could still be nice to her."

"I was nice to her!"

"Obviously not."

What is the world coming to when even my own mother thinks I'm a big old bully? "I wouldn't bully someone, Mom."

"Well, obviously you would." She sniffs. "You *have*. Remember how you and that friend of yours, Tara, used to…you know…"

What does it take to get your mother to realize that you're not a high school cheerleader anymore? "I was nice to Dawn. I swear it."

"I know you, Natalie. I know what you can be like. Don't you remember when…"

As my mother drones on, I hear a beep in my ear. I pull the phone away—Caleb is calling. Thank God. "Mom, I have to go."

"Why? Where do you have to go?"

"I've got another call. Something for work." I'm not about to tell her about Caleb. Not now, when everything seems so tenuous.

She grumbles a bit, but I'm not listening. I end the call and switch over to Caleb. He hasn't called a moment too soon.

"Tell me you're on your way over here," I say.

"Natalie, we have to talk."

Oh no. Again? This is not leading anywhere good. "What? Why?"

"Look…" He heaves a long sigh. "That detective came to see me again."

I can see where this is leading, and I don't like it. "Caleb…"

"He kept pushing me." He sounds anguished. "He kept asking me if I was sure I was with you the whole night. He kept talking about the penalty for lying to a police officer. That guy is scary."

"Please tell me you didn't—"

"I had to tell him the truth, Nat." His voice cracks. "I told him that I left at 9:30. I'm so sorry."

I want to reach through the phone and strangle him with my bare hands. "How could you do that to me? Do you know how this is going to look?"

"I'm sorry—I really am. But what was I supposed to do? Lie to a cop?"

"You already did it once. It's not like he was going to find out."

"He could have found out!" He's just short of shouting. "I live in an apartment building. I've got a bunch of neighbors on my own floor. I saw somebody in the elevator on my way up. He could've easily found out I was lying."

"He never would've found out."

"You don't know that. I could have gotten in a lot of trouble. Honestly, you shouldn't have asked me to do it in the first place. It wasn't right."

I'm squeezing the phone so tightly, I'm shocked that it doesn't crack in my hand. "You could've at least given me a heads-up. That detective already has it in for me. If you had told me, I could have told him first at least. Instead of looking like a liar."

He's quiet for a moment on the other line. "You're right. I'm sorry. I promise you, I wasn't planning to tell him. He just…he got it out of me."

As furious as I am with Caleb right now, I believe him. I know how persuasive and frightening Santoro can be. I can imagine Caleb cracking under the pressure. Especially since he didn't feel great about lying in the first place. He's right—I never should have asked him.

But in my defense, I thought he was utterly infatuated with me. Now I'm not so sure. And I had no idea how weak he is.

"I'm so sorry," he says for what seems like the millionth useless time. "I mean, this hurts me too. I don't have an alibi either now."

Right, but so what? Santoro doesn't think he's the killer. That honor has been bestowed on me and me alone.

"Do you still want me to come over?" he asks in a small voice.

"Please don't. I'd rather be alone."

I don't actually want to be alone, but I don't even want to look at Caleb right now. My chest aches, and it hits me that the person I want to see most in the world right now is Seth, but then I remember he hates me.

It's amazing how quickly I've become isolated from my entire social network. My boyfriend has betrayed me. My former lover thinks I'm a thief. And even my best friend was looking at me funny.

"I'll come to the 5K tomorrow," he says. A peace offering. "I've got my T-shirt all laid out on my dresser."

"Fine."

"I'm sorry, Nat." Every time he says it, it's a knife in my heart. "But I'm sure this will all blow over. I mean, you didn't do anything wrong. How could you have? That detective is just giving you a hard time."

"Yeah."

Except there's something more going on. I haven't told Caleb about that ceramic turtle I found in my laundry hamper, and after he snitched on me to the detective, there's no way I would consider it. But there's a reason Santoro keeps hounding me. I don't know what it is, but somebody has it in for me. I just don't know who. Or why.

The doorbell rings, and I almost jump out of my skin. Even from the sofa, I can see the red and blue lights flashing behind the front door.

Oh no.

"Caleb," I gasp. "I've got to go."

"Are you sure you're all right?"

"I...I'm fine. I have to go."

Before he can answer, I end the call. I rise from the sofa, facing the lights of the police vehicle. Except it's not just the one light on top of the detective's car. It's more than that. There are a bunch of police cars outside my house.

Something terrible is about to happen.

CHAPTER 42

I stand at the door for several minutes, shaking too hard to work the lock and get it open. Part of me wants to make a run for it. I could go out the back door and then…

Well, what could I do? My car is parked in front of the house. There's nowhere to go. And I'm hardly the type to be on the run from the police.

Finally, I turn the locks and crack open the front door. It's no surprise that Detective Santoro is standing in front of my door. It's hard to remember a time when I used to be able to open the door and he *wasn't* standing there.

"Hello, Miss Farrell." He doesn't even crack a grim smile. His lips are a straight line. "We have a warrant to search your house."

I don't doubt that the warrant was obtained after my stupid boyfriend informed him that I did not, in fact, have an alibi.

"I see." I feel like I'm choking. "I guess then… Come in."

I step aside to allow the detective and his crew into my house. This seems like the deepest violation. These police officers are in my home. But what can I do? They obviously had enough evidence to get a warrant to search the place. I don't know how though. I mean, half of Boston probably doesn't have an alibi for last Monday night.

"Should I wait in my car?" I ask in a tiny voice.

"We gotta search your car too," he says without a hint of apology in his voice. "I need you to open the locks on the door."

I don't have much choice but to cooperate. I grab my car keys, point them in the direction of my car, and hit the key fob to unlock the doors. The lights flash as the doors unlock.

"Where am I supposed to go?" I ask Santoro.

He looks at me thoughtfully. "You can sit on your couch in the living room. I'll stay with you."

"Can I stay with a friend?" I could call Kim and crash at her place. If she'll let me.

"I'm afraid not. I need you to stay on the premises."

We head back into my living room, Santoro leading the way, and I follow wordlessly. I searched the house pretty thoroughly last night, but not as thoroughly as these officers seem to be looking. I can hear loud noises coming from upstairs in the kitchen. The sound of a dish breaking.

Thank God I got rid of that ceramic turtle. I even ran all the clothing in the laundry hamper through the wash.

I sit gingerly on the sofa, and Santoro sits beside me. His black eyes are trained on mine. The room feels unbearably stuffy, like I can't even breathe. I wish I could go outside, but it's really cold out. Still, I'd rather be anywhere but here.

"How long will this take?" I ask him.

"Depends on what we find."

"There's nothing to find."

"I guess we'll see, won't we?"

I squeeze my knees together. It hits me that even though I know Caleb told him the truth about Monday night, he doesn't know I know. Maybe I could play dumb and pretend I'm fessing up on my own free will.

"Listen," I say, "I just...I wanted to tell you that I was mistaken about Monday night. I remembered my boyfriend did go home before bedtime. I got it wrong."

"Funny. He just told me the same thing."

I'm too late. I should have told the truth while I could.

"You know," Santoro says, "I got bullied when I was in school."

I pick at a loose thread on my skirt. "Oh?"

Even though I'm not looking in his direction, I can feel his gaze washing over me. "It got pretty bad. Those kids made my life miserable."

"Kids can be really cruel sometimes."

"Kids don't know any better." He cracks his knuckles. "But adults—they do. They ought to know better at least. But plenty of adults out there are still bullies."

I keep my eyes down. I don't know what to say.

"I'm sure you know all about that, Miss Farrell."

There's another crash from the kitchen. These people

are destroying my house, but that's the least of my problems. After that ceramic turtle turned up in the laundry hamper, I don't know what those people are going to find. But there's a decent chance I could leave this house in handcuffs.

This is the point when I should be calling a lawyer. For reasons I don't quite understand, I've become a suspect in Dawn's murder. But lawyers cost money that I don't have right now, and I still feel like getting a lawyer will make me look guilty.

I didn't do anything. I'm innocent. I don't need a lawyer to prove that.

CHAPTER 43

MONDAY

To: Natalie Farrell
From: Dawn Schiff
Subject: Important

To Natalie,

There is a matter of great importance that I need to discuss with you urgently. Please come to my cubicle at the conclusion of the workday today.

Sincerely,
Dawn Schiff

To: Natalie Farrell
From: Caleb McCullough
Subject: Tonight

Still on for dinner tonight? I'm cooking! Can't wait to see you.

To: Caleb McCullough
From: Natalie Farrell
Subject: Re: Tonight

I'll be there! There's one other thing I need to take care of tonight but I don't think it will be a problem.

To: Mia Hodge
From: Dawn Schiff
Subject: Re: Greetings

Dear Mia,

I am just writing a quick email because I've got company coming over. It's the first time since I've lived here that I'm entertaining a guest! Unless you count the maintenance people I've had over, which I guess you really can't.

Even my mother hasn't been here yet. Of course, you'll be here next month during your vacation! I've already set up the extra bedroom for you and George to stay in. I'm glad you got a good price on the tickets!

Telling Natalie was the correct thing to do. I sent her an email asking to meet at the end of the work-day, and she came by my cubicle just before five. When I mentioned there was a discrepancy in the accounts from last year, she agreed to come with me to the empty conference room.

Then when we were alone, I told Natalie about the missing money from each of her sales transactions. I told her how much money it was, and when she heard the number, she sucked in a breath.

Then she started quizzing me. She had about a million questions. She asked how far back in the records I had looked. Then she asked who I thought took the money, and I told her that I wasn't sure, even though it seemed to me that she was the only person who could have taken it. Then she asked me who else I told about it.

"I didn't tell anyone," I told her, although that's not entirely true. I've told you, but she didn't need to know that. It's not like you work for the company.

I was hoping Natalie would confess to taking the money and promise to return it before I had to turn her in. But that's not what happened. Instead, she started talking about other people who might have taken the money and framed her. "Does anyone else have access?" she asked me.

"Only Seth," I told her, but why would he steal from his own branch and make himself look bad? And why would he frame somebody who he likes so much?

But weirdly, Natalie didn't dismiss the possibility that Seth could have done it. In fact, the idea of it got her excited. She said we needed to get together and Nancy Drew this mystery to figure out who took the money and why. That's when she suggested coming over later tonight.

That part was exactly what I wanted to hear. She wasn't blowing off my accusations. She was concerned and wanted to figure it out. Together.

We made plans to get together tonight. She reminded me not to tell anyone, because of course they would try to cover their tracks. Then she told me she was counting on me.

241

I asked her when she wanted to get together, and I was disappointed when she suggested not meeting till ten. She said she already made plans with Caleb, and he'd be so devastated if she canceled. She giggled and mentioned he was completely obsessed with her, which I believe. She has him wrapped around her little finger.

I had been hoping Natalie and I might be able to have a nice dinner together at my house. But then I would have to worry about what I was going to serve. Natalie has very high-end taste in food, and it's hard to satisfy those kinds of tastes while maintaining a monochromatic meal. Of course, I could have served her a meal that was more than one color, but that would have stressed me out too much.

I have been cleaning ever since I got home. Not that my place is messy, but I want to make sure everything is perfect! I even dusted the surfaces and scrubbed down my basketball-sized ceramic turtle. I have fed Junior, and now all I've got to do is wait for Natalie to come.

We're going to have a really nice night together. I have a bottle of red wine, and we can each have a glass while we talk about the situation at work. We'll get to know each other. I'll introduce her to Junior. And we'll figure out who took that money.

Oh my gosh, the doorbell just rang. That must be her!

Wish me luck!

Sincerely,
Dawn Schiff

CHAPTER 44

PRESENT DAY

NATALIE

This is my second day with practically no sleep.

The police finally left my house at some ungodly hour. I didn't see them carrying out any bloody clothing or dismembered limbs, so I'm thinking they didn't find anything. Thank God. I can finally get back to my life again.

This morning is the 5K. I was adamant about keeping it going, but right now, I would seriously consider giving up one of my pinkie fingers if I didn't have to do it.

The weather has held up. It's brisk out, but there's no rain, and it's not unseasonably cold. After running for twenty minutes or so, it will feel perfect. I decide to take the weather as an omen. If the weather is nice, the race is going to go perfectly.

Instead of the T-shirt and shorts I wear when I run around the neighborhood, I've got skintight running pants to wear for the 5K as well as the special T-shirt I ordered. When I toss it over my head, I realize it's a little tighter than I thought, but that's fine. The T-shirts running small is a minor problem.

I've been organizing this 5K for the last five years now, so I've got it down to a science. I recruited some students from Boston College to help out, and I put them in charge of various tasks that need to be done, like manning the water stations, posting the signs for where to go, and making sure everybody running is registered. I went over everything they need to do in advance, but I usually call each of them the night before. I was in no position to do that last night, so I'm just going to have to hope everything goes to plan.

Before I leave the house, I check out my appearance in the bathroom mirror. I've pulled my blond hair back into a high ponytail, and I have on far too much makeup for a 5K, but it's all sweatproof. I got a local news station to cover the race, so I want to be camera ready. And after the last few days, I would never consider being filmed without makeup on. When I stumbled into the bathroom this morning, I looked like the bride of Frankenstein. I certainly haven't had a chance to touch up my roots this week, but it will have to be good enough.

I take an Uber to Florian Hall an hour before the start time for the race. I am expecting the worst, but to my relief, Cleo from Boston College is already at the front of the building with a table of registration clipboards and a jug of water with a bunch of little cups. She helped me out last year too, so she knows exactly what to do.

"Hey, Natalie!" Cleo waves enthusiastically. "We're all set!"

Cleo is all of twenty years old, and she looks so

bright-eyed, it somehow makes me even more tired. And she's not even going to be running the 5K. But I'm grateful to have her help. She has a cousin with cerebral palsy, so she's a big supporter of the cause.

"Everyone came?" I ask.

"Just about." She squints off into the distance. "Eli thinks he's coming down with the flu, although I think he's being a baby. But we've got enough people. All the signs are posted. We're good to go."

"Thank you so much." My knees feel weak with relief. "You've done an amazing job. I'm sorry I didn't call to check in on you. I...I got busy yesterday."

Cleo drops her voice a notch. "I heard what happened to your coworker. I'm so sorry. I hope they find the monster who did it."

So do I. She has no idea how much.

Since everything has been taken care of, I wait around at the start of the race and do some stretches. While I am stretching out my hamstrings, the phone I have strapped to my biceps starts to ring. I pull it out of the holster and look at the screen.

It's a blocked number.

I never got a phone call last night. I was waiting for it, especially while Santoro was at my house. I wanted him to see how somebody was harassing me. But of course, they never called. Just as well, since I suspect he wouldn't have been that impressed.

I hold the phone to my ear. "Hello?"

No answer. Again.

The other night, I started yelling into the phone when this happened. But thanks to Greg Lowsky, I know exactly what to do.

I use the TrackCall app to retrieve the number of the blocked caller. I wasn't entirely convinced it would work, but then a number shows up on the screen, just like Greg promised it would. I grab a pen off the table Cleo set up and scribble down the number on one of the registration sheets.

I stare down at the number I wrote down. The area code isn't local. I think it might be Rhode Island. I bring up a reverse number lookup on my phone, and I type in the ten digits.

I was right. The phone number belongs to a motel just outside Providence.

What the hell?

"Nat?"

Caleb is behind me, wearing a pair of gray shorts and the extra large T-shirt I gave him earlier in the week. I want to be furious at him for what he did to me, but since he showed up here to support me and it doesn't seem like I have a lot of support right now, I can't stay mad. Especially because he looks really hot in his running outfit—his muscles bulge under the T-shirt, which is a bit snug on him as well.

"You made it," I say.

He gives me a lopsided smile. "I couldn't let you down again."

"Yeah."

"Nat…" His Adam's apple bobs. He has the same purple circles under his eyes that I covered up this morning with makeup. "I'm so sorry about everything. I feel awful about it."

"It's not your fault." It's not. It wasn't right of me to ask him to lie to the police. That's not the kind of thing you ask your boyfriend of less than two months to do for you. That's more of a six-month relationship request. "And it's fine."

"Yeah?"

I nod. "The police came by last night and looked around." That's a very diplomatic way to describe the way they trashed my house. "But they realized I don't have anything to do with Dawn's murder. Maybe now they can focus on actually finding out who really did it."

"I hope so."

"Also..." I hold up my phone. "I've been getting these weird calls from blocked numbers the last few days. Ever since I was in Dawn's house. I finally used this app to figure out the number, and it turns out the calls are coming from some motel in Rhode Island."

"Really? That's weird."

I show him the address on my phone. "This doesn't look familiar to you, does it?"

"Nope." He squints down at the address. "Why would someone in a random motel be calling you?"

"I have no idea, but..." I look back at the phone number and address. "It's got to have some connection to what's going on. After this race is over, I'm driving out there."

"Good idea." He nods in approval. "I'll come with you."

I arch an eyebrow at him. "You want to go all the way out to Rhode Island with me?"

"Sure." He grins. "If you wouldn't mind letting me tag along."

I can't help but smile back at him. It would be nice having his company. And after the way Seth treated me yesterday, things are truly over for good in *that* relationship. There aren't going to be any other one-offs, that's for sure. I can't believe I was wasting my time with that jerk *who is still freaking married* when I've got a boyfriend who obviously cares about me a lot.

I tug playfully at the hem of Caleb's T-shirt. "And maybe tonight we can have a makeup dinner for the dinner we missed last night?"

His eyes light up. "You're on."

Out of the corner of my eye, I see the news crew setting up the cameras. Fantastic—the crew has arrived just on time. I have plenty of time to do a quick interview to explain the goals of the charity, and then they can catch the beginning of the race.

About a dozen people have shown up to run today. I initially had nearly fifty people expected, but it looks like the Dawn situation has kept people home. It stings, because a larger number of participants helps to spread more awareness of the charity, but we still get the money to donate either way. This is for Amelia—I can't forget that. And even though some of the runners stayed home, a considerable crowd is forming to watch the beginning of the race.

As I face the crowd, I force my lips to form a smile. I'm not exactly in a smiling mood, but if I keep it on my face, maybe I'll start to feel better. I wave at the spectators, and a heavyset man wearing one of our T-shirts waves back at me.

That's when I notice somebody behind the man. Somebody familiar. I recognize that stringy brown hair and horse face.

Is that Seth's *wife*? What is she doing here?

"Hi, Natalie!" Maria Monteiro from the news team waves to me, and I'm forced to rip my eyes away from the crowd. Maria covered the race last year as well, and she looks perfectly made up in a dress suit, her black hair shiny and her lipstick blood red. "Do you have time for a quick interview before the race?"

"Absolutely!" I hesitate. "But I just want to say, I'd rather not talk about my coworker, Dawn Schiff. I know she's been all over the news lately, but I don't want to detract from the reason we're running today: to raise money for cerebral palsy."

Maria can't hide the disappointment on her face, but to her credit, she quickly recovers. "That's fine. I completely respect that."

"Thanks, Maria. I appreciate it."

I glance back at the crowd, my eyes searching for Seth's wife again, but she seems to have vanished. Or more likely, it wasn't her to begin with, and I'm just being paranoid. I reach behind my head to straighten out my ponytail, and I smooth out the creases on my T-shirt so viewers will be able to see the writing. Maria gestures to her cameraman, and he points the lens in my direction. Maria gets out her microphone, and I know from last year that she'll probably record a little intro later and then splice the whole thing together.

"So, Natalie," she says, "this is your fifth year running this 5K, isn't it?"

I nod and feel my ponytail swish behind my head. "That's right. We'll be raising money for cerebral palsy."

"And that's a charity very close to your heart, isn't it?"

I nod again. "One of my best friends growing up had cerebral palsy, so this race is in Amelia's honor."

Maria takes back the microphone and is asking me another question, but my attention is again drawn away by something in the crowd. It's not Melinda Hoffman this time though—I wish it were. Two of the spectators step aside to allow a large man with black eyes to come to the forefront of the crowd.

It's Santoro.

Maria has pushed the microphone back in my face, and I realize I have no idea what she just asked me. "Um," I say. "Sorry, I…"

How embarrassing. Thankfully, none of this is live. When this video gets edited, she can cut out the part where I wasn't listening to her question.

"It looks like things are getting started soon," Maria observes. "I'll let you get to it then. But thank you for what you've done."

"Yes…"

Santoro is moving forward, coming closer to me. What's going on? He doesn't want to grill me again right before the 5K, does he? This is a *charity event*. Doesn't the man have any *respect*?

"Caleb!" I crane my neck, searching for my boyfriend. I spot him a few yards away. "Caleb, can I talk to you?"

Maybe Caleb can deal with this detective till we're done here. I've got way too much to do. The race is starting in less than fifteen minutes, so I don't have time to answer the same questions over and over. They even searched my house. What more do they want from me, for God's sake?

When I turn my head back to look, Santoro is right in front of me. Less than a foot away. His eyes look like endless pools of darkness. Instinctively, I take a step back.

"Detective, this isn't a good time—"

"Natalie Farrell." His voice is flat. "You're under arrest for the murder of Dawn Schiff."

What?

I feel like I can't breathe. Those damn cameras are still pointed at me. Not to mention that half the crowd has gotten out their phones and is filming me. That bastard Santoro did this on purpose. He chose the most public moment possible to arrest me. He wants to humiliate me, even though I've done nothing wrong.

Maybe he's the one who planted that ceramic turtle in my laundry.

"You're joking me," I sputter. "How could you... I didn't do anything! What is this based on?"

But Santoro isn't offering an explanation. And this is not a joke. He takes out his handcuffs, and before I know it, he's snapping them on my wrists. The cold metal bites into my skin, and my legs turn to liquid beneath me. I'm vaguely aware of the fact that he's reading me my rights.

Caleb has sprinted over. I catch his eye, and he looks completely horrified. "Natalie!" I hear him yell.

"Caleb," I gasp. The crowd is growing louder, and dozens of cameras are trained on me. "That address I showed you. You've got to go there for me. Please!"

"Natalie..."

"Please!" I manage.

Santoro jerks me by the arm. He's leading me to a police car to bring me back to the station and toss me in jail. There's nothing I can do to stop this anymore. I don't know why, but somebody has framed me, and they have done a really good job.

My life, as I knew it, is officially over.

PART II

CHAPTER 45

DAWN

One of the scariest animals in the world is the soft-shelled turtle.

They don't look that scary. They don't even have the traditional turtle shell. They look a bit like a pancake with a head and legs sticking out. But don't be fooled—they can be deadly. They hide in the sand, not moving an inch, waiting patiently for their prey. Ready to strike with their razor-sharp beak.

That's what it takes to catch your prey. Patience.

We can all learn a lot from the soft-shelled turtle.

I've been watching the news all morning. Over and over.

I can't get enough of it. That moment when the detective steps out of the crowd and tells Natalie she's under arrest. The horrified look on her face as he snaps the cuffs onto her wrists. The camera crew was there to record the 5K, but they got more than they bargained for. They got the biggest story on the South Shore.

I wish I still had my phone. I bet there are videos

of Natalie's arrest all over YouTube, and I could watch them over and over and over until my eyes bleed. But I had to leave my phone behind at my house. There was no other choice.

It had to look real.

I sit up straighter on the double bed, hugging my stuffed turtle to my chest. The turtle's name is, quite simply, Turtly. What can I say—I named him when I was four. This turtle is one of the few things I brought with me from my house. It was a risk, because somebody might have noticed it missing, but it was worth it. I have slept with this turtle every night since I was a preschooler. I wasn't leaving it behind.

It was bad enough I had to leave Junior behind. I hope she's okay.

This bed is extremely uncomfortable. At home, I have a memory foam mattress with 270 thread count sheets and a down comforter. I knew the beds at a motel wouldn't be as comfortable as what I am used to, but what bothers me most is not the low quality of the sheets…or the plastic coating on the mattress that makes it hard as a rock and yet also lumpy.

No, what keeps me awake at night is the fact that the sheets and the pillowcase are *two completely different colors*. Yes, you heard me correctly. The sheets are white and yet the pillowcase is an off-white color that is practically *tan*. And even more horrifying, the blankets are blue! It makes my skin crawl just to look at it.

But it's not like I can ever go home again.

I miss my house. I miss my bed with the white sheets, white pillowcase, and white blanket. But again, it's worth it. It's worth *anything*.

Anyway, this bed is surely better than wherever Natalie sleeps tonight. Jail cells aren't known to be particularly cozy. It worked out so perfectly that she got arrested on a Saturday. She's going to be stuck in a cell all weekend.

I pick up the pad of paper I left lying by the bed. I handwrote a letter on it to Mia, since email is not an option right now. There were some things I still had to say, and I wanted to get them down on paper. For practical reasons, this will be the last letter I write to her.

I reach for the remote control and flip around to find another news station. I want to see Natalie get arrested again. When I get my hands on a computer again, I'm going to make that shot my wallpaper.

My stomach growls. All I've got to eat is the small amount of food I've been stashing in the mini fridge in the room, although they do have a few vending machines outside. My door leads right outside, and I don't have to pass any other people to get to the machines. My breakfast was a bag of Doritos. I'm not looking forward to having cheese doodles for lunch.

I'm trying not to venture too far out of the motel. I do have a nondescript brown wig that I use to conceal my hair. Some people cut off their hair when they don't want to be found, but mine is already slashed off half an inch from my skull. So my only choice is a wig. A *cheap* wig that itches intensely if I have it on for more than five minutes. I wear a baseball cap on top of it so it looks more realistic.

Still, my face has been all over the news lately. Especially today, since Natalie was arrested this morning. It's too dangerous to walk around, even in disguise. That's a risk that isn't worth taking.

I can't let myself be found. It was hard enough to get Natalie arrested. I can't blow it all when I'm so close.

She needs to pay. If I don't do it, nobody else will.

The news switches to a segment about me. About the life of Dawn Schiff. Not that they really know anything about me, but they know the basics. Where I grew up, where I went to high school and college, that I'm not married and have no children. There are a few unflattering old photographs of me, undoubtedly provided by my mother.

The main photograph they always show on the news is the one from my ID photo at work. I've never photographed well, but that one is particularly awful. My hair is plastered to my skull, because I had recently showered, and my eyes are wide open like I've just seen a ghost. It looks like a bad mug shot.

I wonder what Natalie will look like in her mug shot. Even she can't pull off a good mug shot photo. Even though she's beautiful. She's always been beautiful. Maybe if she weren't, she would be a better person.

Now the television is showing my mother. I can't believe my mother agreed to go on camera and admit that she and I are related. She's tearfully talking about how she wants justice for my murder.

I stare at my mother's face on the television screen, waiting to feel something. Guilt or remorse.

No. Nothing.

My mother has never been supportive of me for one day of my life. When I was a kid, all she wanted was for me to stop embarrassing her. And as an adult, all she cared about was that I sent her those checks every month. If I never come back, she might feel a little bit sad occasionally, but she'll be happy to get the money I

258

left in my bank account. She doesn't care about me any more than I care about her. And if she knew what I was up to, she would turn me in herself.

I push myself up in bed, and my left wrist throbs. I've kept it bandaged since Monday, when I made the cut that created all that blood on the floor of my living room. I had to be very careful about it. If I cut too deep, that would have been the end of me.

I sit up straighter at a loud noise coming from outside my room. I'm on the second floor, but the walls are paper-thin and the windows may as well be made of Saran Wrap. There's no heat either, and I spent all last night shivering under that flimsy (blue!) polyester blanket. Nobody said revenge was easy.

I shut off the television and walk to the window. A green Ford is pulling into a spot just outside the main office. I push my glasses up the bridge of my nose and peer through the glass.

The driver's side door to the Ford opens up. Someone gets out of the car. I recognize him immediately.

It's Caleb McCullough.

I tug on the shades to partially conceal my face as I watch him. He goes straight to the main lobby and disappears inside. I stand at the window, wondering what's going on in there. What is he doing in there?

My stomach churns. I've been so careful.

About ten minutes later, Caleb exits the lobby. He takes a left and moves in the direction of my room. He pauses in front of the stairs that lead up to the second floor. Then he starts to climb.

I take a step away from the window. What's going on? What is Caleb doing out there?

And then he disappears from my line of sight. He must be on the second floor. I can hear his footsteps on the walkway, growing louder. And then...

Three loud knocks on the door to my room.

He's here.

CHAPTER 46

I don't answer immediately. I back away from the door, wiping my hands on my blue jeans. I glance around the room anxiously.

He knocks again.

"Dawn!" His voice travels through the thin door like he's in the same room as me. "Come on, Dawn. Open up!"

I walk over to the door. I flip open the dead bolt, then I turn the lock. Caleb is standing there, his brown hair tousled by the wind even though he never ended up going on that 5K run, and he's holding a white paper bag I hadn't noticed him carrying. He thrusts it in my direction. "I brought this for you," he says.

I step aside as he enters the motel room. I shut the door behind him, lock it, and throw the bolt again.

"Did you see her get arrested?" I ask him.

He grins at me. "Yeah, I was *right there*. I wish you had seen her face, Dawn. It was epic."

"I've been watching it on the news all morning." I glance at the television screen, which is now dark. "I wish I had it on repeat."

Caleb digs around in his pants pocket and pulls out his phone. "It's all over the internet. Let's eat, and then you can go nuts."

I want to watch it now, but I'm too hungry to argue. I rip open the paper bag and pull out a turkey sandwich with mayonnaise on white bread. Caleb knows I like monochromatic meals. He even made sure the bag was white. He knows me so well.

The color of food is more important than people think. Green sea turtles get their color from what they eat. They are primarily herbivores and consume mostly seagrass and algae. The food gives their cartilage and fat a green color.

"Just one sandwich?" I ask. "You don't want anything?"

"I grabbed a burger on the way over." He shrugs. He doesn't care about things like food color. He's not like me. He's normal. Well, as normal as any guy plotting to frame his girlfriend for murder can be. "Go ahead. Eat. You must be starving."

I tuck into the sandwich, nearly ripping it apart in my eagerness. I haven't been eating very well this week. I brought some food with me and I've been stashing it in the mini fridge in the room, but as I said, I'm afraid to go out much. Caleb only dared to come here once this week to bring me food. So I've been eating a lot of vending machine meals. My nutritional status is suffering.

Caleb hesitates at the foot of the bed, looking around the room with his forehead scrunched up. "This place looks different."

"I reorganized."

He does not ask me why, although I would be happy to explain that the furniture in this motel room was arranged completely incorrectly. I moved the dresser, the mini fridge, and the lamp to be in ascending order of height. I also did quite a bit of cleaning, as it's clear the janitorial staff of the motel has been quite negligent in their duties. If he were to enter the bathroom, he might appreciate the way I reorganized all the toiletries he brought me.

But he also might not.

"Why were you down in the main lobby?" I ask around a mouthful of turkey and white bread.

He frowns. "Did you *call* Natalie?"

My cheeks grow warm. I didn't know he knew about that. I knew I shouldn't do it, but I wanted to hear the panic in her voice. I loved it when she was screaming at me to leave her alone. "I blocked the number before I called."

"Dawn." He lets out an exasperated sigh. "That's not foolproof. She traced the call back here. She was telling me about it this morning. If she hadn't been arrested, she was going to be driving out here this afternoon. Do you know how screwed we would've been?"

"Oh."

Perhaps it was impetuous of me to call her. But then again, Caleb is not blameless. He told me about how he tormented her all week with that turtle figurine on her desk, even though it would have ruined everything if she had caught him in the act.

"It's not safe to be here anymore." He runs a hand over the back of his neck. "I checked us out and settled the bill. We'll find another place today."

"Okay."

I'll be glad to be out of this seedy motel, although I'm sure the next place won't be any better. Really, I want to get out of New England altogether. Head south. But Caleb thinks it's too dangerous to be driving around right now. Plus, it would look suspicious if he suddenly quit his job. He's got to stick around a little longer, then we can go.

I'm not sure where. I always wanted to live in the south. People are nicer down there.

As I chew on my sandwich, Caleb climbs into bed beside me. I could never have done this without him. He played his role perfectly—he deserves an Academy Award. And it was so much better than I hoped. Natalie shot herself in the foot by trying to convince him to be her alibi.

I don't know how he managed to pretend to be her boyfriend for that long. But he never slept with her. He swore he wouldn't.

While I finish the sandwich, I turn the television back on. They're talking about the body that was found in the woods in Cohasset, brutally beaten. The body of Dawn Schiff. Or so they think.

"They're going to figure out it's not you sooner or later," Caleb remarks.

"I know."

"Christ," he mutters. "What are the chances, you know?"

He's talking about the coincidental fact that a body turned up of a woman approximately my age, and apparently, her face was so badly beaten, they assumed it was me. The news mentioned most of her teeth had been knocked out, so they could not use dental records. It facilitated Natalie's arrest, but ultimately, it won't matter. Eventually, the DNA will reveal that the dead body is somebody else. This random dead body won't send her to prison.

Caleb's eyes are still on the screen. "What kind of sick person would do something like that?"

"There are a lot of sick people out there," I say. "You should know that by now."

"Yeah. But to be beaten so badly, they can't even recognize who she is…" He turns slightly green. "And nobody is even looking for her."

I stuff the last of my turkey sandwich down my throat, and I nod in the direction of the phone in Caleb's hand. "Show me the video," I say.

He's got one already to go, which makes me think he's been obsessively watching them the same way I have been. He hates her as much as I do. He's been waiting for this as long as I have. We're both soaking it up.

In this video, you get a close-up of Natalie's face as that detective reads her her rights. You can see her lips contorting in an ugly way. Her face turns bright red, and then she's yelling something.

"She's calling your name," I observe.

"Yeah," he says quietly. "She is."

The detective jerks on her cuffed arms and she stumbles. He leads her to the police car and shuts her inside. She's crying now. Big ugly tears. And snot is bubbling under her nose, but she can't wipe it away.

"Oh my God." I stare up at Caleb. "We made this happen."

"We did."

We sit there for a moment, staring at each other. Caleb is the first one to lean forward and press his lips against mine. I grab two fistfuls of his shirt, pulling him even closer. He pushes me down onto the plastic-wrapped mattress with the white sheet and the *tan* pillowcase, climbing on top of me, careful not to touch the bandage on my wrist.

"We did it," I gasp as his lips make their way down to my neck. "We did it."

"We did it," he breathes in my ear. "I love you so much, Dawn."

"I love you too."

Caleb is kissing me and unbuttoning my shirt and I don't even care anymore that the sheets are a completely different shade of white from the pillowcases. He fumbles for the remote control to turn off the television, but I grab his wrist to stop him. "I want to watch," I tell him. "In the background. Okay?"

Caleb gives me a look, but I've made plenty of strange requests of him over the years. This is not the strangest—not by a long shot. The man has agreed to sleep in a bed with no less than a dozen stuffed turtles. "Yeah. It's fine."

What Caleb is doing to me feels so good, and I want it so badly, but I can't help but keep one eye on the television. Natalie is on there again. She's facing the camera, a smile plastered on her lips. This must be before she got arrested.

"This race is in Amelia's honor," she's telling the reporter.

Despite everything, her words fill me with white-hot rage. How could she say that? That lying bitch. How could she tell the world that Amelia was her best friend and all this is in Amelia's honor?

266

I look over at the table by the bed, where the pad of paper with the letter to my own best friend is written in my neat cursive, which Mia would know instantly. I close my eyes, remembering the words I scribbled on the paper in ballpoint pen:

Dear Mia,

You would have been so proud of me today.

The police arrested Natalie Farrell. She was at her stupid 5K race, and right in front of dozens of cameras, they snapped handcuffs on her wrists and took her away. You should have seen the look on her face.

I have dreamed of this day for so many years. Caleb and I dreamed about it together. There were times when he started to go soft on me, asking if it was worth it to go through with it, but I didn't let him give up. I wouldn't. And together, we made this happen.

Now Natalie will go to prison for the rest of her life. That's what she deserves, although she will technically be going for a crime she didn't commit. Still, since she is guilty of murder and was given a free pass, it feels justified.

I told you I would get vengeance. I told you I wouldn't let Natalie get away with killing you. I made a promise on the day you died, and today, I honored that promise.

I love you. I will never forget you.

Sincerely,
Dawn Schiff

CHAPTER 47

Amelia was her given name, but her friends called her Mia. Natalie wouldn't know that, because she was never Mia's friend. Natalie's view of the world is very Natalie-centric. If something isn't happening in her own personal little bubble, she doesn't know about it.

That's how she managed to work in a cubicle next to mine for nine months without realizing that the two of us went to high school together, albeit briefly. I always thought she was going to eventually figure it out and my cover would be blown, but she never did. To be fair, I looked very different in high school. I wasn't as thin as I am now, and I had longer hair then. I was also a year ahead of her, because in sixth grade, Mia was out most of the year after a bad case of pneumonia put her in the hospital for months and she was held back. And Natalie transferred from another school at the beginning of her junior year, so we were only at the same school for a single year, in two different grades.

Even though she was the new girl, Natalie was the queen of our high school. Any surprise there? And Mia…wasn't. Her mother gave birth to her ten weeks early, and she had lived with cerebral palsy her whole life. Her mind was fine, but she needed braces and crutches to walk. Her speech was slurred, especially when she got excited, which embarrassed her terribly.

I met Mia in first grade. We were supposed to pick buddies for a class trip, and I watched as the kids paired off as always, leaving me to be assigned to be buddies with another loser who nobody liked—or worse, the teacher. So I was surprised when the new girl with braces and crutches came straight over to me. *Dawn, will you be my buddy?*

I was so astonished, I didn't know what to say at first. Even at age seven, I was used to being excluded from everything. Nobody ever invited me to their birthday party unless they invited the whole class, and even then, they often found a way to exclude me. At first, I thought Mia might be teasing me. But then I saw the earnest, wide-eyed expression on her face, and something happened to me that had never happened ever before:

Another girl wanted to be my friend.

Of course, I said yes.

Mia was the greatest friend who ever was—she made my life worth living. Before she came along, I was utterly alone. People always made fun of me, and Mia had the same experience. It was just part of life for both of us. My mother told me I deserved it for being so weird. Mia was lucky enough that her parents were more supportive, and she had a big brother who looked out for her. We hoped things would get better as adults, but we accepted that kids can be cruel. And when we were together, it didn't seem so bad.

Especially because we defended each other.

For example, in third grade, when Jared Kelahan wouldn't quit making fun of Mia, I pushed him right off the monkey bars—you can bet that stopped the teasing. And when Duncan Albright wouldn't stop calling me Turtle Girl, Mia threw some water on the crotch of his pants and started a very popular rumor that he wet himself. We had each other's backs, always.

But when I was away at college, that's when things deteriorated.

I couldn't be there for my best friend. I couldn't defend her anymore. All we could do was talk on the phone while I would reassure her that she was going to be okay. But that wasn't enough.

Mia had a disability, and she was never apologetic or ashamed about it. So it was painful to watch her change in that way. The other kids giggled about the way she walked on crutches. Kids would try to trip her up—make her fall. On one occasion, she took such a bad spill in the hallway that she chipped her front tooth. And then they made fun of her for her marred smile.

But the worst part was the way they made fun of how she talked.

I loved Mia's voice. I would give anything to hear it again. We used to talk on the phone for hours, and even though it took a little getting used to, I never had trouble understanding her. But she used to garble her words—especially when she was nervous or excited—one syllable slurring into another.

Natalie came up with a particularly nasty way to

make fun of Mia. They shared a math class together, and every time Mia would answer a question, Natalie and her best friend Tara Wilkes would mimic the answer in that same slurred voice. Low enough that the teacher couldn't hear it, but everyone around them could.

It gave other kids ideas. It started happening in all her classes. And when Mia complained about it, the teachers wouldn't do anything. *Natalie and Tara would never do anything like that*, they would say.

After a couple of months of this torture, Mia stopped raising her hand in class.

We mostly communicated on the phone because I was long-distance, but it was hard not to notice the change in her personality. Mia had always been a strong person—stronger than me. She was the one who told me not to let myself cry in front of anyone else. But Natalie and the other girls *broke* her. I could hear the pain in her voice.

Hang in there, I told her. *High school is almost over.*

I know, she said. *Believe me, I'm trying. I won't let Natalie win.*

I didn't know what to do. I thought about calling Mia's parents to let them know what was going on, although she would have hated that. I even went so far as to type an email to Mia's brother, hoping he might be able to do more than I could. But in the end, I believed Mia would get through it. It was, after all, more than halfway through senior year. Soon, she'd be in college and would leave all this behind.

Then there was the Valentine's Day incident.

For as long as I knew Mia, she had a crush on a boy named George. We went to school with him since kindergarten, and she used to fantasize about marrying him someday, even though she laughed when she talked about it. George was a nice kid, as far as I could tell. He wasn't particularly handsome or popular or athletic, although he wasn't an outcast like we were. He never laughed at Mia or made fun of her. He said hi to her in the hallway. He was kind.

In the days leading up to February 14, Mia received a series of notes from George. She read them to me on the phone. They were exactly the sort of sweet notes that I would have expected from George, and I was so happy for her. It felt like things were finally turning around for my best friend. Even though I desperately wanted a boyfriend of my own, which seemed like an impossibility, I wasn't jealous. I only wanted Mia to be happy.

It wasn't until Valentine's Day arrived that Mia approached George when she saw him carrying a red rose. She thought the rose was for her, but it was for some other girl who he had a crush on. He was never interested in Mia—not now, not ever. The notes were all from Natalie and Tara, playing a joke on her—George had no idea about any of it. Natalie masterminded the whole thing. And while George tried to be nice about it, he made it painfully clear he had zero romantic feelings for Mia and never would.

Two days later, Mia took her own life.

She took a bunch of pills, then slit her wrists in the bathroom. By the time her parents found her, she was already gone. They called me that night to break the news to me. I loved her as much as they did. I would never have another friend like Mia.

Mia was gone. And it was all Natalie's fault.

I wanted vengeance. I tried to convince Mia's parents to do something—press charges against Natalie. But there was no evidence Natalie did anything wrong. It was Natalie's word against a dead girl, and everyone loved Natalie. Mia's parents just wanted to forget about it. *Let her rest in peace, Dawn.*

I couldn't though. I was too angry. My hatred for Natalie Farrell burned inside me. I watched as she went off to college and dated the hottest guys and made a zillion new friends and did all the things that Mia would never do. Because of *her.*

There was nothing I could do about it. Nobody cared except me. Even Mia's own parents were willing to let it go.

And then one day, I found somebody who hated Natalie as much as I did. Someone who blamed her for killing Mia the same way I did. Who wasn't willing to let it go as easily as her parents were.

Caleb.

Mia's brother.

CHAPTER 48

NATALIE

Since I've been arrested, I am entitled to have an attorney provided for me. The smart thing to do would be to hire a lawyer of my own, but I am incredibly short on funds right now, and whatever I do have, I'd like to save it to bail myself out. So I consent to use the freebie lawyer.

Right now, I'm supposed to be having a meeting with my lawyer. They have led me into one of the interrogation rooms lit by an overly bright bulb right over my head, and I've been sitting in an uncomfortable plastic chair for the last forty-five minutes waiting for an attorney named Archibald Ferguson who I'm increasingly certain will never show up. If only I had money to pay for my own lawyer. But I am pretty sure the constitution or something says that I have a right to an attorney. They can't just say they gave me one and wash their hands of it.

Finally, the door to the interrogation room swings

open, but my heart sinks when I see that it's just some teenager. Probably a high school intern working at the police department, dressed in one of his father's oversized suits. But I may as well make the best of it.

"Could I have some water?" I ask the intern. "My throat is really parched. And do you think you can ask them how much longer till my lawyer shows up?"

The boy clears his throat. "Actually, I'm your lawyer."

I stare up at the kid, all thoughts of my parched throat flying out of my head. This has got to be some kind of joke. This is a *child*. He doesn't even look like he's old enough to grow facial hair. How could he be a *lawyer*? How could he be *my* lawyer?

"What?" I sputter.

"I'm your lawyer," he repeats, although it doesn't seem more plausible the second time he says it. "I'm Archie Ferguson."

He holds out his smooth white hand, but I don't take it. "How *old* are you?"

He flinches. "I'm twenty-five."

I suppose that's better than what I first took him for, which is sixteen. But not much better. This kid does not look like he is in any position to be defending somebody in a murder trial. He looks more like he should be working the drive-through at McDonald's.

"You're a lawyer?" I ask.

He nods proudly. "I graduated this past June."

Great. He's been a lawyer for five months. I want to bury my face in my hands and burst into tears. But somehow, I manage to hold it together.

Ferguson settles into the chair across from me. His suit is at least two sizes too big for his skinny frame—it must belong to his dad or a big brother. He'll grow into it, I suppose. By then, I'll be serving twenty-five years to life.

"So let's talk about your case, Ms. Farrelly," he begins.

"*Farrell.*" I glare at him across the almost comically tiny table. "My name is Farrell."

Ferguson frowns. He looks down at a stack of loose papers in front of him and starts shuffling through them. "Farrell? Are you sure? I thought—"

"*I know my own name.*"

"Right. Right, of course." Ferguson's voice cracks because he's apparently still going through puberty. "Sorry. Ms. *Farrell.*"

I don't say anything to that.

"So…" he says.

I raise an eyebrow. "Yes?"

He clears his throat, which turns into a cough, then a series of coughs. Finally, he jumps up, explaining that he has to go get some water. He runs out of the room, grabbing his sweaty stack of papers, and then he returns about ten minutes later.

"Sorry about that," he says as he plops down in the chair across from me.

I just stare at him.

"So…" He coughs again, and I swear to God, I am going to lose it if he has another coughing fit. "Let's discuss your, um, case."

"Listen," I say, "no offense, Mr. Ferguson, but this case is kind of a big deal. This is a *murder* trial. Is there anyone else who could help me? Like, somebody with a little more experience?"

Ferguson's cheeks turn bright red. "I've been doing

this for almost six months. I've tried lots of cases. Don't worry. You're in good hands."

"I *am* worried though." I chew on my thumbnail. "This is a murder charge, you know?"

He nods slowly. "Yeah, this is a tough one. They have a pretty good case against you. A lot of stuff."

A lot of "stuff"? How could that be? How much "stuff" could they possibly have against me when I haven't done anything? "Like what?"

"Like they got into that Schiff woman's emails and she wrote all about the things you did to her." He tugs at his tie, which doesn't seem to be knotted correctly. "She cataloged the way you bullied her at work and that she caught you embezzling money from the company where you both worked. And that the two of you were supposed to meet that night."

"That's complete fiction." My heart is pounding. "I was nice to Dawn. And we weren't supposed to meet that night. I don't know what she could possibly be talking about."

"Also," he says, "your fingerprints were on the handle of a knife in her house."

"I explained that. I picked up a knife to defend myself in case there was an intruder in the house. And it wasn't like she was stabbed to death."

Ferguson smiles apologetically. "Also," he adds, "the police found blood and hair in the trunk of your car. It matched up to what they found in Schiff's apartment."

My mouth falls open. They found Dawn's blood and hair in my *trunk*? I can't even begin to explain that one.

"Not to mention," he goes on. Oh my God, there's *more*? "Your boyfriend's statement is extremely damaging. That's going to be a hard one to rip apart."

"Is it really that bad?" I ask. "I mean, yes, we weren't together that night."

"And you lied about it."

I wince. "Yes, I did. But have you *seen* that detective? He's terrifying. And I didn't make a statement under oath. I just didn't have an alibi for that night. There are plenty of people who don't have an alibi for Monday night."

Ferguson gives me a funny look. "That's not all your boyfriend said."

"This completely isn't fair." I squeeze my right hand into a fist. "Santoro was harassing Caleb. He found him and forced him to say a bunch of things he probably didn't mean."

"No, that's not what happened at all. Caleb McCullough came to the station voluntarily. He told them he wanted to make a statement, and they recorded it. I saw the transcript."

I blink at him, wondering if I heard him right. "Caleb *asked* to make a statement?"

"That's right."

"But…" My thoughts won't stop racing. This doesn't sound right. "What did he say?"

"It's, uh…not good." Ferguson riffles through the pile of papers in front of him until I want to rip them out of his hands. "He said that you pressured him into lying about being together that night. He said that he left your house at around nine thirty after you asked him to leave. Apparently, you told him you had somewhere to be."

"What?" I cry. "That's ridiculous! That's a complete lie."

"Well, that's what he said. He also said that you and Dawn didn't get along. That you were constantly picking on her. That the two of you hated each other."

My head is spinning. Caleb said that about me? Why would he say that? He barely knew Dawn, and he wasn't even around work that much. And even if he did think I was bullying Dawn, why would he say that to the police? That's a pretty awful thing to say about your girlfriend.

"As you can see," Ferguson says, "they have a strong case against you. But there is some good news."

"Like what?" I choke out. At this rate, I'm looking at life in prison.

"Well," he says, "they don't have a dead body."

My head snaps up. "What? I don't understand. The detective said they found Dawn's body." *Beaten to death.*

"Actually..." He shuffles through the papers in front of him again. "They were having trouble identifying the body because she was beaten so badly and her teeth were destroyed, so dental records couldn't be used. But DNA testing has now revealed that it was not Dawn Schiff."

My head is spinning. Another girl about the same age turned up dead right in our neighborhood? It seems like a crazy coincidence, but I suppose a good number of people are murdered in big cities, and some percentage of them are going to be young women. "So...she might not even be dead?"

He gives me a look. The amount of blood on the floor of her house, the blood in my car, and the fact that she has not resurfaced all indicate that she is almost certainly dead. And I am still very much the prime suspect.

"Can I be convicted of murder if there's no body?" I ask.

"It's harder but still possible. I think you have a good chance of getting bail."

That would be great news if I had any chance of

being able to afford the bail. "But what about a conviction?" I press him.

He hesitates. "These are some really serious charges, Ms. Farrell. And the DA has a super strong case, like I said. Given the circumstances, your best bet is to confess and take a plea bargain."

"Confess!" I cry. "But I didn't do anything!"

Ferguson flashes me a skeptical look. "You know, we have that attorney-client confidentiality thingy. It's better if you tell me the truth so I can help you. I'm not allowed to tell anyone, so you should be honest with me."

"I didn't," I insist. "I swear."

Ferguson frowns. He might be young, but apparently five months of defending criminals have already made him jaded. "Fine," he says. "But either way, it might be worth taking a plea bargain. Go to prison for a few years, then you'll be out. If we take a chance and go to trial, especially if the body surfaces, you'll be looking at life in prison."

Life in prison.

Life in prison.

Ferguson starts talking about the bail hearing on Monday, but I can barely focus on what he is saying. *Life in prison.* Those three words keep repeating in my head over and over. If this goes badly, I could be living in a cell until the day I die. Behind bars. That's even worse than a cubicle.

Life in prison.

I can't let that happen to me. I *can't.*

If it looks like I'm going down for this, if it looks like I might spend the rest of my life in prison, I'm going to end it all. I'll drive back out to Wollaston Beach, and I'll throw myself off the pier in the middle of the night at high tide. Nobody will be able to save me.

But I hope it doesn't come to that. There was a girl in my high school who committed suicide, and it was so incredibly tragic—something I couldn't stop thinking about for years to come. Except now I get it. I finally understand the hopelessness that girl must have felt when she took her own life. The feeling that it would be better to be swallowed up into the abyss than continue to live life as you know it.

I can't let that happen to me. I *can't*.

CHAPTER 49

DAWN

Turtles have interesting mating habits. The male turtle often follows the female around, sniffing near their cloacal opening before starting a courtship ritual. While the male and the female are going at it, they twist their tails together as the semen passes from the male to the female. But the female doesn't have to lay her eggs right away. She can hold on to the sperm for several years before laying her eggs, if she so desires.

Caleb always gets sleepy after we have sex. Do all human men do that? I'm not sure. Caleb is the only man I've ever been with. I'm sure he's the only man I ever will be with. If not for him, I would almost certainly still be a virgin. I wouldn't have lost it to a turtle, as Natalie helpfully pointed out.

I am watching more videos on his phone, my head propped up with the pillow, and he's lying next to me, his arm slung across my chest. When he first came here, it seemed like it was urgent that we get out of this motel, but now he says we've already paid up for the rest of the evening, so we don't have to rush. I suppose with Natalie in jail, things are at a standstill.

"Do you want to watch it too?" I ask him, tilting the phone in his direction.

He yawns. "That's okay. I was there, remember?"

He squeezes me with his arm, cuddling closer to me. I reconnected with Caleb about a year after Mia died. I came to see her parents, and he was there. I knew Caleb from when we were younger, but I never paid much attention to my friend's big brother back then—although I always liked him because I knew he was protective of Mia. When I saw him all those years later, I was taken aback by how tall and cute he was. I got crushes on boys sometimes, but I had learned to ignore them. I knew by now that none of the boys would ever like me back.

Caleb is Mia's *half* brother. His father died when he was young, and his mother remarried. That was why they had different last names. He adored his baby sister, and he had spent the last year blaming himself for letting this happen to her. He didn't even know about Natalie— not all of it anyway. Not until I filled him in.

He was beyond furious. When I went back to college, we vowed to keep in touch. Mostly, we talked about Natalie, and to a lesser extent, her friend Tara. What Natalie had done to Mia and how to get her to pay. We never had any concrete ideas though. Well, I suggested cornering her in a dark alley, but Caleb wouldn't go along with that idea. He was adamant about not wanting to hurt anyone physically, and that limited our options. Mostly, it was just fantasies.

We can't just let her get away with it, Caleb would say. *It's not right.*

I can't remember exactly when it seemed like our friendship was evolving into something different. We never had the same sort of friendship that Mia and I had—I never expected that—but I noticed he was looking at me in a different way than most people. I didn't quite understand it.

Three years from the time of Mia's death, Caleb and I were at a restaurant together and having quite a nice evening. For once, the silverware was clean and the glasses didn't have any smudges on them that required them to be replaced. When the check arrived, Caleb grabbed for it.

No, I protested, *it's my turn to pay.* Caleb and I always took turns covering the check when we went out. If there was a significant discrepancy between that evening's check and the last time, I would offer him money to cover the difference.

I want to pay, he told me as he tugged the bill out of my fingers. When I started to protest, he added, *I got a raise at work.*

All right, I finally agreed, albeit reluctantly, *but let me at least make sure it's correct.*

I looked over the numbers, and sure enough, there was a major error. They charged us for two beers, but only Caleb had ordered one. *I saved you six dollars,* I told him rather proudly. *What would you do without me?*

You're right, he agreed. *I don't know what I'd do without you.*

And then I noticed he was looking at me with a lopsided smile on his face. I didn't quite know what he was thinking until he blurted out, *Dawn, would it be okay if I kissed you?*

I was stunned. I noticed he had been treating me differently, but this was something entirely unexpected. Nobody had ever kissed me before. And yet I was oddly touched that he asked permission, which was what inspired me to say yes.

It was my first kiss. And it was so much better than I ever imagined it would be. It was the first of many, and it wasn't until we had kissed at least a dozen times that he stopped asking permission.

And then I somehow fell in love with him.

He loves me too. Before all this, he was talking about getting married. He wants to marry me, even though I am...me. Ultimately, I am certain he will be disappointed. Mia accepted me for exactly who I am, but I suspect Caleb sees something in me that isn't there.

More concerning, the deeper he fell in love with me, the more his hatred of Natalie seemed to dissipate. He didn't talk about her much anymore. He didn't want to get revenge. *It was a long time ago,* he started saying. That was when I knew. We had to do it now, before he completely lost his desire.

"We should hit the road in about an hour," he says in that same sleepy voice that makes me think he isn't going to want to get on the road at all in an hour. "I found another motel we can go to about thirty miles south of here."

"Okay," I agree.

He props his head up on his elbow. "I thought maybe I could spend the night with you. I think it's safe."

"You think?"

He bats his eyes at me. "Let's live dangerously."

I can't very well argue with him after I made the stupid move of calling Natalie from the motel. And I *would* like him to spend the night. These motels are frightening after dark.

"I wonder if they figured out that dead body isn't me," I muse. "I haven't seen it mentioned on the news."

"If they haven't, I'm sure they will soon," he says. "I guess they had to do DNA tests since her face was so damaged. That takes time."

"I guess so."

He rubs the stubble on his chin. "It's such a crazy coincidence, isn't it? I mean, a girl the same age as you turns up at the exact same time."

He keeps saying that. He keeps talking about what a strange coincidence it is. But it's not *that* strange. Thousands of women are murdered every year in this country. It's a *coincidence*. He doesn't need to give me a funny look when he says it.

"How long do you think she'll go to jail for?" I muse.

"A long time, I'll bet."

"You think?"

"Sure. I mean, it's a murder charge."

I chew on my lower lip. "But as soon as the DNA tests show that the dead woman isn't me, there won't be a body. They can't lock her away for life if there's no dead body, can they?"

"Well, there's nothing we can do about that, is there?"

"I guess not."

Caleb tilts my head so he can kiss me. My stomach churns as I push away the thought that's been intruding on my brain for the last month or so, as much as I try not to let it bother me. It's hard not to think about it though.

He kissed her. He kissed Natalie.

At first, I didn't think it was a big deal. But now every time his lips are on mine, I imagine him kissing her. I *saw* the two of them kissing. And if I didn't know better, I would've thought he was enjoying it. He probably was enjoying it on some level. I'm sure she kisses very well. She's had lots of experience.

"What was it like kissing her?" I blurt out.

His lips part slightly. "Excuse me?"

"When you kissed Natalie," I clarify. "What was it like?"

His face darkens. "What do you think? It was awful. I hated it."

"Really? Because it didn't look like you hated it that much when you were doing it." I quickly add, "I'm just wondering. I'm not mad."

Caleb sits all the way up in bed. There's a muscle twitching in his jaw. "This is the last thing I want to talk about."

"Well, it just seems like you didn't mind playing the part that much. Just an observation."

I don't know why I'm doing this. We got exactly what we wanted. And a large part of it is because Caleb went out with Natalie. But I can't help the way I'm feeling.

"You have *got* to be kidding me, Dawn," he growls. "You *know* I didn't want to go out with her. I didn't want to do any of that! I told you *no*. But you kept pushing and pushing."

That is not inaccurate. Caleb did not, in fact, want to date Natalie. He thought it would be enough to just be friendly with her. But I felt like he could incriminate her so much better if he were her boyfriend. So I talked him into it. It actually took quite a bit of work, because he really, really didn't want to do it. But I was relentless. I wouldn't give up until he agreed.

"You didn't have to do it," I point out. "You could have refused."

"Have you ever *met* you?" he shoots back.

"I'm just saying…"

"You made me do it! You begged me! You *cried*!"

I did put on quite the performance. And it wasn't an act. It's that important to me to get Natalie behind bars. So yes, I did tear up a bit. But deep down, I was still hoping he would refuse. Because, you see, Caleb is supposed to love me and only me. And if you really love a woman, you would never agree to kiss another woman. Not under any circumstances.

Caleb frowns. "You know, I didn't even sleep with her. And believe me, that wasn't easy."

"Oh, I'm sure."

"I didn't mean it like that! I'm just saying, I didn't do anything with her."

"Except kiss her."

"Yes. But that's it. And I hated it. I wanted to throw up after."

He's lying. He doesn't hate Natalie the way I do. He was going to let the whole thing go. When I suggested getting jobs at Vixed to set her up and send her to prison, which is what she deserves, Caleb looked at me like I was crazy. Ten years ago, he would've been happy to go along with it. But I had to force him to do it now. Kicking and screaming.

Mia has been dead for thirteen years now. And it feels like I'm the only one who truly cares anymore. Even her own brother has forsaken her.

I still care, Mia. I did all this for you.

Natalie is going to pay. Those emails left on my computer were a stroke of brilliance. Who is stupid enough to leave their computer password on a sticky note under their mouse pad? But I'm sure the police bought it. Those emails I composed to Mia were a work of art. I'm so glad Mia could play a little part in the plan to take down the woman who killed her. Caleb even set up an untraceable fake account from Mia to "reply" to the emails and make it all seem more real. Caleb composed dozens of fake emails allegedly from Mia, and we gave her the life she always wanted. She always dreamed of living on the West Coast and, of course, being married to George.

In my emails, I painted Natalie to be a psychopath. And it all but says she was at my house on the night of the disappearance. Then there's the bloody ceramic turtle Caleb planted in her laundry hamper. And her fingerprints strategically scattered throughout my house. And one more damning little surprise.

She's finished. There's no way she isn't going down for murder.

Caleb reaches for my hand. He laces his fingers into mine. I saw Natalie hold his hand like that once. "You're not really upset over this, are you?"

"No, it's fine," I lie. "We should get on the road soon."

Caleb nods. We both get out of bed and start getting dressed. It's lucky Natalie told him that she had traced my calls. If she hadn't, it could've ruined everything. That was a very close call.

I'm not going to take any chances anymore. This has to go exactly to plan.

CHAPTER 50

NATALIE

I've never spent the night in jail.

Obviously. I'm not the sort of person who gets hauled in by the police. I don't get drunk and make a spectacle of myself in public. I don't do drugs. In general, I follow all the laws to a T.

Yet here I am.

There's something inhuman about being kept in a cage this way. It makes me feel less like a person and more like some sort of animal. It's stifling. Claustrophobic.

I'm in a tiny cell with one other woman. She's not much bigger than me, but she's absolutely terrifying. She has pockmarks all over her face and a jagged scar splitting one of her eyebrows in half. She has tattoos everywhere. She even has them on her neck. I once tried to get a tattoo, and I chickened out—and that was going to be a tiny heart on my shoulder blade. How gutsy do you have to be to let somebody tattoo a giant skull on your *neck*?

They shut off the lights inside the cell when it was

time for bed, but they're still on in the hallway right outside the bars. It's these fluorescent lights that keep flickering—it's even worse than the ones at work. I can't sleep with that going on, but it's not like I can ask them to shut the lights out—plus this cell would be far more terrifying if it were pitch-black. And the stench of urine is almost overpowering, to the point where I want to breathe through my mouth. The gray mystery meat I ate for dinner churns in my stomach.

When I got here, they gave me the option of changing out of my 5K T-shirt and running pants into a jumpsuit. At the time, it seemed like a good idea. But now I regret it. This jumpsuit is itching like crazy. I don't know if it's the detergent or what. At home, I use a hypoallergenic detergent, but I'm guessing the jail laundry doesn't have that.

At least there's a bed in the room so I don't have to sleep on the floor, but I might as well be. There seems to be a mattress on the bed, but it's not much better than a sleeping bag.

Also, it's freezing. All they have given me is a paper-thin wool blanket that's possibly itchier than the jump-suit, yet I'm obscenely grateful to have it. I don't even know how it's so cold. The winter hasn't even started yet. It's got to be colder in here than it is outside.

I just want to sleep. Is that too much to hope for?

"Hey. You."

I roll my head in the direction of the other bed in the cell. It's the woman with the neck tattoos.

"What?" I say.

"It's cold in here," she says.

"I know." I shiver under the itchy wool blanket. "It's freezing. Do you think we should tell the guard?"

The woman laughs. "Yeah, what do you think he's going to do? Turn up the thermostat?"

"I don't know."

"Listen, I need your blanket."

I shift on the poor excuse for a mattress. "What do you mean?"

"I mean, I'm *cold*. I need your blanket."

"But then I won't have a blanket."

"Like I give a shit."

"But…"

The woman climbs out of her bed. She straightens up and crosses the small cell, and now I am absolutely terrified. She bends down close enough to me that I can smell her stale breath. She reaches out one arm, and I flinch, sure she's going to punch me in the face and break my nose. But instead, she grabs my blanket and yanks it clear off me.

If I was uncomfortable before, it's a lot worse now. I didn't realize how much warmth that skimpy blanket was providing me. Without it, I'm practically shaking. But my cellmate doesn't care. I'm lucky she left me with my pillow, even though it's flat as a pancake.

I lie on my back, still shivering, trying to get some sleep. This is going to be my life from now on. I don't have enough money to make bail, so I'm stuck here until my trial. And if the trial goes as badly as my attorney has warned me it will, this could be the rest of my life.

Before I know it, tears are streaming down my cheeks. I don't cry easily, but this last thing has broken me. Losing my itchy, crappy blanket has broken me. I wipe the tears away with the back of my hand, because it would be too much to hope for a tissue.

"Hey!" my cellmate snaps. "Keep it down over there! I'm trying to sleep."

How did my life get to this point? I never laid a finger on Dawn. How could they think I would kill her? Why won't anyone believe me?

CHAPTER 51

DAWN

Caleb decides it's safer to wait until late to leave the motel. So it's well into the evening by the time we arrive at the new motel.

It looks exactly like the other one. Identical. It's like we just drove around the block for forty minutes and arrived exactly where we started. But Caleb is the one who picked it, and I don't feel like complaining. It's not like some other place would be better. Any place nicer than this is probably going to pay more attention to who is checking in, and that's the last thing we want.

Caleb goes into the main lobby to get us a room. I am wearing my wig and baseball cap, and my spare tortoise-shell glasses are in my coat pocket. I duck down in the seat, but it's not like it matters. The outside of the motel is very poorly lit, and there's hardly anyone around anyway. I probably look more suspicious crouching down.

About ten minutes later, he returns to the car, a key jangling in his hand. "Second floor again," he tells me.

I grab the small bag containing the meager belongings I chanced bringing with me. It's a few pairs of jeans, underwear, some shirts, Turtly, and that's about it. If I took too much, the police might think I went on a trip instead of coming to the conclusion we want them to reach. I sling the bag on my shoulder and follow Caleb out of the car and up to the motel room.

The motel room has the same dingy look as the last place. Everything seems to be covered in a layer of grime. Not the kind of grime that will come off on your finger if you touch it—grime that's built in from years of overuse of already second-rate furniture. When Caleb flicks on the light, there's even grime on the lampshade.

I scrutinize the bed. The thin blanket is brown, and when I yank it loose, the sheets underneath are a pale yellow color and the pillowcase is *gray*. Does anyone even make the slightest attempt to match the linen? I can't even fathom pairing a gray pillowcase with yellow sheets.

He notices the expression on my face. "Sorry it's not nicer."

"It's fine." It is far from fine. There's nothing I can do about the sheets, but I will spend all day tomorrow scrubbing this room until the level of grime becomes acceptable. "It's good enough."

"It's only for a few days."

Right. A few days and off to the next place, which will be exactly the same.

I pull off my wig and baseball cap, and then I spend a good minute scratching my scalp. That wig is awful. I should probably try to grow out my hair, but I hate having long hair. I hate the way my hair feels against my skin. "Can I have your phone?" I ask.

Caleb reaches into his pocket and pulls out his iPhone. He hands it over to me, and I immediately look up news updates. I'm searching for articles about Natalie. I want to know if there's anything new in the case. My heart sinks when I discover an article announcing that police have "confirmed that the identity of the dead body found in Cohasset was not, in fact, Dawn Schiff."

"They found out the body wasn't me," I say.

He doesn't seem particularly concerned. "It was going to happen sooner or later."

"Do you think Natalie will get out on bail?" I wonder aloud.

"I don't know."

"She probably will." I put down the phone on the bed, face up. "I'm sure the judge will fall in love with her and go easy on her."

Caleb snorts but doesn't comment. I'm not sure what that means. I have asked him in a casual sort of way if he finds Natalie attractive—he did kiss her, after all—and he always reacted like I was being ridiculous. But she *is* attractive. He would have to be blind not to see it.

I always wondered what his type is. I am not anyone's type. I believe that he does love me, but it's despite the way I look rather than because of it. I don't know what sorts of girls Caleb dated before he dated me. I wonder if he has a thing for blonds. Most men do.

If Mia were around, she could answer that question. She adored Caleb and knew absolutely everything about him. She used to constantly mention him casually in conversation, like to tell me the TV show we were watching was his favorite or that he taught her to hide the icky lima beans from dinner under her pillow. At the time, I wasn't terribly interested, but now I wish I had listened closer to the things she told me about him. I wish I had come to dinner that Thanksgiving night she invited me, when Caleb was home from college and had brought his girlfriend.

That girlfriend was long gone by the time Caleb and I got together, but I wonder what she was like. He liked her enough to bring her home for Thanksgiving. I wonder if, like Natalie, she had blond hair and blue eyes and no soul.

I lie back against the mostly flat pillows on the stiff motel mattress. "Do you think she could get sentenced to life in prison?"

Caleb rifles around in the backpack he brought with him. "I don't know. Maybe. Probably."

"Maybe or probably?"

"Probably."

"But…" I shift on the uncomfortable mattress. "There's no dead body. Do you think they can convict her without a dead body?"

"We looked it up. Prosecutors can convict someone if they have enough evidence to show that the victim has died. Like lack of communication, lack of recreational and bank activity, abandoning their home. And obviously, signs of a crime scene. We got all that going on."

"Right, but it will be harder to convict her without a dead body."

"Harder, but there's a very good chance."

"But there would be a better chance if there were a dead body."

Caleb stops rifling around in his bag and looks up at me. "Dawn, it's really starting to upset me that you keep talking about this. There's no dead body because you're still alive."

"But—"

"There's not going to be a dead body. *Ever.*"

I can't argue that he hasn't made a valid point. But I can't help but feel he's not as invested in this plan as I am. He didn't even want to do it in the first place. When I suggested it, he looked at me like I was crazy. Natalie drove his sister to kill herself, and he was willing to just *let it go*. If I said the word, he would probably happily bring me back to Dorchester and tell the police I'm alive and well.

"I just want to make sure she pays for what she did," I murmur.

Caleb sits beside me, and the mattress makes a crunching sound. "I know. I do too. But we've done all we can. I don't think it's worth taking any other risks."

"Yeah."

He picks up my hand in his. "You agree, right?"

"Um…"

"Dawn." He applies firm pressure on my hand. "Tell me you agree. You're not going to do anything stupid."

"Caleb…"

"Promise me. Promise me you're not going to do anything else. *Promise me.*"

"Fine. I agree." I pull my hand away. "What do you think I'm going to do anyway?"

He gives me a look. "I don't want to think about it."

He goes back to his bag, and I pick up his phone again, scrolling through the articles. The truth is, I'm just telling him what he wants to hear. He doesn't get it. There's nothing more important to me than this plan. *Nothing* is more important than avenging Mia's death. Even him.

Even me.

CHAPTER 52

NATALIE

I feel like a walking zombie and am in no mood to talk to my parents. But according to one of the guards, they are on the phone.

In some ways though, my parents are my only hope. I don't have enough money in the bank to bail myself out of jail. So if I don't convince them to lend me some money, I'll be stuck here until my trial.

That's not an appealing thought.

The guard leads me to a bunch of phones set up on the wall. I look at the row of phones, not sure what to do. I glance over at the bald guard, who isn't giving me any instructions.

"Um," I say. "What should I do?"

"You pick up the phone and talk," he barks at me.

I want to snap back at him that I know how a phone works, but I suspect that won't make my situation any better. Then I notice that one of the phones is off the hook and the receiver is lying on a counter beneath it. I reach for the receiver, which feels sticky in my hand.

"Hello?" I croak into the receiver.

"Natalie!" My mother's voice is far too loud, as usual. "Natalie, are you okay?"

I'm in jail. What the hell does she think? "I'm okay."

"Are you eating? Is there food there?"

"Yes, there's food. This isn't a death prison."

My mother is used to my sharp replies on the phone, so it surprises me when she bursts into tears. Which in turn makes a lump rise in my own throat.

"Natalie, how could you do this?" she sobs.

I stare at the receiver, stunned. How could she think that I'm guilty? It was bad enough that Seth thought I stole money from the company. Now my own mother thinks I'm a murderer?

"I didn't do it, Mom," I whisper.

"Oh, Natalie."

"I didn't! How could you even think that?"

"You have to admit," she sniffles. "It's the sort of thing you would do."

I don't even know what to say to that. *It's the sort of thing I would do?*

"I mean," she goes on, "there were all those incidents when you were younger. Remember that girl you and your friend Tara bullied…and she *killed* herself?"

She always brings that up. It doesn't seem to matter that I have set up a charity to honor Amelia. I'm still the girl who drove her to her death. But it should be said that the police didn't even consider bringing charges against me. I was barely even questioned.

I have tried to make amends. When Tara and I were

writing those fake Valentines to Amelia, I never for one second believed they would make her kill herself. She seemed so much stronger than that. A fighter. Everyone was so shocked when she killed herself. And I've been trying to make it right ever since. Trying to make up for the stupid thing I did when I was too young to know better.

"I was just a kid," I point out.

"You're lucky they didn't throw you in prison back then."

"Mom…"

"Daddy says there's a prison in South Walpole. I think that would be the most convenient location for us to come visit you."

She's already talking about prisons and I haven't even gone to trial yet. "Listen, I need to talk to you about money. Do you think you can lend me money for bail?"

"Well…how much?"

"I'm not sure. It's going to be a good amount. Five figures, probably."

"Oh, honey."

"Please, Mom." My voice cracks. "I need your help. I don't want to stay in here. It's awful."

There's a long pause on the other line, followed by shuffling. After a few seconds, my father's deep voice booms, "Natalie, you know we don't have money for this sort of thing. We live on a fixed income."

"Yes, but—"

"Don't make us feel guilty about this," he snaps at me. "Whatever you did, you need to deal with the consequences."

"But I didn't do anything!"

The guard notices the volume of my voice rising. He shoots me a look. "You got one minute left, Farrell."

"Please!" My voice cracks. "I can't do this. I really can't."

"I'm afraid you're going to have to get used to it. According to your lawyer, you're going to be in there a long time."

"But, Dad—"

Before I can get out the entire sentence, the guard walks over to me and hits the button to end the call. I shake my head. "You didn't even let me say goodbye."

"I told you to wrap it up." There's no sympathy in his voice. This is how I'm going to be treated from now on. "Now get back to your cell."

I allow him to march me back to the square room with the cellmate with the neck tattoos. I am completely screwed. I don't know how I'm going to get money to make bail, especially if it's the amount that Ferguson warned me it could be. My parents can't give me the money. Kim and I don't have that kind of relationship where I could ask to borrow the money, even though she could give it to me if she wanted to since her husband is loaded. Seth is off the table—I'll be lucky if he speaks to me again.

There's no chance the bail will be less than what I have in the bank, even accounting for the fact that I only have to pay 10 percent to the bondsman. It looks like I'm going to be in jail for a while to come.

CHAPTER 53

DAWN

The motel room is dark and Caleb is sound asleep next to me.

I was right—this new motel is no better than the other one. The bed is just as hard and uncomfortable. The television is even worse. It's mostly static. This is the kind of place to stay for one night. Maybe even just an afternoon. It's not the kind of place you live for weeks or even months.

This is a necessary sacrifice though.

I clutch Turtly while I watch Caleb sleep. I do that sometimes. He doesn't snore, but he breathes deeply through his mouth and sometimes there's a little whistling sound. His hair is mussed by the pillows, falling almost into his eyes if it were a little longer. He has long eyelashes for a man, and they flutter slightly as he sleeps. Maybe he is dreaming.

I wonder what he dreams about. He told me once that he never remembers his dreams. But he must have them. Everybody dreams. Maybe he's dreaming about Natalie.

The truth is, I was already in love with Caleb the first time he kissed me. We were so close by then. We saw each other constantly, and while at first we mostly talked about Mia, we had started to talk about other things. The other things were always his idea. But I never dared to imagine he might feel the same way about me that I felt about him.

That first kiss was wonderful in a way I hadn't expected. I had never been kissed before, not by a man. It wasn't one of those gross kisses from the movies where a guy's tongue is practically in her stomach. It was a nice kiss. Just his soft lips on mine—he had popped a mint after dinner so even his breath smelled nice. It was almost a chaste kiss, although when I looked at his face, there was no doubt about his intentions. It turned out he felt the same way about me that I did about him.

He took things so slowly, for my sake. He was satisfied for a long time just holding hands and kissing. He bought me thoughtful presents, like a gold chain with a turtle charm on it. We were together almost a year before we made love. I won't lie—I was terrified. He was really slow and careful about it though. He made it special.

Before Caleb, I had crushes on boys, but I was realistic that none of them could ever really like me. But it isn't like that for him. When Caleb asked Natalie if she wanted to go to dinner, she gave him a quick yes. He didn't even have to talk her into it. She *liked* him.

I remember once I saw them in the break room together, having lunch. They looked like such a normal couple. They were having an easy conversation that had nothing to do with turtles or revenge. He made a joke and she laughed—a genuine laugh. That never happens to me. When I'm with another person and they laugh, either it's polite laughter or else they're laughing *at* me.

It was at that moment that I realized Caleb is *normal*. He isn't like me at all. We both got caught up in getting justice for Mia, but aside from that, we have nothing in common. Mia is our only bond. And eventually, he will realize it.

He was lying when he said he felt nothing for Natalie. The image she puts forth is extremely likable. She's the sort of person everybody gravitates toward. She's always been that way. A golden girl.

Not everyone realizes what a snake she is. That she will smile to your face and then stab you in the back. She invites everyone to parties but schedules them for times that she knows only her favorite people will be available. She lies to customers. She slept with another woman's husband and destroyed his marriage.

Tomorrow morning, they will probably have a bail hearing for Natalie. She's been in jail all weekend, which is a good start, but not enough. I'm hoping that all the evidence Caleb planted—her fingerprints on the glasses, the hair and blood in her car, the ceramic turtle in her laundry hamper—will mean she's stuck in jail until the trial, even now that the DNA evidence has shown the random mystery body wasn't mine. Natalie doesn't have much money—she lives beyond her means, and her parents are as broke as mine.

Ultimately though, there's one big problem. They're trying to convict Natalie of murder, but there's no dead body. There's no solid evidence that a murder has even been committed.

My left wrist throbs under the bandage, but there's no fresh blood on it. Caleb was against me cutting myself that way. He thought it was too risky, especially since that's the way Mia died. But I was careful about it. I didn't cut too deep. There had to be blood on the floor. Otherwise, the police might just think I went away on vacation. There had to be convincing evidence of foul play.

I climb out of bed as quietly as I can. Caleb stirs briefly on the mattress, but then he goes back to sleep. He's a very sound sleeper. I know everything about him, maybe even more than Mia knew when she was alive. I know that he loves to belt out rock songs in the shower, even though he can't hold a tune. I know his least favorite food is pickles—he can't eat anything that has even *touched* a pickle. I know his shoes are a size 10. And I know that he has spent the last thirteen years beating himself up for not protecting his little sister.

Caleb's jacket is hanging on the coat rack by the door. I stick my hand into one of the pockets, searching for his phone. I pull out a couple of crumpled napkins, which I throw in the garbage. I hate it when he sticks napkins in his pocket—he always does that. I feel around in his pocket again, and my hands close around a rectangular object.

I pull out the object. It's a small blue velvet box.

Oh no. He bought a ring.

I don't open it. I *can't*. He's been talking about getting married when this was all done, although I don't know how we're going to do it if the police are supposed to think I'm dead. He's very logical about most things, but he hasn't thought this through at all. He just wants to marry me, but he doesn't see how much of a mistake that would be.

Not just because of Natalie. In general, it would be a mistake. He doesn't want to be stuck with me for the rest of his life. He's gotten all mixed up in his head because he feels so awful about what happened to Mia. He feels responsible for me.

I stick the ring box back in his pocket. I'm going to pretend I didn't find that.

His phone is in his other pocket. I type in the six-digit code to unlock the screen—he is comfortable enough with me to entrust me with this information. I wonder if Natalie knows it too. I wouldn't be entirely surprised, even though it would have been a big risk. There were things on that phone we wouldn't have wanted her to discover. Like the recording he took of me crying "*help me*" in a tearful voice. That was Caleb's idea—he figured that phone call would get someone investigating my house faster. And it worked, although it would have been better if she hadn't gone over there herself, because that gave her a way to explain all the fingerprints.

We planned this out so well. There's only one missing piece.

It's finally clear to me how this is all supposed to end. Really, I knew all along—I just didn't want to admit it to myself. When Caleb and I first discussed this plan, I liked the idea of starting over again with a new identity—not having to be Dawn Schiff anymore. I should have known from the start it would never go that way. Caleb and I didn't get together so we would fall in love. We got together so that we would get justice for Mia. To make Natalie pay for driving her to suicide.

There's only one way that can happen. There's only one way that Natalie will go down hard.

There needs to be a dead body.

And it needs to be mine.

CHAPTER 54

NATALIE

The bail hearing goes as well as it possibly could. Meaning the judge grants me bail as long as I surrender my passport. Unfortunately, it's a stupidly high amount that I could never afford. Even the 10 percent bond is a higher amount than I can afford.

Which means I will remain incarcerated until my trial. At which point, I will almost certainly be sentenced to some sort of prison time. I'm going to spend the next several years behind bars. If I'm *lucky*.

However, the overwhelming likelihood, Ferguson has assured me, is that the DA will go after a murder one charge. He updated me this morning that they don't seem interested in seeking a deal. This has been a very high-profile case, because of the accusations in Dawn's emails, and they want to make sure I receive the punishment I deserve. They feel confident there's enough evidence of foul play that they can convict me without a body.

They want me to go to prison for the rest of my life. They want me to die behind bars.

As I sit in my jail cell, all I can think about is how badly I want to go home. I want to take a shower in my own bathroom. I want to eat a giant, juicy cheeseburger. I want to lie in my own bed all alone with a cozy blanket and sleep as long as I want in the morning.

But I have a sick feeling that's never going to be my life ever again. At least not for a long time.

So I am nothing short of shocked when one of the guards calls out my name. "Farrell! Your bail has been posted."

"What?" I leap off the bench in my horrible cell, where I have been sitting and feeling sorry for myself. "By who?"

The guard just shrugs, and it's not like I'm going to interrogate him. I just want out of here. Even if it's for a few weeks until my trial.

It's only after I get back my phone and wallet and other belongings that they lead me to the waiting room and I discover who my benefactor is. It's the last person I expected.

"Hey, Nat," Seth says.

He must have come straight from work, because he's wearing a dress shirt and tie. He looks tired, but I'm sure I look much worse. My hair feels like a rat's nest. I'm scared to even run my fingers through it.

"What are you doing here?" I ask. "I thought you hated me."

He offers me a crooked smile. "Let's talk in the car, okay?"

I'm not going to say no. I'm tired and hungry, and all

I want is to go home, so even if he's going to berate me for the entire ride home, I'll still take it.

I follow Seth out to the parking lot, where his Audi is waiting for us. I get into the passenger seat, rest my head against the headrest, and shut my eyes. If I'm not careful, I'm going to fall asleep right here and now. I never want to go back in there. Ever.

Seth climbs into the car beside me. He starts up the engine and we're off. I watch his profile, wondering what his game is. The last time I saw him, he was furious and hurt, accusing me of stealing money from the company. But he doesn't seem angry anymore.

"So," he finally says. "I…I checked through all the accounts, and there was no money missing."

"What a shock."

He frowns. "I'm sorry. I should've believed you. But that detective came in, and he sounded so sure of himself."

"Uh-huh."

"I'm really sorry." His voice cracks slightly. "He just…he got to me. I should've known you would never do something like that."

He feels bad about it. And he's here, which means a lot. Nobody else is here for me. Yes, he was awful to me, but I can forgive him. "I can't believe you paid the bail. That was a lot of money."

"I've got the money." He lifts his shoulder. "You did me a favor. It's less in my bank account for Melinda to get her hands on. Also, you need a decent lawyer. That Ferguson guy I talked to was awful. What is he—twelve years old? I'm going to help you out with this."

I don't want to owe Seth anything, but at the same time, I'm in no position to refuse. He's right. I need a decent lawyer. One who graduated from law school more than six months ago.

"I didn't do anything to Dawn, you know," I say.

"I know. This whole thing is ridiculous. We'll get it all sorted out."

He believes me. It feels like he's the only person who does. Even my parents think I'm guilty. They think I'm a terrible person. All because of that incident in high school with that girl. Amelia.

"Are you hungry?" he asks. It's nearly lunchtime. "We can grab some food."

I swallow a lump in my throat. "I just want to go home."

"You got it."

While he's driving, I check the messages on my phone. There are about five billion messages and voice-mails. I don't have the energy to deal with all these. Not now.

Then I notice a text from Caleb. He sent it on Saturday evening.

> Checked out the motel. Nothing there. Seems like a dead end.

I stare down at the text message. A few days ago, I would have felt grateful to him for driving all the way down to Rhode Island for me. But now I'm not sure what to think.

I thought Santoro bullied Caleb into ratting me out. But it turns out it was the opposite. Caleb went to the police himself. He voluntarily told them my alibi was a lie. And he said a lot of other things.

"Was Caleb at work today?" I ask.

Seth shakes his head. "Didn't see him. But I'm sure he'll come over and see you. If that's what you want."

It's not what I want though. I don't trust Caleb anymore. He turned on me, and I'm not sure why.

"What do you think of Caleb?" I blurt out.

"Well, I think you could do better. Obviously."

"Seriously, Seth."

"I don't know." He pushes his palm down on his horn as a Subaru cuts him off. "Selfishly, I don't like him. I don't think he's been very supportive of you through this whole thing. But he seems like a nice enough person. I guess. And I'm sure he's just worried about Dawn."

"Why would he be so worried about Dawn? He hardly knows her."

Seth glances at me. "What are you talking about? They know each other. She was the one who recommended him to me for the website job."

"*What?*"

My world has suddenly gone on tilt. Dawn was the one who recommended Caleb? How could that be? They never spoke to each other, except for a polite hello. A few times, Caleb even got her name wrong, which now seems increasingly suspicious.

"Oh yeah," he confirms. "She went on and on about him. You know how she does that. Gets stuck on some topic and won't shut up about it."

Holy crap.

It suddenly occurs to me that Caleb had easy access to my house—more than practically anyone else. Could he have planted that turtle in my laundry hamper? And he could easily have gotten into my trunk. Since he was at the office, he could have put those turtles on my desk every day. And how many times have I drunk from wineglasses in his apartment, then left them behind with my fingerprints on them?

It hits me that when Caleb took away my alibi, he also eliminated his own. He has no alibi for the night Dawn was killed. Moreover, he was the one who told me he was tired and wanted to head out early. I was trying to get him to stay.

Is it possible that Caleb murdered Dawn and is trying to pin it on me? It seems crazy, but in a strange way, it makes sense. It's the *only* thing that makes sense.

But *why*?

That motel. I've got to get over there.

CHAPTER 55

During the rest of the drive home, I explain the situation to Seth. Whatever else I can say about Seth, I trust him. He'll give me sound advice.

"I just need to take a shower and change." I'm still stuck in the clothing I wore to the race on Saturday morning. I can't wait to peel it off my body. "Then I'm going to head out to the motel."

"I'm coming with you."

I raise my eyebrows at him. "Don't you have to work?"

"I'm the manager. I'm entitled to an afternoon off for something important. I'll drive you there."

"You don't have to—"

"I'm driving," he says more firmly this time. "You probably barely slept the last few nights. I wouldn't even trust you behind the wheel. Let me drive."

I start to protest again, but I don't know why I'm fighting him on this. I'm exhausted. I'm scared I really might fall asleep at the wheel. I'd love to take a nap, but I'll be tossing and turning until I get to the bottom of this.

When we pull up in front of my house, there are a handful of reporters crowded on my front lawn. My stomach clenches at the sight of them. Videos of my arrest have gotten all over the news—Detective Santoro could not have picked a worse moment to arrest me. Or a better moment, depending on how you look at it.

"I can't deal with this," I mutter.

Seth glances up at the rearview mirror. "Don't worry. I'll take care of it."

He gets out of the car, and I watch in the side mirror as he speaks to the reporters. I don't know what he says to them, but they all take off. I am almost ridiculously grateful to him.

When I get into my house, I just stand in the living room for a moment, drinking in the quiet. In addition to the flickering lights and freezing cold, the holding cells were always noisy. There was a woman in the cell next to mine who seemed to be going through some sort of drug or alcohol withdrawal, and she was screaming about seeing bugs the entire night last night. I never realized how wonderful it is to have complete silence.

Seth hovers in the doorway. "I can wait in the car if you want."

"No, it's fine. I'm going to hit the shower, then we'll go."

"You got it."

When I get up to my bedroom, my phone starts ringing. It occurs to me that I never even let my parents know I had gotten out of jail. But I think I'll wait on that. I don't want to deal with them right now. If it's my mother calling, I'll let it go to voicemail.

But it's not my mother. It's Caleb.

I stare down at his name, flashing on the screen. Caleb McCullough. A week ago, I had been thinking to myself that he might be the one. Now I don't know what to think. He definitely hasn't been completely honest with me. I wonder what he's got to say.

I swipe to take the call. "Hello?"

"Nat! Hey, I heard you got out on bail."

Word travels fast. I sit down gingerly on the edge of my bed, gripping the phone. "Yeah. My parents helped me out with the bail money." The lie rolls off my tongue.

"That's great." He sounds normal. Concerned but not too concerned. Just the right amount of concerned. *This man may be a cold-blooded killer.* "How are you feeling? Are you okay?"

How does he *think* I'm feeling? I just spent three days in jail! But I bite my tongue. I'm not going to snap at him. I don't want him to know what I know. "Just tired, that's all."

"Did you get my message about the motel?"

"Uh, yeah."

"I drove over there," he says. "There was a guy at the desk, and I asked him if he noticed anyone suspicious. I showed him that photo of Dawn from the papers."

"And?"

"Nothing. He didn't know what I was talking about."

"I see." I cough. "Well, thanks for going down there."

"No problem. This is all so awful what you're going through."

A hundred thoughts are running through my head.

I want to ask Caleb if he knew Dawn before working at Vixed. I want to ask him why he went to the police about me. I want to ask him if he was the one who planted that hair and blood in the trunk of my car.

I want to ask him if he ever cared about me or if the whole thing was just an act.

"Can I do anything for you?" he asks.

"I just want to be alone for a while," I say.

"Of course. Call me later?"

Does he want me to call him because he's concerned about me? Or because he wants a window into what I'm thinking? "Sure."

What is Caleb's game? I know that he knows Dawn, but that's all I know for sure. He doesn't seem like he could possibly be a murderer. I can't wrap my head around it.

There's something at that motel he doesn't want me to know about. I'm sure of it now.

I'm going to find out what it is.

CHAPTER 56

An hour later, I am freshly showered, changed into jeans and a sweater, and feeling like an entirely new person. I feel so good, I hate the idea of getting into the car and taking a long road trip. But it won't be so bad. Seth will be driving, and I have to get to the bottom of this. Somebody from that motel was calling me over and over. I need to know why.

Seth stands up when I come down to the living room. "Ready to go?"

"Yes. Definitely."

"You feeling okay?"

I rub my eyes. "Just a little tired. I'll be fine."

"Maybe you should take a few Collahealth capsules?"

Then we both laugh.

We get back on the road, but I still haven't eaten much since the awful breakfast they served me in jail. We stop off at a fast-food drive-through, and I order food I would never ordinarily indulge in. But I'm *starving*. All I want is a big, greasy fast-food burger.

Seth laughs when I demolish about half the burger in three bites. I remember when we were hooking up last year, we ended up eating a lot of fast food in the car. After all, we could hardly go to a restaurant. Sitting here in the car with Seth, stuffing fast-food fries in my mouth, gives me a sense of déjà vu.

"How are things going with Melinda?" I ask.

"Awful. This may come as a shock, but getting divorced sucks."

"I'm sorry."

"Don't be."

I squirm in the leather seat. "I feel responsible."

"You're not," he says flatly. Yeah, right. "Look, I'm not going to say that what happened between you and me didn't make the whole thing a lot more contentious. But it was going to happen either way. We didn't even *like* each other anymore. You know Melinda and I haven't had sex in over three *years*?"

He said something like that when we were together, but I always thought he was exaggerating. I don't think so anymore.

"It's not your fault," he says. "Or if it was, it was only because you reminded me that I was actually capable of being happy."

I don't know if he's saying that to let me off the hook or if he means it. But right now, I'll take it. I already feel bad enough about myself. I don't need to add home-wrecker to the list of horrible things I've done in my life.

Seth turns on the radio while we drive. He's really into classic rock, which is not my favorite, but I don't care much right now. I remember when I told Caleb my favorite singer was Celine Dion. His face lit up. *Celine*

Dion is my favorite too! Now I wonder if he was making that up as another way to get close to me. What man's favorite singer is *Celine Dion*?

It's an almost ninety-minute drive to get to the motel. It's a large place—two stories sprawled out over a large lot—with dozens of rooms that open directly to the outside. And it's in the middle of nowhere. It's a perfect place to hide out.

A neon sign denotes the main office for the motel. Seth parks right outside, and we sit in the car for a moment. "You ready?" he asks.

I nod wordlessly. There are butterflies in my stomach—I'm terrified of what Caleb doesn't want me to know about this place. What has he done? Is my boyfriend a cold-blooded killer? Is Dawn lying dead in one of these motel rooms, sprawled out on a plastic-covered mattress?

We march to the front door, which is hanging on its hinges. This motel is a dive. A man is sitting behind the counter, his eyelids sagging shut, his brown hair long and scraggly. This entire lobby looks like it hasn't been cleaned in a decade. If I sat on the sofa in the room, a big puff of dust would come out of it.

"Help you?" the clerk asks lazily.

"Yes, thank you." I dig my phone out of my purse and bring up a picture I've got of Caleb. Well, it's Caleb and me. It's a selfie I took of the two of us, back when I thought he might be the one. I hold it up for the man. "Have you seen this man?"

The clerk barely glances at the photo. "I don't know. We get a lot of people coming in and out."

Seth digs out his wallet from his back pocket. He

pulls out a couple of bills and slides them across the table. "Do you think you could look again for us?"

The man looks down at the cash on the table. He scoops up the bills and tucks them into his front pocket. Then he leans in to take a better look at my phone.

"Oh yeah," he says. "Now I recognize him. He was here. On Saturday."

My heart sinks. That doesn't help me at all. Caleb already told me he drove here on Saturday. So this only proves that he was telling the truth.

"Did you talk to him?" Seth asks the guy.

He nods. "Yeah, he was checking out."

I suck in a breath. "Checking out?"

"That's right. He got a room, I think on Monday night, and he came in here to check out."

Seth and I exchange looks. There it is. Solid evidence that Caleb is full of it. My boyfriend has been lying to me all week. Except…why?

"Was he with anyone?" Seth asks.

The clerk hesitates. "I'm pretty sure he had a woman staying with him in the room. But I'm not absolutely sure. I try not to pay too much attention. You know? Unless I hear screaming or gunshots, I look the other way."

A woman?

On a whim, I type the name Dawn Schiff into my search engine. It brings up that awful ID photo of Dawn. I hold up the image. "Was this the woman who was staying with him?"

"It's possible. She had more hair than that, but it could've been a wig. And no glasses. She was skinny as a rail like this woman though."

Holy crap.

Is it possible Dawn is still alive?

"Did she look like she was being held hostage?" I ask.

The clerk lifts a shoulder. "Didn't seem like it. She wasn't tied up or anything. But like I said, I try not to pay too much attention."

We thank the clerk and get out of the motel. Caleb was definitely here, but it's obvious he's long gone. But it doesn't matter. Caleb isn't planning to disappear like Dawn did. He'll show up at work sometime this week, pretending everything is fine. That's when I'll confront him with what I know.

"That asshole," Seth mutters as we get back into the car. "What the hell is he up to?"

"I have no idea."

"Look what he's putting you through." He hits the steering wheel with his palm. "And for what? Why is he doing this?"

I wish I knew.

"I'm sorry I didn't believe you at first." The sun has dropped in the sky, and his eyes look shiny in the shadows. "I should never have doubted you. I know you wouldn't steal."

"I don't blame you."

"When I get my hands on Caleb, I'm going to punch him in the nose."

For some reason, his words make me laugh, and he grins back at me. It's the first time I've laughed in what feels like forever. But it's beginning to feel like there's a small chance this could all work out. Caleb is the key to everything. And he has no idea what I know.

We start on the drive back to Dorchester. As buzzed

as I am from the events of the day, the motion of the car eventually lulls me to sleep. Seth gets how tired I am, and he shuts off the music and drives in silence. He doesn't even hit his horn, which is unusual behavior for him because he's a typical Boston driver who loves to lean on his horn. Sitting in the passenger seat of his car, this is somehow the best sleep I've gotten in a week. It's only interrupted by Seth's hand on my arm, shaking me awake.

"Natalie," he says.

There is an urgency in his voice that makes my eyes shoot open. "What?"

"Look."

I blink a few times and rub my eyes. The sun has gone down completely now, but I can tell we're back in my neighborhood. On my block. In fact, my house is only a stone's throw away from the car. Seth is pointing at the house.

It's very dark out, so I have to squint to see what he's talking about. That's when I notice there's a man in front of my house. Sitting on the front steps. And when he sees our car, he rises to his feet.

Oh my God.

It's Caleb.

CHAPTER 57

"Stay in the car," Seth says. "Lock the doors."

He means well. Caleb isn't who we thought he was, and he's certainly been lying to me. But at the same time, I don't think he's dangerous. In my heart, I don't believe he killed Dawn. I don't think he's capable of it. Even with all the lies, I can tell he's not the sort of person who would do something like that.

And even if he is, he's not going to kill me right in front of Seth, right on the street. If nothing else, he's smarter than that. He's certainly not impulsive. Whatever he's done was planned over months—maybe *years*.

So I unlock the car doors and get out, despite Seth's protests. Caleb is walking toward me but there's nothing threatening about him. He doesn't have a weapon. This is going to be okay. I need to know what's going on. I need the truth.

"Hey, asshole!" Seth yells. He's getting out of the car just behind me. "You need to stay away from Natalie."

Caleb is about three feet away from me now. He looks up at Seth, shakes his head, and looks back down at me. I notice now that his brows are knitted together. "Natalie," he says in a shaky voice. "We need to talk."

"Damn straight," I say. "You've been lying to me all along. You planted that hair and blood in my car, didn't you?"

Caleb looks taken aback. He didn't expect me to say that. He stands there for a moment, not sure how to respond.

"Well?" I prompt him.

"Fine." His voice is gruff. "I did it. I put the hair and blood in your trunk. Okay?"

I stare at him, stunned he admitted it. Even though I had suspected it, I can't believe he would really do it. And *why*?

Seth jogs over, joining me next to Caleb. "You killed her, didn't you? You killed Dawn, you bastard."

Caleb's face turns bright red. "No. *No*, of course not. I would never do that. I would never hurt her. She—"

He stops himself midsentence.

"She what?" I press him. "What is it?"

He shakes his head. "I…nothing. I can't…"

"Caleb, *tell me what's going on here*." A vein throbs in my temple. "I deserve an explanation."

Caleb looks at me for what feels like an hour, but it's probably more like a few seconds. He lets out a long breath. "Dawn isn't dead."

"How do you know that?" Seth shoots back.

Caleb holds up his hands. "It…it's a long story. But she's not dead, okay? I promise."

"Then where is she?" I ask.

"I…" He rakes a shaking hand through his hair. "I don't know. That's why I'm here. I need your help."

"No chance." Seth glares at Caleb through the darkness. "You put Natalie through the wringer. She was in *jail* because of you. Why did you do this to her? What the hell is the matter with you?"

Caleb's Adam's apple bobs. "Listen, there's no time. Dawn—"

"Bullshit. You need to tell us right now why you did this. Otherwise, we're calling the police on you."

Caleb takes a step back. "No, please."

Seth opens his mouth to say something else, but I hold up my hand to silence him. This isn't about him. This is about me and Caleb. I need the truth.

"Caleb," I say, "I'm just trying to understand why you did this. I need to know. I don't think I deserve to be treated this way."

I watch as his chest rises and falls, considering my statement. "I've watched you these last few months," he says. "Organizing your little 5K. Getting on all the podcasts and local news stations. Talking about how you were raising money for your *good friend Amelia*. But she wasn't your friend, was she?"

There's venom in his voice now. I have a sinking feeling in my chest. "Caleb…"

"I'll tell you who she was," he spits at me. "She was my *sister*. And she was Dawn's best friend. Not that you ever even thought of her as a *person*."

My legs feel like Jell-O. I'm scared if I don't grab on to something, I'm going to fall flat on my face. "Amelia was…"

"My sister is dead because of you!" He is shouting

loud enough for the neighbors to hear, but he's beyond caring. "And you just moved on. Like she meant *nothing* to you. Like she *was* nothing. Worse—you're *using* her to promote yourself. How could you? Are you really that heartless?"

I dig my thumbnail into my palm. "I'm trying to raise money for charity."

"Yeah, whatever. You're just doing it because you like the attention. It helps promote the company. I get it. You used her back then, and you're using her now."

Caleb's eyes are burning with hatred. He hates me. He really and truly hates me. How could he have kissed me and joked around with me and taken me to dinner when he hated me this much?

"I was seventeen years old," I manage. "Yes, I was awful to Amelia. But I was a *kid*." I look over at Seth, who appears thoroughly confused. "She was a girl I knew in high school. I was mean to her. I know I was—"

"Mean to her!" Caleb bursts out. "You drove her to slit her wrists! My baby sister is dead because of you!"

I can't believe Caleb is Amelia's brother. I didn't even know she had a brother. They have different last names. Hers was Hodge. It's hard to forget what happened that year. Things just got out of control. I'm not going to deny any part of that.

I don't know why we were so mean to Amelia, in retrospect. I guess because she was different. And because we *could*. When you're seventeen and you're pretty and popular, it makes you feel good to pick on somebody weaker than you are. It makes you feel powerful.

"What do you want me to do, Caleb?" I say. "What can I do?"

"I want you to rot in prison for the rest of your life," he hisses at me. "Like my little sister is rotting in the ground."

His eyes bore into me, smoldering with an anger that he will never be able to let go of. He can never forgive me for this. He will never stop believing that I should be punished for the rest of my life. There's nothing I can say or do to make this right.

"So why are you here, Caleb?" I finally say. "To tell me how much you hate me?"

My question seems to take some of the fight out of him. "Look," he says, "I hate you for what you did, but you need to know that this whole thing—Dawn planned the whole thing out. It was *her* idea. And she's taking it too far, because…well, you know Dawn. That's how she is."

Clearly, he knows Dawn very well. Much better than I could have imagined.

"Damn straight she's taking it too far," Seth chimes in. "You sent an innocent person to jail."

Caleb shoots him a withering look. "Right, but she doesn't think the charges will stick if there isn't a dead body. *Her* dead body—not whoever they found in the woods. She kept talking about that. And…now I don't…I don't know where she is. She used my phone to call for a Lyft back to the South Shore, and now I don't know where she went. She called me from a phone somewhere and left this crazy message. She was giving me all these instructions for how to take care of her turtle and it sounded like…like she was going to…"

I gawk at him. "What are you saying?"

His face crumbles. "I'm pretty sure she's planning to kill herself. To make sure there's a dead body."

I clutch my chest. "Oh my God."

Caleb is crying now. He buries his face in his palms, his shoulders shaking. It's at that moment I realize something shocking. Caleb *loves* Dawn. He truly loves her. When he was with me, it was all an act, but he's not acting now. He's terrified of losing her.

He pulls his hands away from his face, and his eyes are red and puffy. "Natalie," he croaks. "You've got to help me find her. I've been driving around for hours, and I don't know where she is. Please. You owe me this. You owe *her*."

"How could we possibly find her?" I say.

"It's impossible," Seth says. "We've got to call the police."

"No." Caleb's voice is unwavering, despite his puffy face. "You can't do that to her. Do you know how much trouble she'll be in?"

"As much trouble as Natalie was in this week?" Seth retorts.

"Seth, stop." I raise my eyes to look at Caleb. "Do you have any idea where she could be?"

Caleb looks down at his watch. "If I had to guess, I'd say she has been hiding out near one of the beaches. It's high tide tonight." He grimaces. "She probably figures if she drowns herself, she won't be found for long enough that they won't be able to place the exact time of death."

It's the same thought I had while I was sitting in jail. Wait for high tide, throw myself in the ocean.

"We can find her," I say. Too bad there are about a million beaches around here, depending on how far she went. What if she's all the way in Cape Cod? "We need to split up. How far do you think she could've gone from here?"

"She took all the cash in my wallet," Caleb says. "But there wasn't a lot. Maybe a hundred bucks. So she couldn't have gotten very far."

"We're going to find her," I say with more authority than I feel. "We'll stop her before she does anything stupid."

I hope I'm right. I need to stop Dawn from killing herself. I need to make this right.

CHAPTER 58

The three of us split up.

I take Wollaston Beach, where I disposed of the pieces of the ceramic turtle the other night. It's the beach I know best. Seth grumbled about me wandering around the beach by myself at night, but I'll be fine. I bought some Mace for my purse after getting freaked out on Monday night when I arrived at my unlocked house.

Unfortunately, the beach is very large, stretching all the way down the coast. And it's very, very dark out. I don't know why it always seems so dark after daylight saving time. I put my high beams on whenever I dare, but I can't see anything.

Dawn could be anywhere.

For all I know, she's already drowned herself and we're too late.

I pull over for a moment to think. I have to be strategic about this, or else it's like trying to find a grain of sand on this gigantic beach. Dawn isn't just going to jump into the water and drown. It doesn't make sense. Her natural instinct will be to kick and flap her arms to save herself. Moreover, her body would quickly be found, and if they knew she was alive for a week after her disappearance, it could eliminate me as a suspect. When I had contemplated jumping into the water, I knew there was another element I needed.

Something to weigh me down.

I start driving again, but this time I'm looking for something different. I'm looking for places where they're doing construction.

After another ten minutes of slowly driving along the coast, I spot it. A construction site, abandoned for the night. Full of bricks and mortar and wooden planks and one other thing.

Cinder blocks.

I park my car and get out. If Dawn raided this construction site for a cinder block, she couldn't have gone far from here. Those things are *heavy*. If my instincts are right, she's probably somewhere around here. Of course, I'm just guessing. She might not even be at the beach. But I also think she would stay close to where I live, in keeping with her strategy of pinning this whole thing on me.

It's dark when I get out of my car. There are streetlights, but they only illuminate the street. The beach is pitch-black.

I turn on the flashlight function on my phone. There's a pier right around here, and that would be the most logical place for Dawn to jump. That's what I would've done.

The pier is to my left. I took my shoes off the other

day, but I leave them on now. I need to be able to make a quick exit. I step into the sand, squinting into the distance, directing my phone at the pier. And then I see it.

A figure hunched over at the very end of the pier.

CHAPTER 59

DAWN

The average human lifespan is under 80 years. But a lot of turtles live longer than that. Sea turtles especially can live to be 150 years old. Some large turtles can live over 400 years, in theory.

I can't imagine anyone wanting to live 400 years. I've lived thirty years, and it has been utterly exhausting. I'm done. I have experienced everything I need or want to experience. I have had true friendship, even though it didn't last as long as I would've liked. I have had an enjoyable career. I have been in love, until the man I loved betrayed me with another woman. Although to be fair, I did ask him to do it.

Mia once told me she thought she was going to live to be 87 years old. I don't know how she came up with that number, but she liked to be very specific about things. She told me she was going to move to the Pacific coast and have three children and eight grandchildren. She also had a list of places she wanted to visit before she died. It was a long list.

We'll go together, Dawn, she used to say. *We'll travel the world, just the two of us. Okay?*

The idea of traveling the world was terrifying to me—all those new places and things. I don't do well with novel experiences. What if you go to a new country, and they can't serve you food that's all one color? What if I went into a restaurant and ordered a dish without knowing what it was because I didn't speak the language, and then it turned out I was *eating a turtle*?

Yet the idea of traveling with Mia was exciting. I wouldn't have been scared to be in a new place if she was with me. She would make sure we would have a good time and that I would feel safe. She always did.

Now that she's gone, the world seems terrifying again. I don't want to leave Massachusetts. The idea of being pregnant and having a baby growing inside me is frightening to me. I don't like to travel either. If I can't experience these things with Mia, I don't want to experience them at all. I thought there was a chance I could do those things with Caleb someday, but unfortunately, that didn't work out like I thought it would.

I have experienced everything I care to experience. The best parts of my life are over. So there's no reason to keep going.

And I'm going to make sure my death counts.

I borrowed a small cinder block from a construction site nearby. I took the smallest one I could find, which should be more than heavy enough to hold me underwater. It weighs around thirty pounds. I bought some cord at a drugstore with the cash I took from Caleb's wallet. I've tied one end to my ankle and the other to the cinder block.

I've been watching the tide come in for the last hour. When the water gets high enough, I'm going to jump with the cinder block. Nobody is in the water in the middle of November, so there's an excellent chance I won't be found for at least a few weeks. The appearance of my corpse will be the final nail in Natalie's coffin. She will spend the rest of her life in prison.

We did it, Mia. We're finally going to make her pay.

I wonder if she would have done the same for me. Mia and I defended each other, but I always defended her more vehemently than she defended me. Like that time in third grade when I pushed that boy Jared Kelahan off the top of the monkey bars because he wouldn't quit teasing her. I remember sitting at the top of the monkey bars, staring at Jared on the ground, watching the pool of blood forming around his head as one of the teachers at the playground started screaming. Mia told me I went too far that time—she sounded a lot like Caleb does sometimes now. But the fact is, Jared never made fun of her again. Actually, he never made fun of *anyone* ever again.

As the water levels rise, I wonder what Caleb is doing right now. I left him a message, mostly to make sure he knew how to take care of Junior, but he's smart. He may have figured out from the message what I was planning to do to myself—he's probably panicked right now. But he'll come to realize this was for the best. If not now, someday.

The waves crash against the beach. Over and over. It almost sounds like the water is calling my name. It's ready for me. *Dawn, Dawn, Dawn…*

It's time to jump.

"Dawn!"

Okay, that sounded a bit *too* much like my name.

I whip my head around. For a second, I am blinded by a flash of light. I shield my eyes, and I realize that it's a phone flashlight. Somebody is standing on the other end of the pier.

"Dawn!"

I scramble to my feet. I squint into the mist and can barely make out a figure walking toward me. At first, their face is in the shadows, but it's not Caleb. Wrong build. It looks like a woman, and the voice is female.

"Dawn!"

She takes another step forward, and her facial features become clear. My stomach turns.

It's Natalie.

What is *she* doing here?

She shuts off the flashlight on her phone. She sticks her hands up in the air like I've got a gun. If only. If I had a gun right now, she would be dead. And there would be no witnesses.

I thought about that. I considered a simpler plan. *Kill Natalie.* Then I wouldn't have to fake my own death and go on the run. Except death is too easy for her. I wanted her to suffer the way I have suffered. The way Mia suffered before she decided to end it all.

"Please don't jump." Natalie's eyes flicker down to the cinder block at my feet. "Please don't do this."

"Don't tell me what to do." I clench my teeth. "How did you find me here?"

"Caleb told me what was going on."

If I wasn't angry before, I'm furious now. How could he? How could he go to her after all we went through

338

to frame her? Why couldn't he just let this happen? "He had no right."

"I'm glad he told me." The wind whips at Natalie's face, and she picks strands of blond hair out of her eyes. "I had no idea you knew Amelia."

I hate the sound of my best friend's name on this woman's lips. "*Knew* her? She was my best friend. My *only* friend."

"I know. I'm sorry."

"You killed her! You and your buddy Tara tormented her until she slit her wrists!"

Natalie flinches. "I know. And I'm so sorry. All I can say is that I was only seventeen years old. I didn't know better."

"No, I don't accept that. Seventeen is old enough to know better."

She takes a step toward me, and I take a step back. Although I need to be careful about that—I don't want to fall yet. "Listen to me," she says. "You hate me, but don't you think I feel terrible about what happened to Amelia? I do. Of course I do. Every single day since then, I have blamed myself. Why do you think I started this charity run? I've been trying to make it up to her."

"Too late."

We stare at each other for a moment. I'm wearing just a light jacket that belonged to Caleb, and I'm shivering in it. We didn't want to risk taking any of my own coats out of the house. The sleeves are far too long on me. I rolled them up, but they're still almost down to my fingertips.

"Look," Natalie says, "I know everything. Seth does too. If you jump, it won't do any good. You can't frame me for murder anymore."

It's the first thing she's said that's gotten through to me. She's right. If Caleb blabbed about our plan, she'll never go to prison for this. He has ruined everything. Everything we worked for. How could he do this to me? He couldn't possibly love me if he would betray me this way.

Natalie knows who I am now. She's ready for me. I had a chance to get revenge, and Caleb blew it. I wanted to make Natalie pay for what she did to Mia, but it's not going to happen. There's only one way left to make her pay.

I have to kill her. Caleb would never let me do it, but he's not here right now. He can't stop me. I have to end this.

Right here. Right now.

CHAPTER 60

NATALIE

I can't tell if I've gotten through to Dawn. She's difficult to read. She doesn't show anger on her face the way Caleb did. She still hates me, but I don't know what she'll do next.

Will she still try to kill herself? Did anything I say resonate with her?

She bends down and picks up the cinder block. I'm not sure why, but there's nothing good she could be doing with it. I step closer, scared she's going to toss the block into the water, and then it will pull her in. I don't think I can save her easily if she does that. But I'm ready to jump in if I have to. I'll try.

But she doesn't do that. Instead, she heaves the cinder block into the air, holding it above her head. She lifts her eyes to meet mine, and all of a sudden, I realize what she's doing.

She's planning to beat me to death with the cinder block. Oh God.

It wouldn't be hard. That thing has got to weigh at least thirty pounds. A few good clocks on the head, and that would be the end of me. She would finally have her revenge.

"Dawn," I gasp. "What are you doing?"

"What I should have done years ago." Her voice is flat, her eyes dull. "I'm going to make sure you can never hurt anybody ever again."

"Dawn, please don't do this." I clutch my purse to my chest and stumble backward. "I told you, I'm so sorry for what I did to Amelia. But killing me won't change anything. It won't bring her back."

"And you stole the man I love…"

"Stole him?" I shake my head. "I didn't steal Caleb!"

"It wasn't enough that you killed my best friend. You also had to have *him* too."

She has really lost it. I'm not sure I can talk her down anymore. "Dawn, Caleb was the one who asked *me* out. I thought he was single, for God's sake!"

"I loved him." A few flecks of saliva hit me in the face. "He was the last good thing in my life—the *only* good thing—and you *took* him from me! And now he likes you better."

"That's not true!"

"Yes, he does! Of course he does!"

"He doesn't! He hates me, just like you do."

"Liar! He used to hate you. But not anymore. He's fallen under your spell, like everyone else… Why else would he betray me this way?"

Her eyes are wet. It hits me that as angry as she is about Amelia and what I did all those years ago, she's just as furious that I "stole" Caleb from her. Maybe even more so. I'll never forget the anguished look on Caleb's face when he thought Dawn might kill herself. It turns out she feels the same way about him.

Apparently, Caleb *is* the one. Just not *my* one.

But she refuses to believe he has no real feelings for me. She's lost her grip on reality, which was tenuous to begin with. She doesn't care anymore what's true. She only cares about getting revenge. Dawn is small and skinny, but her arms aren't even shaking as she holds up the cinder block. That thing will do damage no matter where it lands.

I've got to do something to stop her.

I fumble around inside my purse. My fingers close around the spray bottle of Mace, and I yank it out. Dawn's eyes fill with confusion, and then a second later, I hit the nozzle. The chemical comes spraying out in a thick cloud, and then her eyes are filled with Mace (whatever that is).

She screams. She drops the cinder block onto the ground, thankfully missing all four of our feet. She clutches her eyes and doubles over. "You bitch!" she hollers.

Damn, I got her good. She's writhing around on her knees, still clutching her face. I hope I didn't somehow blind her. I don't need to add that to the list of crimes I have committed against Dawn Schiff.

When she finally stops screaming and looks up at me, her eyes are bloodshot and watery. On the plus side, she doesn't seem to be blind.

"Fine," she says. "You win. He's yours."

I crouch down beside her on the pier. I'm going to get splinters, but I try not to think about that. "Dawn, I don't want Caleb. And he doesn't want me. Trust me on that."

She buries her face in her palms, just shaking her head.

"He loves you," I tell her. "You and only you. I was throwing myself at him, and he always kept me at a distance. Now I understand why. And you know what he did tonight?"

She shakes her head again.

"He cried." I think back to the tears in Caleb's eyes. No man has ever felt like that about me before. Sometimes I wonder if it will ever happen. And yet Caleb feels that way about weird Dawn. "He couldn't bear it that something might have happened to you."

"He would have gotten over it."

"I don't believe he would have. It would've destroyed him."

Dawn considers this for a moment as she sits on the pier, wiping away the chemicals I sprayed into her eyes.

"What I said before is true, you know." I look out at the ocean, watching the waves crash against the shore. "There hasn't been a day that goes by when I don't think about Amelia and hate myself for what I did. Yes, I made up the part about us being friends, but I was always running in her honor. It was all for her. My penance."

"That doesn't erase what you did."

"I know. I wanted you to know it though."

Dawn's eyes go down to her ankle. The cord is still secured to her right leg. She starts working on the knot, attempting to untie it.

"Caleb really cried?" she asks as the knot pops open. I nod.

"He didn't even cry over Mia," she murmurs.

She doesn't say anything else. Neither do I. We just sit together, watching the tide come in, both of us glad it's not pulling us into its clutches as we realize how close each of us came to suffering that fate tonight.

CHAPTER 61

My phone is buzzing in my purse. It's a text message.
I pull it out and realize that I've missed several messages. Two from Seth and five from Caleb, all asking where I am. I text them both that I found Dawn, but not our exact location. I'm not even entirely sure how to describe where we are.

"Hey," I say to Dawn, "Caleb and Seth are looking for us. We should head back."

She frowns. "What happens next?"

That's a great question. The first thing I would like to do is march Dawn right back to the police station so Santoro can see she is still alive—that I'm not a cold-blooded murderer who bullied my coworker and killed her when she discovered I was allegedly stealing money. I want to hear him tell me that all the charges have been dropped.

Unless he plans to pin the murder of that stranger on me. Frankly, I wouldn't put anything past him.

"Caleb just wants to see that you're okay," I tell her. "And then we'll figure out what to do from there."

Dawn considers this for a moment. Then she struggles to her feet, wobbling a little bit before she finds her balance. Part of me is scared she might throw herself into the ocean at the last second, but she doesn't.

"He's going to be mad at me," she murmurs.

"He won't be mad. He's just going to be relieved you're okay."

I turn on the flashlight on my phone so we don't accidentally walk off the pier before we get back to dry land. I also shoot off a quick text message to both Caleb and Seth:

We are on the pier right near the Angry Crab restaurant.

Just as we get back to the main road, a pair of twin headlights approaches us. Both Seth and Caleb are here. Caleb pulls over first in his green Ford and leaps out of the driver's seat while the car is almost still moving. His hair is disheveled and his coat is hanging open as he runs down the street to where we're standing. Before we can even acknowledge his presence, he throws his arms around Dawn, holding her close to his chest.

"Jesus Christ." His voice cracks. "I was so worried about you. How could you think of doing something like that? How could you, Dawn? I'd never..."

Dawn doesn't say anything, but she hugs him back. Her skinny little fingers cling to him so tightly, I can see how white they are even on the dimly lit street. They just stand there like that, holding each other.

It makes me tear up a bit if I'm being honest.

"Nat!"

Seth has parked behind Caleb, and he's getting out of his own car now, at a lot more leisurely pace, but he still sprints the rest of the way over to me. I'm not going to kid myself that Seth loves me the way that Caleb loves Dawn, but he's gone out on a limb for me today. He bailed me out of jail. He drove me out to Rhode Island. He was going to foot the bill for a lawyer if it came to that. I may have underestimated Seth Hoffman.

"You okay?" he asks when he gets within comfortable earshot.

I nod, although when I wrap my arms around my chest, I realize I'm not as fine as I thought. I was in *jail* this morning. Dawn was about to clock me on the head with a cinder block about twenty minutes ago. I am far from okay.

But I will be.

"Are you cold?" Seth tugs at the zipper of his coat like he's going to take it off and give it to me. "You look like you're freezing."

"I'm a little cold," I admit. It's got to be thirty degrees out here—maybe less when you factor in the breeze from the ocean.

Seth doesn't take off his coat, but he unwraps the scarf that was around his neck. He gently places it around my own neck—it's a black fleece scarf that has a hint of Seth's aftershave. It radiates his warmth.

"Thanks," I say.

"You're welcome."

His eyes linger on mine, and I wonder if it would be inappropriate to ask if he would come home with me tonight. It's not just that I don't want to be alone. I want to be with *him*.

"Oh, hey," he says. "Guess what? I was listening to the radio on the way over, and apparently they identified the dead body of that woman in Cohasset."

I nod. "That's good for her family."

"Yeah, and I bet Santoro is going to get a lot of shit for arresting you for the murder of somebody who turned out to still be alive. They should've waited for the DNA to come back—they really jumped the gun."

Yes, Santoro should have waited. But he was just too eager to nail me. All because he got bullied as a kid.

Caleb and Dawn have finally disentangled themselves. He's got his arm around her shoulders, keeping her warm with his body heat.

"So who was the woman in Cohasset?" I ask Seth.

He lifts a shoulder. "Some woman…uh, Kara something?" He cocks his head thoughtfully. "No… Tara, I think? Nobody we know anyway."

Tara?

No…it couldn't be…

My hands are shaking slightly as I reach into my purse and pull out my phone. I bring up a search engine and look up news stories about the identity of the body found in Cohasset. It's breaking news, and the name comes up instantly.

"Tara Wilkes," I choke out.

Tara Wilkes. My old best friend from high school. The one who sat with me writing fake valentines to Amelia Hodge all those years ago.

Seth snaps his fingers. "Right, Tara Wilkes. That was it."

My eyes dart over to Caleb's face. He heard me say the name Tara Wilkes just now, but he didn't react.

There's not even a flicker of recognition. The name means nothing to him.

But when my eyes reach Dawn's, I see something completely different.

The girl found in the woods was not a coincidence. All those years, Dawn hated me for being the mastermind, but she hated Tara too for the part she played in Amelia's suicide. Death was too good for me, but it wasn't too good for Tara.

Oh God.

"That poor woman," Seth is saying. "They were saying on the radio that the reason they thought it was Dawn was that her hair was all hacked off, and her face was so badly beaten, she was unrecognizable."

"Oh geez," Caleb says, squeezing Dawn tighter in his arms. "That's awful."

Dawn's eyes stay on mine. "Yes," she says. "Awful."

A chill goes down my spine that has nothing to do with the freezing temperature. Dawn wanted more than anything to get revenge on the people she felt were responsible for Amelia's death. She was willing to do anything. She was willing to take her own life. She was willing to kill.

She's a very dangerous woman.

And nobody knows but me.

EPILOGUE

DAWN

Turtles have a reputation for being slow, although it's not entirely fair. Most walk at a speed of about 2 miles per hour, approximately half of the normal human walking speed of 3 to 4 miles per hour. But they can swim at a speed of 10 miles per hour. And the fastest turtle in the world can reach speeds of over 20 miles per hour. That means the fastest turtle in the world could finish a 5K in about ten minutes.

It took me half an hour.

I spent the last two months training. Caleb and I did it together. We ran around the neighborhood together, side by side, working on my endurance and speed. The first day, I could barely run a mile. By the last quarter of a mile, I was huffing and puffing, my lungs on fire. But today, I burst through the finish line of the 5K, sweaty and achy but filled with adrenaline.

Caleb is right by my side. Even though his legs are so much longer than mine and he could have been done with this 5K ten minutes ago, we ran the whole thing together. He cheered me on.

Mia would have been so proud of us.

"Great job, Dawn!" Caleb holds up his hand so I can high-five him. "You okay?"

I nod, still trying to catch my breath. "That was awesome."

"Wasn't it?" He grins at me. "I told you."

My heart swells as I look up at Caleb, even though he is just as sweaty and disheveled as I feel. When Caleb held me in his arms that night at the pier, when I nearly killed myself, I realized at that moment how stupid I was to be jealous of Natalie.

He loves me. He will always love me.

I still had my reservations about saddling him with me for the rest of his life, even though he has assured me that's what he wants. We've been taking some baby steps to move our relationship forward. We moved in together a couple of months ago. I had to spend several days rearranging all his furniture to my liking as well as the contents of all the cabinets in his kitchen (he had three different colors of plates, all stacked haphazardly—it was awful). But after some growing pains, it seems to be going well. Still, I've been hesitant to talk about the next step after that. Marriage. That's a big one.

Although more and more, I'm beginning to actually believe it might work out.

Natalie waves to me from the registration desk. She looks beautiful as always today, in her 5K T-shirt and skintight running pants. I still remember the way the color drained out of her face when she found out the

351

dead body in the woods belonged to Tara Wilkes. When she realized what I had done.

I wasn't certain if she would keep her mouth shut. I was ready to do whatever it took to silence her, but as it turned out, she is good at keeping secrets. Which is fortunate for her, because I know a lot of secrets about her too.

For starters, Natalie went along with the story that I told to Detective Santoro, that the ceramic turtle accidentally fell on my head and I spent several days disoriented and wandered away from home. That I hadn't the slightest idea that half the South Shore was searching for me.

And she never told the police about our link to Tara. Nobody looked into it, and I was very good at covering my tracks. Her murder is still unsolved. I was fortunate that she had grown up to be a miserable human being who had isolated herself from most of her family and had few close friends, so nobody was pushing too hard for answers.

Then a few months ago, Natalie asked if I would be interested in helping her organize the 5K this year. Both Caleb and I quit Vixed a long time ago—it would have been far too awkward to keep working there—but the idea of helping to raise money for a charity that Mia would have really cared about was appealing to me.

With Natalie's blessing, we made the race even more about Mia this year. I even went on podcasts and talked about her. It was cathartic. I talked about some of the struggles she went through with her mobility and how important this money would be. Natalie said donations broke all records this year.

Right next to the registration desk, there's a huge

poster of Mia made from an old photo Caleb dug up. I miss her so much, and just looking at that poster makes me feel happier.

"Mia would be proud of you too," Caleb says as if reading my mind. I don't know how he does that. "For sure."

Mia *would* be proud of me. She'd be proud that I avenged her death by killing Tara Wilkes. I let her down with Natalie though. But I didn't have a choice—Caleb didn't know about Tara, but he would never have let me kill Natalie. He was so *maddeningly* against violence. It got to the point where I was sorry I told him anything in the first place.

Caleb believes I'm a better person than I am. He can never know the truth.

I lay my head against his shoulder. "What do you think she would think about the two of us being together?"

"Her brother and her best friend? Are you kidding me? She'd be over the moon."

He's probably right. It's exactly something that Mia would've gotten a huge kick out of. I wonder what kind of man she would have ended up with. She was so great. It would've had to be someone really special.

"Wherever she is right now," Caleb says, "she's rooting for us to end up together."

"Do you think we will?"

Caleb gives me a funny look. I've gotten better at reading his facial expressions, but I can't read this one. I don't know what he's thinking. Does he think we won't end up together? Because I've been thinking more and more that I can't imagine any sort of life without him. And even though he would be better off without me, I selfishly still want him.

"What?" I say.

Caleb doesn't answer me. Instead, he drops down onto one knee. I stare at him and clasp a hand over my mouth.

"Dawn." He fishes around in the pocket of his running shorts and comes up with a blue velvet box. He must have been holding on to that for a whole year. Waiting for the right moment. "Dawn, I love you so much."

I can't even speak. I don't cry easily, but I feel tears gathering in my eyes.

A crowd is forming around us, now that people realize what's happening. He opens up the blue velvet box. I let out a gasp at the ring inside. Instead of a diamond, he got me an emerald. It's green. Like a turtle.

"Dawn, will you marry me?"

"Yes! Yes!"

Both of our hands are trembling as he slides the green rock onto my left fourth digit. Maybe it's the endorphins from running, but I don't think I've ever felt this happy. I was dead wrong a year ago when I thought I had experienced everything there was. I have so much left. I'm so grateful to Natalie for stopping me before I made the worst mistake of my life.

I'm glad I decided not to kill her after all.

NATALIE

Caleb and Dawn are so cute you could almost puke.

The crowd is going wild about Caleb's surprise proposal. The two of them are going to be really happy together. They're both wicked crazy—it will be a good fit. God help any children they make together.

Of course, Caleb doesn't know quite how crazy Dawn really is. But if he finds out, it's not going to be from me.

Seth comes to join me at the registration table, which is empty now that the race has finished. He throws one of his arms around my shoulders and grins at me. He's been a lot more open about public displays of affection since his divorce went through last month. Melinda put him through the wringer, but she's out of his life for good. And now it's just us.

"You did an amazing job, Nat," he says.

"Thanks. This is our best year yet."

Dawn catches my eye from her spot in the crowd, where everyone is offering her congratulations. She looks a little overwhelmed like she always gets in large crowds, but she's dealing with it. I give her a little happy wave, and she waves back. Dawn was a huge part of organizing the 5K this year. I wasn't sure she would agree to it, but she loved the idea of honoring her best friend, who took her own life all those years ago.

Now it's fourteen years later, and Amelia is still making a difference in our lives. We have raised a ton of money over the years from the 5K, breaking records this year. Even Detective Santoro made a sizable donation—a peace offering, I suppose.

And of course, I have skimmed my usual share off the top.

I'm careful though. I never take more than a small amount. Enough to help me pay for my lifestyle but not so much that anyone will notice. Amelia owes me after all the trouble she got me into after her suicide. So many people blamed me for that, and I had to resign as class president—one teacher even threatened to fail me! It wasn't my fault she took her own life—she was *weak*. My God, it was just a stupid *joke*.

Last year, I had to siphon off a little more than usual from the donations. I had to transfer the money back to the Vixed account before Seth figured out I had stolen from the company. If he had done a more thorough audit, I would not have been able to hide my tracks. But of course, I knew he wouldn't. If he were more careful, I never would have gotten away with it in the first place.

I don't feel guilty about it. Vixed is a huge company that's earning record-breaking profits—our products are selling like crazy. Well, except for Collahealth, which had to be recalled a few months ago due to unexpected side effects.

Seth squeezes my shoulders, looking out at Dawn and Caleb, who are now holding hands. "Is this giving you any ideas?"

"I don't know," I say. "Is it giving *you* any ideas?"

"Maybe." He winks at me. "I'm a free man now, you know."

Things have gotten fairly serious between Seth and me over the last year. He had been devastated after I broke things off with him and was desperate to get me back. It's flattering. Of course, the first time we were together, he was reluctant to break it off with his wife. He was meticulously careful to make sure we didn't get caught.

So I helped move things along. I sent Melinda a little note about her husband's extracurricular activities. She was devastated, but she didn't leave him like I hoped she would. So I faked a few threatening phone calls from her, some scarily worded notes. I got Seth to believe his wife was crazy.

And then to my surprise, she really did go a little crazy. Started threatening me for real. I had to back off, at least temporarily.

But she's out of our lives now. I even managed to get a restraining order against her, not that little Melinda Hoffman is any real danger to me. She can't hurt me.

I'd like to see her try.

And thanks to the generous donations to the 5K this year, I will have a little nest egg set aside to pay for my wedding dress. When we get married, I can give Seth the child he always wanted. It's a happy ending for everyone. Well, aside from Melinda.

I stand with Seth, watching Caleb kiss Dawn yet again. They really do make a nice couple. And I'm glad Dawn came to her senses that night and didn't jump in the water. It's amazing how close that little mouse came to taking me down. She's craftier than I gave her credit for.

She and I have an unspoken agreement now. I keep my mouth shut about Tara. And she keeps her mouth shut about all the money she knows I embezzled from Vixed. After all, Seth might be careless, but she isn't. I knew the second I got that email from her asking to speak with me after work that she knew what I had done. *A matter of great importance.* That was why I was so desperate to speak with her. So desperate that I went to her house looking for her the next afternoon, which is where I discovered Dawn had vanished and there was all that blood on the carpet.

She wanted me to get caught for embezzlement. She wanted that to be my motive for killing her. But now I know one of her secrets too.

We will keep each other's secrets to the grave.

Dawn may be dangerous.

But so am I.

READING GROUP GUIDE

1. Why is Natalie so worried when Dawn doesn't show up to work? What does she do to try to get in touch with her? Put yourself in Natalie's shoes. What would you have done?

2. What role do emails play within the story? How did they change, and what do they reveal as the story progresses?

3. What's the office dynamic like at Vixed, and how does it change as the story progresses? Did the corporate environment of Vixed remind you of places that you've worked?

4. Early in the story, Detective Santoro begins to treat Natalie like a suspect. What are some reasons for this? Did you also believe she was guilty?

5. Dawn states at one point that secrets bind people close together. Do you think this is true? What secrets do each of the characters have that bind them to one another? Discuss whether any of these characters are truly honest with one another.

6. What actually happened to Dawn? How did your feelings toward her change after this was revealed?

7. This story is packed with twists and turns. Which of them surprised you the most?

8. Who is Mia? What happened to her, and what role does her presence play throughout the entire story?

9. How does the theme of vengeance play out in the novel? Do you think Dawn and Caleb had the right to do the things they did?

10. Discuss the end of the story. What did you think was going to happen?

ACKNOWLEDGMENTS

I've been working on this book for fifty years.

Considering I'm not fifty years old yet, that's probably not accurate, but it feels that way. I've been working on drafts of *The Coworker*—referred to in shorthand as "the turtle book"—for several years and several extremely different drafts. I have to be honest: the original beginning was boring. Everyone said so. It took like four rewrites just to make it not-boring (I hope).

Thank you to my mother, who has read this book in every single iteration. Thank you to all the other people who beta read drafts and gave suggestions: Pamela, Nelle, Kate, Maura, and Emilie. And thank you to Val for the proofreading. I am so appreciative!

A very big thank you to my agent, Christina Hogrebe, as well as all of JRA, for your support and faith in me, as well as helping to make this the best draft possible. And thank you to Jenna Jankowski and Anna Michels at Sourcebooks for helping to bring *The Coworker* into the world!

I always end my acknowledgments by thanking my readers. I have to, because wow, I have just about the best and most dedicated readers ever. I am so extremely thankful, and I hope you enjoyed this most recent fruit of my labor!

ABOUT THE AUTHOR

#1 Amazon, *USA Today*, and *Publishers Weekly* bestselling author Freida McFadden is a practicing physician specializing in brain injury. Freida's work has been selected as one of Amazon Editor's best books of the year, and she has been a Goodreads Choice Award nominee. Her novels have been translated into more than thirty languages. Freida lives with her family and black cat in a centuries-old three-story home overlooking the ocean.